THE

BUZZ

BOYS

A NOVEL

By
EDWARD IZZI

D1525031

THE BUZZ BOYS

ISBN 979-874-48333986

AUTHOR'S DISCLAIMER

This book, "The Buzz Boys," is a complete work of fiction. All names, characters, businesses, places, events, references, and incidents are either the products of the author's imagination or used in a fictitious manner to tell the story. Any references to real-life characters or incidents are used purely as a fictional means of reciting a narrative for enjoyment purposes only.

The author makes no claims of any real-life inferences or actual events other than to recite a fabricated story with a fictitious plot. Any resemblance to natural persons, living or dead, or actual events is purely coincidental or used for entertainment purposes.

ABOUT THE AUTHOR

Edward Izzi is a native of Detroit, Michigan, and is a Certified Public Accountant with a successful accounting firm in suburban Chicago, Illinois. He is the father of four grown children and one all-too grown-up granddaughter, Brianna.

He currently lives in Chicago and will always be a 'Buzz Boy.'

For Ernest Izzi

My uncle, my 'big brother' and my best friend.
For a Buzz Boy, who never lost faith.
Thanks for your unconditional love.

You are forever missed.

"Quando arrivano i demoni, la morte segue sempre."

When the demons come, death always follows.

A Roman Proverb.

CHAPTER ONE
The Dante Alighieri Club – October 2019

It was a warm, autumn evening at the Dante Alighieri Club as several older men played in an intense bocce ball tournament. The club in Franklin Park had several bocce courts with tournament-style courtyards that were ideal for bocce contests. There were four long bocce courts that were thirteen feet wide and one hundred feet long, following bocce ball legal court dimensions.

The older men who usually played there had promptly begun their tournament at five o'clock. Each team was starting out by throwing out the little ball, or the yellow 'piccola palla' out in the middle of the bocce court, with the red and green balls trying to throw and get closest to the little ball. Each bocce ball is 4.2 inches in diameter and 5.5 ounces each, and the bocce balls are uniquely made with an indented strip around each ball to assist the player with their grip.

One of those men playing was an eighty-three-year-old, retired Local 150 equipment operator who lived in Elmwood Park, a suburb of Chicago not far from the bocce club.

Vincenzo 'Papa Enzo' Pezza was pretty proficient at playing bocce, having started playing as a young boy in Altavilla Milicia, a coastal town about a half-hour south of Palermo, Sicily.

At the age of eighty-three, one would say that Pezza looked great for his age. Besides playing bocce with his friends four times a week, he played cards a few times a week at the local Italian social club on Diversey Avenue. Pezza was also very fit for his age, walking seven miles every day around his neighborhood at 6:00 am every morning. Other than high cholesterol medication, he was extremely healthy. When the weather was inclement, he had a membership to the local park district at Elmwood Park, where he did his exercise on a treadmill. For an older man, he was in good shape. At five feet, six inches tall, he was a lean 150 pounds and still had a full head of white, gray hair. At first glance, one would think that he was in his early sixties, and he prided himself on his seasoned good looks.

'Papa Enzo' Pezza was a widower and had three adult children whom he was estranged with for one reason or the other. He had a daughter and two sons that he hadn't spoken with for several years. Enzo had his selfish motives.

They were always asking him for money, he always said. They were always accusing him of one reason or another of making their lives extremely uncomfortable.

It was no secret that Papa Enzo was not a kind, loving father and husband to his family. He was a difficult man to understand and get along with, and everyone at the bocce club was very familiar with his loud, ferocious temper. Pezza was highly opinionated and very judgmental. He took issue with everyone who had a different belief, whether it was sports, religion, or politics.

He played bocce with three of his 'paesani,' and after several hours of intense play, finished the tournament in third place. Papa Enzo hung around with his friends at the bar inside the club, enjoying a few more Peroni beers until almost ten o'clock. He then said goodbye to his friends and walked outside of the club to his car in the parking lot.

As he remotely unlocked his older model Buick Skylark, he heard a familiar voice calling him.

"Pop," the voice shouted.

It was his estranged son, Marco, calling him from behind.

Marco and his father had not talked to one another in several years for different reasons, and Papa Enzo was rather shocked to suddenly see him in the parking lot of the Dante Alighieri Club.

"Marco?" the old man surprisingly said.

8

"What are you doing here?"

"Get into the car, Pop. We need to talk."

Papa Enzo looked at his son for several long moments, wondering what it was that his son wanted at such a late hour. He had always asked him for money in the past.

The two of them then got into his Buick, with the old man sitting in the driver's seat and his son Marco sitting directly behind him in the back seat of the car.

"If you're here to ask me for money again, my answer to you will never change. The answer is still no," Papa Enzo defiantly said in a stern voice.

Enzo spoke with a slight Italian accent but made his point very clear to his oldest son, who had asked him for money several times before. Marco's lifetime troubles, tormented upbringing, and psychological issues had all come to a head-on that evening. Marco Pezza was a very angry man who had come to the end of his proverbial rope.

"Why are you sitting in the back seat," he asked his son.

Marco didn't say a word to his father at that moment. He grabbed his father's keys away from him, making sure that the two of them were locked inside. He then took out his Apple iPhone and dialed 9-1-1.

"Franklin Park Police," the dispatcher answered.

"Yes...I would like to report a double murder, please."

A silent moment.

"There are two dead bodies inside of a Buick Skylark, mine and my father's, parked on the north side of the parking lot of the Dante Alighieri Club. Thank you."

Marco then abruptly pushed the 'End' button of his Apple iPhone.

Papa Enzo was still confused, trying to look over his shoulder to his oldest son, sitting in the back seat. The old man was almost incoherent, not understanding what was about to happen. At that moment, Marco withdrew his 9mm Beretta 92 pistol and jammed it hard against his father's head.

"For all the times you beat up Anthony and Rosaria, for all the times you beat up Mom, driving her to her death...." Marco loudly exclaimed.

"You made her crazy, Pop. You made her sick. You fucking killed her!" he loudly accused his estranged father.

"What the hell are you talking about," the old man loudly protested.

"For all the times you made me bleed, for every black eye, every welt across my back, for every belt beating you ever gave me..."

The old Sicilian just sat there, silent.

"For all the fucking times you pulled my pants down and fucking molested me when I was a little boy, years ago when Mom wasn't home..."

Another silent moment.

"For the time that you fucking raped Rosaria when she was a little girl..."

"For every time that you fucking made us cry..."

Papa Enzo was now shaking, and he began to urinate all over himself in the front seat of his car.

"I'm now going to send you where you fucking belong, you rotten bastard."

"For ruining my fucking life...I have dreamed of splattering your fucking brains all over the front of this windshield," as he turned off the gun's safety.

"I HOPE YOU ROT IN FUCKING HELL," he loudly screamed at his father.

With the gun pointed up against the back of his head, he suddenly pulled the trigger.

There was a loud bang as blood and brain matter spattered all over the vinyl seats, the steering wheel, and the front windshield. Blood was gushing everywhere as Marco felt his face get suddenly sprayed by his father's blood. Papa Enzo immediately slumped over the wheel as the horn started to go off loudly. By that point, several members from the Dante Alighieri Club had started to come outside to see what all the commotion was in the parking lot.

Two police cars from the Franklin Park Police suddenly pulled into the parking lot with their sirens and bright blue lights flashing. Two patrolmen immediately exited the squad car and, with their guns drawn, pointed at the man in the back seat of the Buick.

Papa Enzo was still slumped over the steering wheel. While his estranged father's dead body was still lying up against the horn, Marco Pezza began to put the barrel of his Berretta pistol inside of his mouth. As his final act of defiance, he flipped his middle finger to one of the patrolmen.

He then pulled the trigger.

CHAPTER TWO
A Successful Attorney

The greying clouds of the Chicago skyline were within arm's reach of my high-rise office as I was preparing for my two o'clock deposition. It was another divorce case. With the high volume of publicity-drenched divorces I was handling in my office, I was fast becoming the point person for many of the upper class, north shore power couples with the unwavering desire to dump their spouses.

I had just celebrated my sixtieth birthday last July, and I was in the process of taking inventory of my life. In looking at everything, I would have to say that I have been very blessed. I have enjoyed a very successful career as a divorce attorney here in Chicago. My sky scrapper office at the top of the John Hancock Building encompasses my twenty-two-employee staff, including many law clerks and several junior law partners.

My law firm, Robert Mazzara and Associates, LLC, has become very well known within the Chicagoland area for our high-profile divorce and family law litigation. This firm was started on my kitchen table back in 1985. Thankfully, I have developed quite a respectable reputation among the Chicago elite and Gold Coast couples, with a status that has fast become a bargaining chip for any scheming spouse wishing to play hard ball with their former, significant others.

The 'We'll Take Your Side When You Dump Your Bride,' and the '1-800-DumpHim' slogans were well thought out advertising campaigns that I created many years ago. Our marketing strategies have allowed us to enjoy an exclusive position as one of the top five family law firms within the city. We have been accused of practicing a kind of ruthless, no-holds-barred style of law that has made many of our opponents and several judges cringe whenever we walked into a courtroom with our clients. And with our reputation, we've been able to enjoy large upfront retainers and a billable hourly fee from our clients that justifies our 'down in the trenches' kind of law practice.

To get to this point over the last thirty-five years has not been an easy road by any means. The demons I've battled over the years have been a constant struggle, thanks to the many issues I suffered early on. My personal life had undoubtedly been impaired.

I became a widower when my wife of twenty-one years, Anna Maria, died of glioblastoma nine years ago. I have two daughters. My oldest, Diana, is a medical student in her final year at the University of Illinois, and Annette, is a law student at Loyola University. My hot and cold relationship with both of my daughters has always been amply fueled by their bad attitudes and self-proclaimed feelings of entitlement. Although I am very proud of both of them, they only seem to reach out to me when my ATM machine is plugged in and in good working order.

I am a former alcoholic. I attend Alcoholic Anonymous meetings every other Wednesday evening. I was also in psychological therapy twice a week for almost ten years, having suffered from extreme bouts of manic depression that has led to severe, suicidal thoughts. On top of all of this, I was diagnosed with stage three prostate cancer four-and-one-half years ago and will celebrate my fifth anniversary as a cancer survivor this December.

In part, I attributed my cancer diagnosis to all of the physical and emotional stress that I've had to absorb throughout my whole life. Since I was the oldest of three boys from a very strict, very domineering Italian family, my turbulent childhood seemed to be the catalyst to all of my problems throughout my life. My personal life was always in a constant state of turmoil.

My 2:00 deposition in my conference room was done and finished by 4:00 pm. By the time the court reporter packed up and left, I was exhausted. I walked into the kitchen of our office and went into our refrigerator to grab a Diet Coke. We usually left the television in the kitchen on all day for anyone who wished to listen to the extra noise in an otherwise tranquil office. As I grabbed my beverage, I heard on the news an announcement of a gruesome discovery in the western suburbs that put me into a complete and total state of shock:

"This is Chaz Rizzo, Channel Eight Eyewitness News. There has been a gruesome murder-suicide in Franklin Park last night at the Dante Alighieri Club on West Belmont Avenue. The gruesome discovery occurred approximately a little after 10:00 pm last evening. The victims have been identified as Vincenzo Pezza, 83, of Elmwood Park, and his estranged son, Marco Pezza, 60, of Wood Dale. There was an apparent confrontation in the older man's vehicle when the son shot his father in the back of the head before turning the gun on himself. The alleged shooter notified the Franklin Park Police Department within minutes before killing his father, then killing himself. This parking lot has been roped off with yellow crime scene tape, pending the investigation by the Franklin Park Police Department."

I felt my whole body turn numb as the blood running through my veins temporarily stopped flowing. I felt my heart stop beating and fall into my stomach. I felt my face turn several shades of white as I almost dropped my just-opened soda on the floor. I kept staring at the news blaring from the kitchen television as I slowly sat down at the kitchen table and tried to absorb the terrible news.

"Mr. Mazzara...are you okay?" my secretary and administrative associate, Sandra wanted to know as she walked back into the kitchen. I only managed to shake my head.

"No."

There were now tears in my eyes, and I was having difficulty responding to her simple question. I only stoically sat there, listening to the news, attempting to make sense of this very sudden, very tragic, very real nightmare.

Realizing that something was wrong, Sandra handed me a tissue from the Kleenex box and then, momentarily, listened to the terrible news with me on the kitchen television.

"I'm so sorry," she said, as she rubbed my shoulders as if to try to comfort me. She then got up from the table, walking out of the kitchen after closing the door behind her.

As I sat there alone at that table, I broke down and cried. For several long minutes, I was loudly grieving and inconsolable. I was in physical pain, and my heart was utterly broken.

Hearing about Marco's sudden death was like hearing about the death of a very close brother, and it hit me very hard. I struggled to think about the last time I had talked to him, which was unfortunately over two months ago. I had known about Marco's difficult times that he was recently experiencing and recalled the many times that I had reached out to help him. Marco was a victim, succumbing to his terrible, past experiences that he psychologically never got over.

15

Marco Pezza was a childhood friend whom I had known and grown up with since the fifth grade at St. Angela's School in Elmwood Park. We were the best of friends when we were kids, having gone to grade school and later Holy Cross High School in River Grove, graduating together in 1977. I had known his parents, Papa Enzo and his mother Cira, who practically helped raise my siblings and me while we were growing up in the old neighborhood together. I had known his brother and sister very well for many years. They had lived next door to our family on Cortland Avenue, and his parents were very close to my mother and father.

As I sat at that table, I was physically and emotionally paralyzed, as I was trying to cope with my intense state of shock. I just couldn't believe it. Flashbacks of our past, of our childhood, of the intensity of our growing up and practically growing old together over these last fifty years overwhelmed me, and for several long minutes, I couldn't move.

Marco was once my very best friend. He was once a huge part of my personal life. Marco was my grade school and high school classmate, and we had spent a considerable amount of our childhood together growing up in the old neighborhood. Marco Pezza and I, along with Billy Kozar, Petey Rodriguez, and Johnny Orozco, were as close as five childhood friends could be throughout most of our lives.

My first instinct was to reach for my bottle of comfort in the kitchen, which I had, fortunately, removed from my kitchen cabinets over two years ago.

Jack Daniels was my poison of choice, and I had spent many years with my best friend Marco, trying to cope with our personal problems over the innumerate glasses of our favorite drinks. We had spent many hours sitting at the bar over at

Diamond Lil's on North Milwaukee Avenue, sucking down tumblers filled with 'JD on the Rocks.' Marco and I were intense alcoholics, drowning our troubles away, sitting at our favorite 'gin mill,' feeling sorry for ourselves, and blaming our abusive fathers for our current problems.

After my wife's death and being busted on a second DUI, I had entered an alcohol rehabilitation program over two years ago. At first, Marco had joined with me. We had both been dry for almost six months until Marco had a relapse. After that, it was all downhill for him. He had lost his wife. He had lost his house. He had lost his job as a detective at the Chicago Police Department. Marco had lost everything.

While watching the news, I realized that Marco had finally confronted the very person he felt was the culprit of all his problems. He dealt with that the only way he knew how. One of Marco's biggest downfalls was that he had a violent, uncontrollable temper and went on the attack whenever he felt threatened. His temper and violent way of thinking not only got him into trouble but eventually destroyed his life.

We were once a small fraternity of five boys who had each other's backs, who shared a common thread of being raised in very intense, unhappy, sometimes violent family environments. We rebelled against our families, and especially our abusive fathers, together, with some of us not yielding a positive result. The five of us had screwed up, unhappy childhoods, which included horrific experiences that no young boy should ever have to live through. Those tragic events within our young lives adversely shaped our futures, none for the better. For me, struggling and succeeding beyond the terrible events of my childhood has been nothing short of a miracle.

Marco Pezza, who was also sixty years old, was divorced and was an extreme alcoholic. He was fiscally irresponsible, having filed bankruptcy twice in his life. He was currently a Chicago policeman and detective who had been recently suspended from the Chicago police force for his excessive drinking and using unnecessary pressure on many of his arrested victims. Marco was also accused of shaking down several of his perpetrators for money after taking them into custody many years ago. Still, the Chicago P.D. couldn't prove any of those accusations. Because of his many other violations and his excessive misconduct, his police pension was forfeited. By all definitions, Marco was a troubled, former 'dirty cop.'

Marco had fallen on hard times. He had been unemployed for the last two years, having been terminated from his security job at a local jewelry store in Northbrook. To say that he had a difficult life was an understatement.

He blamed his father for all of his personal, lifetime problems, and he was finally at his breaking point. Marco was penniless, having lost his home in Addison to his ex-wife in his last divorce and being evicted from his apartment.

We all learned to read and write together. We learned to fight together. We chased girls together. We went to driver's education classes together. We played sports together in high school. We stood up at each other's weddings, some of us baptizing each other's children. We experienced our lifetime hardships, our setbacks, and with some of us, experienced many intense, personal tragedies together.

We all were affected by our difficult childhoods in one way or another, but I was the only one of the five of us who gotten help and had pursued intense psychological therapy. I tried so hard to convince the others to get help, knowing that our terrible childhood experiences would eventually destroy us.

One by one by one...by one.

Unfortunately, I was right. By some means or another, we were all destroyed by those intense, terrible, abusive experiences that no young boy should ever have to go through. It was probably through the 'Grace of God' that I have psychologically survived this far in my life.

With the suicide death of my long-time best friend, I slowly realized that I was now...the only one left.

Once upon a time, a long time ago, Marco and me, along with Billy, Petey, and Johnny...were once called 'The Buzz Boys.'

CHAPTER THREE
Cortland Avenue - 1965

The huge swing set erected in front of the old school building looked like a skyscraper to me, and I walked in front of St. Angela's School in Elmwood Park for the first day of first grade. It was a bright September morning, and I was already trying to pull off my clip-on tie, which my mother had securely fastened onto my white, short sleeve shirt. At that early stage of my life, I thought everyone had to wear uniforms to school.

Sister Cecilia was standing by the doorway of our classroom as we all walked single file the way we were trained to the prior year in morning kindergarten. I had heard rumors on the playground about what a 'mean' and 'nasty' teacher Sister Cecilia was, so I knew that I had to be on my best behavior. We were assigned desks in our class, and the boy next to me became the first of my lifetime best friends. I remember that day like it was yesterday because one of the first things we had to learn was how to write our complete names in cursive. The boy next to me seemed to have trouble because his name was quite long.

His full name, 'Pedro Juan Carlos Rodriguez' was a long, twenty-four-letter name that he probably never learned how to write in cursive until he was in high school. Because his father's name was 'Pedro,' his nickname was 'Petey,' which he insisted everyone call him, including Sister Cecilia. The nun tried to get him to write his full name but realized early that her attempts at his learning how to formalize his name were futile, and she eventually gave up.

After about the middle of the year, she finally accepted his 'Petey Rodriguez' name on the top of all of his homework papers.

I don't think Petey liked his name. I remember his getting into a fight in the playground once with someone who had called him by his real first name, inserting a few swear words in between. Petey was a dark-haired, dark-skinned little boy who looked Latino but didn't appreciate being called a 'wet-back or the 'beaner' nicknames that the other Latino little boys in the neighborhood were called. Because most of the boys in my neighborhood and my class were Italian or Polish, Petey wanted to assimilate with the rest of us. To him, the name 'Petey' sounded more Italian than 'Pedro,' and as far as he was concerned, that was his name.

Petey was also an Italian wanna-be his whole life. I remember his coming over to our house almost every day after school and my mother making him pasta and meatballs with Sunday sauce. It got to a point where he didn't want to eat any of his mother's Mexican cooking anymore because he liked my mother's Italian cooking so much.

We would play in our backyards, everything from 'Hide-N-Seek' to 'Pickle Baseball.' He was the one who taught me how to throw a baseball and football since my father was always working, as I was the oldest of three boys. We would play pick-up baseball and touch football on Cortland Avenue in the middle of the street and knew that we had to be home for dinner when the streetlights came on, usually around 7:00 pm.

Petey also taught me how to colorfully swear like a truck driver. He taught me swear words that I had never heard before, putting them together in sentences that would make any hardened criminal blush. On Saturdays, when his mother was out shopping and his father was at work, we used to go to his garage and peruse through his dad's Playboy magazines. Petey knew precisely where his father had hidden his stash, and we were more than happy to go through and critique all of Hugh Hefner's adult, sophisticated modern literature.

By then, Billy Kozar started coming around. He was the Polish kid who lived down the street on Cortland Avenue. He watched the two of us throwing a baseball around in our neighborhood and figured he could teach us a few things. He was always a little bit bigger and taller than all of us, and it took us a few years to figure out that he had been held back by the nuns. Billy had flunked out, and was re-doing the first grade. But he could hit the ball, throw the ball, and catch the ball better than either of us. Billy wasn't the smartest kid in the class, but he was undoubtedly the most street-wise.

The three of us were pretty much together during recess and after school, playing either baseball in the middle of the street or going off on our bicycles somewhere far away from home, which in those days was Harlem Avenue. At that time, we were able to walk back and forth to school without any fears or incidents, and there was usually a gang of kids following us from Cortland up 78th Street to West Armitage Avenue. The three of us were inseparable, and after a while, everyone in the neighborhood wanted to be friends with us, thanks to Billy. Because of his athletic prowess, he was pretty much respected by everyone on and off the street, and nobody picked on us.

We hung out at a little store on the corner of 75th Street, and Fullerton called Tony's Deli. There, we would bring our allowances after school or on Saturdays after a game of 'streetball' and get ourselves a soda and a candy bar. For me, it was always a Kit-Kat and an Orange Crush. We would then sit on our bicycles and fantasize about the kind of cars we were going to drive when we all turned sixteen.

There was one incident that I had never forgotten that occurred on a Saturday afternoon.

We were all supposed to get together with the other kids in the neighborhood when Petey and I couldn't find Billy, as he was nowhere to be found. We both went to his house and knocked on his door, but there was no one answering. After repeated knocking, I walked over to his bedroom window and climbed up on the ledge to peer into his window.

All I remember seeing was Billy lying face down on his bed, with his pillow covered in blood. I had gotten scared and told Petey and together, ran home to my house to tell my mother what we had seen. For some reason, my mother dismissed it, telling us to forget what we had seen and 'not to get involved.' We didn't see Billy for several days until one day; he showed up at school.

Billy's eyes were both black and blue, and his face looked like he had bruises on it and was in the healing process. We asked him at recess what had happened, and he only said that he was in 'a car accident' with his father. We came to find out years later what had really happened:

Billy had been caught by the store manager trying to steal a Playboy magazine from Tony's Deli, and the owner called the police. When the police brought Billy home to his father, he beat Billy up so badly that he severely broke his nose and dislodged a few of his teeth. Someone in the family came over later to adhere to Billy's injuries, as he was never taken to the hospital or the doctor. When he finally arrived back at school, the principal at St. Angela's accepted his parents 'car accident excuse', and no one made any more mention of it.

Billy's father, Casimir Kozar, was a seasoned alcoholic. His father used to hang out at the Armitage Lounge on Harlem Avenue daily, often not coming home until very late at night. His mother, Bozena, wasn't much better. She would go out on occasions, leaving Billy to watch his younger sister all alone at home. He would usually pray that his mother would come home before his father did, as his mother would try to stand between his drunken father and Billy receiving another beating.

Billy coming to school with facial injuries that day wasn't the first incident that this had occurred, as his old man used to crack around his oldest son whenever he found an excuse to do so. All of us figured that his father had broken Billy's nose on at least three different occasions, resulting in Billy growing up with a rather 'crooked' nose. It was for this reason that Billy was so tough. He was undoubtedly feared in the neighborhood, and he had to learn very early on how to defend himself.

Billy Kozar was a fighter, and as a result, taught us how to fight as well. He taught us how to block a punch, throw a karate kick, and adequately throw a right cross while blocking with our left.

He also taught us how to play cards, and we would gamble in Petey's garage every Saturday afternoon when it was either too rainy, too snowy, or too cold to play outside. We were probably the only kids in the first grade who could play 'Blackjack' and 'Texas Hold-Em' probably better than most adults.

As six-year-old boys, the essential things in our lives were baseball cards, comic books, MAD magazines, and of course, cars. We would sit around on my front porch and watch all of the cars go by, giving a thumbs down to any vehicle that we wouldn't be caught dead in. At the tender age of six, we already knew what kind of cars we would be driving when we were old enough to get our licenses.

We were all in love with the 1965 Ford Mustang convertible that had just come off the Detroit assembly. Every sixteen or seventeen-year-old kid who had a license to drive back then drove either a red, blue, or white Mustang. My Uncle Aldo had just purchased a brand new, blue Mustang convertible, and he used to come over to visit us on Sunday afternoons. We used to convince him to take us out for ice cream while we all piled in the back seat of his convertible Mustang with a little begging.

'Batman' had just come out on the television, so most of us wore our masks and capes during recess. Petey and Billy would come over to the house, and my mother used to make us hamburgers or hotdogs for all of us to enjoy. After making a big bowl of popcorn, we would then be glued to the TV set on Wednesday and Thursday nights, 'same Bat-time, same Bat-channel.

But Petey's home life wasn't much better than Billy's. Petey came home one day to find an Elmwood Park police car on his driveway. A patrolman was escorting his father in handcuffs outside of his front door, putting him inside the patrol car. When Petey asked his mother what was going on, she only said that the 'policeman had made a mistake and that he would be returning home soon.'

Petey's father finally did return home...three years later. During that time, his mother had to work full-time waiting tables at Mister C's Deli & Diner on West Diversey and didn't come home until nine or ten o'clock. Petey would stay over at our house, and my mother would happily have him over for dinner, which increased his appreciation for authentic Italian food.

We came to find out later that Petey's father, Pedro, was convicted of an attempted homicide charge, where he had severely pistol-whipped somebody who had owed him a lot of money. He was paroled after three years from Stateville on good behavior.

When my mother had purchased one of the 'GAF View Master' slide views with the 3-D circular wheels, I remember an incident. She had bought it for me, and I was so excited to play with it, I had accidentally broken one of the viewer slides that needed to be inserted into the view master.

When my father, Alberto Mazzara, had found out about it, he hit me several times with his belt until I had reddened welts on my back and legs. My father always tried to hit me somewhere other than my face, as he knew that the black and blue marks would not be as visible on different parts of my body. I remember the incident so well that I couldn't walk without the pain of the stinging, blackened bruises on my legs.

These beatings from my father had become so prevalent and happened so often I thought that they were normal and that all children got severely beaten by their parents. It wasn't until later on, as we got older, that we realized that our beatings went far and beyond just 'spankings,' as we suffered some severe physical injuries from being hit with objects like wooden two by fours, open frying pans over our heads, and even the broken legs from a chair. All of these weapons were fair game in not only our household but in Petey's and Billy's house as well.

And then there was the terrible incident that occurred at the end of the first grade. I had come home once from school one day to find that I had been locked out of our house. I went around to the backyard and found my two little brothers, Michael, and Jimmy, sitting outside on the swing set.

When I asked Michael what was going on, they only said that Mom and Dad were arguing inside the house. I tried knocking on the back door, but no one answered. I could only hear my mother screaming and shrilling in a crying voice that I could never get out of my mind. It sounded like she was in terrible distress, as I heard my father screaming and beating her while she screamed at the top of her lungs. I heard some broken tables and chairs in the kitchen and several glasses and dishes being broken. This probably went on for over an hour, until finally, we were all allowed to come back inside of the house.

When we did, the bruised and bloody face of my mother sitting in a chair, all alone in the family room, trying to control her whimpers and crying, brought chills down my spine. That was an image I could never put out of my mind. I came to realize later that my father had beaten my mother several times before when all of us were at school until the police were finally called many years later.

I also realized that it was one of the neighbors who had called the police on my father, not my mother. As much as she was beaten, she was always too intimidated and too scared to report any of her injuries to the police. The bruises on my mother's face lingered for weeks as she desperately tried to apply makeup on her injured face to cover her bruises and swollen eyes.

I remember how angry I was as a little boy but feeling so helpless. I couldn't do anything to protect my mother. I would only watch my father, sitting there in the kitchen, pretending that everything was okay and that nothing was wrong, while my mother tried to control her whimpering and her tears from the other room.

It was in the first grade when we all learned how to hate our fathers.

CHAPTER FOUR
The Playground – 1966

The bright, afternoon September sun was shining brightly on the playground sand as a little girl played alone during the St. Angela school recess. She had some white and pink chalk and was drawing hopscotch diagrams on the black asphalt. As she was filling the number on each square, she was softly smiling and singing to herself contently, enjoying the late summer sunshine. Her long, curly, raven black hair was neatly combed back, not to get in the way of her white blouse and plaid vest and matching skirt.

She couldn't have been more than eight years old but seemed to be undisturbed as the surrounding children played vigorously nearby. There were boys clad in their white shirts and ties, fighting for their turns on the schoolyard slide or monkey bars, while the girls in their Catholic school uniforms were playing jump rope in the middle of the school play area.

As the little schoolgirl played alone on her own, skipping by herself in the playground, she seemed to be ignored by the other children. Boys and girls were walking and running past her as if they wished to leave her to play all alone. There was something uniquely different about her. Her neatly ironed white blouse, her almost perfect dark curly hair, and her laced socks folded neatly above her black and white saddle shoes seemed to stand out among the other children. It was as though she were an animated porcelain doll, playing happily and quietly alone in the schoolyard.

A dark-haired little boy, wearing a grass-stained shirt and loosened tie, began to walk over the brunette little girl playing alone.

"Where is your rope?" the little boy curiously asked.

"What rope?" the girl replied.

"You're supposed to skip rope while playing hopscotch on each of the numbers."

"Well, that's not the way I play. I just throw a small stone into the first square. I put my foot on the first empty square and jump on the numbers with both feet," the little girl replied.

The little boy looked confused. "Yeah, but we do that while skipping rope."

The petite brunette then threw the first rock on the first chalked number on the square. Then she skipped onto each number of the chalked outdoor diagram. She then passed the stone over to the little boy, who skipped on each number until ending the desired diagram.

They continued to play hop-scotch together, laughing and giggling on the playground. Her soft, mellow voice contrasts with the loud, laughing children playing on the adjacent swing sets.

After several minutes of playing hopscotch together, the boy quickly sat down next to her on the grass.

"What's your name?" asked the little boy in earnest.

"Anna Maria," she replied.

"What's that?" he innocently asked.

"My name. It's Anna Maria. But my Mom calls me Annie."

"Oh." The little boy seemed to be undaunted by her explanation as he got up and continued to play hopscotch using the new method which the little girl had taught him. He had dark stains on his white shirt, and there was sand in his shoes from playing in the sandbox. He had thrown the rock on another number and was trying to skip his way across the chalked hopscotch diagram.

"What's your name?" the little girl asked.

"Robby," he said politely, still paying more attention to the hopscotch game.

"Do your friends call you Bob?" she curiously asked.

"Only the ones who want to get punched," he replied.

Little Annie started to giggle as her new friend continued to throw the rock on the hopscotch diagram drawn earnestly on the asphalt ground.

"Let's sing a song while we skip," she exclaimed, as the two of them started singing silly songs that didn't rhyme or make any sense, as the two of them were enjoying playing together until the recess bell began to ring.

Little Robby and Annie became fast friends in the second grade, sitting next to one another at lunchtime every day. Robby would unpack his peanut butter and jelly sandwich from his Hector Heathcoat lunchbox, while Annie would bring along her Holly Hobby lunchbox and would always share her Mortadella and Swiss cheese sandwich with him.

They would talk and share about all of their new adventures together in the second grade. They would play together at recess, usually playing hopscotch or in the school yard's sandbox area. They would make sandcastles in the sandbox, digging deep trenches, and getting themselves all dirty and full of sand before going back into class. Annie would share her Holly Hobby books with Robby while bringing his Superman comic books into class to share with his friends, but mainly with Annie.

Little Robby would tie his jacket around his neck and pretend he was the superhero, flying around the playground with his arms extended, pretending to save the world. Annie would often play along, flying along with him as Robby would call out.

"Fly with me, Supergirl! We have to capture Lex Luther!"

"I'm right behind you, Superman!" she would exclaim, as she would follow him around the school yard with her cape tied around her neck, her arms extended.

When Annie didn't feel like flying around the playground, they would sit down along the wall overlooking the sandbox, and Robby would read his Superman comic books to her. They would pretend to save the planet from evil, as Annie would call Robby "Superman," and they would pretend that he was rescuing "Supergirl" from Metropolis's dark criminals. On some mornings, the two superheroes would begin their mission of fighting crime first thing in the morning.

"Save the world, Supergirl!" as little Robby would chase Annie around the turnabout, their jackets tied around their necks. Their superhero names would often become their moniker, calling each other by their comic book names as they played in the playground and on the way home from school every day.

Soon after, as the fall weather became colder, Robby would walk from his house to Annie's place on the corner of Armitage and 75th Streets. He would pick her up and walk together to school every morning. Along the way, there was a circular, round turnabout in the middle of Forest and Oak Streets, on the way to St. Angela School. Each morning, Annie and Robby would take the time to play tag and chase each other around and around, laughing, giggling, and loudly playing together every day.

During that time, Robby had all but ignored his other friends Petey and Billy, letting them walk back and forth to school by themselves. Robby would only play with his best friends' afterschool but always made sure that he was available for Annie during most recesses and escorted her en route to her house and St. Angela's.

Early one cold November morning, Robby and Annie played on the turnabout when, as Robby was chasing Annie, she fell and badly scrapped her knee. Annie started to cry as she saw the blood, started shaking and began to get scared. The boy, remembering that his mother always packed a cloth napkin in his Hector Heathcoat lunchbox every morning, took out the napkin and turned it into a tourniquet, wrapping it tightly around her knee to stop the bleeding. He then pulled her arm around his shoulder and slowly walked her to school and the nurse's office.

As the Christmas holidays came, they would still meet at the turnabout and have snowball fights when it was snowing and built a snowman in front of Annie's house, complete with a carrot nose and a long, old blanket which the two pretended to be a Superman cape.

It wasn't until Valentine's Day when the two of them took their friendship to a higher level. Robby had brought the new Superman comic book Valentine's edition to recess, and the two of them sat on the wall and pretended to be their favorite superheroes. They were reading each page together as they followed the story of how Supergirl was falling in love with Superman, and finally reading the end of the story where the two superheroes were embracing.

Annie innocently asked Robby that day, "Superman, would you ever marry Supergirl?"

"Married? Are you crazy? Superman can't get married! Besides, he's in love with Lois Lane!" he proclaimed.

"But...what if Supergirl was in love with Superman? Would you marry her then?" she asked.

Before Robby could even respond, Annie quickly planted a kiss on Robby's cheek. Robby looked at Annie, totally surprised. Most little boys in the second grade would have yelled out "Cooties" and began whipping their cheeks profusely with anything they could find. But Robby quietly looked at her and nodded his head.

"Fine, Supergirl. I'll marry you."

It was a bright, warm morning in May, as the school bell began to ring at precisely 8:05. Little Robby was winded from running to school alone, by himself. Annie did not show up to pick her up and walk her to school, and her mother had called his mom to let him know that Annie would not be around for him to pick her up.

As the children began to march through the front door single file, Annie was just arriving at school and had barely got there on time. Robby spotted her at the back of the line and waited for her to take a seat in the back of the class. Her eyes were puffy and extremely red, as if she were crying. He tried to get her attention throughout the morning class, but Annie avoided making eye contact with him. She didn't sit with him at lunchtime and decided to sit with some of her friends instead. It wasn't until after recess that Robby finally confronted her as she was sitting by herself on the playground wall overlooking the school yard.

"Annie? What's wrong" he demanded to know. She was silent and stared straight ahead as he continued to try to get his attention.

"Annie? You're crying! What happened? Is something wrong?" he asked again, only in a louder voice.

"We're moving," she quietly said, as the words could barely come out of her mouth.

"Moving? Where are you going?"

"I have to go to live with my Nonna. My Momma says we can't stay in our house anymore. We're moving in two weeks," he said, as his eyes were starting to well up with tears.

Her mother only told the little girl that they were moving. She did not want to expose and worry her daughter about the complications of a bank foreclosure. Since her father had moved out several months ago and abandoned the family, her mother could not afford the mortgage payments, even with her working two jobs.

"Where does your Grandma live?" he asked inquisitively.

"She lives far. We have to drive over an hour each time we have to go there," she replied.

"Almost a hundred miles," she softly said.

They both sat there together in silence as they tried to figure out how they were going to be superheroes together one hundred miles apart. Who was going to play Superman with him? Who was he going to walk to school and play with in the sandbox? How were they going to stay friends so far, far away?

"Maybe you can come and visit me? You won't need a car, Supergirl. You can fly here."

He was trying to cheer her up as she wiped some of the tears away from her face.

"Maybe my mom will drive me to visit you," he suggested, but Annie was expressionless.

"Come on, Supergirl. We still have two weeks that we can play together. You're not leaving today, right?"

"Yes, I know."

"Let's go play in the sandbox. We can make a magic castle where we can hide away together. And then, maybe when they come to take you away to move, they won't be able to find you because we'll be hiding in our sandcastle together!" Annie looked at Robby, kind of surprised.

"Do you think we could run away together?" she asked him.

"We could find a place where nobody will be able to find us. We could hide in the woods. I will bring my pocketknife and some matches. We could live like the Indians!" Robby's eyes started to perk up with excitement.

"Hmmm. Can I come home at night for dinner at five o'clock? My Nonna gets mad when I'm late for dinner."

"If we are hiding away in the woods, you can't go home for dinner, Annie! Once you run away and become an Indian, you can't go back home to visit."

"I don't think my Mom is going to like that," she slowly said, realizing that being a run-away may not be such a good idea.

"Maybe I could ask my uncle to give your mom a job, so you won't have to move. He's a boss at a factory, you know," Robby suggested, trying to come up with other ideas.

"No.... I don't think that will work. My mom says we have to leave our house and move in with my Nonna."

The two of them sat there on the playground wall in silence, waiting for the recess school bell to ring. They both knew that, once the second grade was over and Annie moved away, they would probably never see each other again.

The following day and every day for two weeks, the two children continued to play their superhero games, walking each other to school every day and playing together at recess. Robby did his best to cheer up Annie and tried to come up with every excuse under the sun to keep her from moving away. He even asked his mom to hide Annie at their house when the day came for her to move. His mother kindly explained to him that kidnapping Annie was not a good idea. She politely told him that kidnapping was a crime and that he was too little to go to jail.

When the last day of school arrived, Robby walked to Annie's house and picked her up. They took their time walking to school together, hoping to make the last morning walk last forever. As they approached St. Angela's School, Annie held Robby's hand and played "skip the sidewalk line" to prolong the school walk. Finally, as they both approached the playground and walked over to the sandbox, Annie wiped the tears from her face.

"Robby.... promise that we will meet once a year at the playground. Promise me that we will come here and meet on the swing set every year on Valentine's Day, okay?"

"Ok, Annie, I promise."

Annie leaned over to Robby and put her hand over her mouth as she whispered into his ear.

"I love you, Robby."

She started to cry and ran up to the front of the school line so that Robby couldn't see her. The little boy's eyes filled up with tears as the school bell rang at 8:05. It was the last day of school, and they were only in class for a few hours. As the final bell rang, Annie's mother was outside of their classroom to pick her up from school and get some paperwork and transcripts for her new school in September.

As Annie was gathering her things from her desk, she took one long last look at Robby. He waved back and then looked away. Annie then exited the classroom, walking hand in hand with her mother down the hallway as they left St. Angela School.

On the following Valentine's Day, little Annie begged her mother to bring her to the St. Angela's playground after school. It was a warm winter day, and the sun was fairly bright that afternoon. They had been visiting friends and family in the area, so it was convenient for her mother to bring her to her old school. As she arrived, she got out of the car and waited in the sandbox for Robby to arrive.

But little Robby never came. Anna Maria's mother knew of the crush and intense friendship that her daughter had for little Robby Mazzara, and bringing her to the St. Angela playground on Valentine's Day after school became an annual ritual. But after three years, it was apparent that

37

little Robby had forgotten about their promise. He never showed up at their old grade school playground.

They never saw each other again.

CHAPTER FIVE
Grandparent's Death - 1967

It was springtime, and Petey and I were looking forward to making our First Communion in a few days. We had been preparing in class for the last several months, doing all the workbooks and answering all the right questions about how important it was to receive the 'Body of Christ.'

Making your First Communion at that time was a big deal. We all knew that there would be a big party thrown in our honor and that there would be friends, goodies, and especially cash envelopes to look forward to.

All of my friends in class, and especially Petey and I, were looking forward to our first communion parties in the garage with a big Napoli Bakery sheet cake, all the expensive gifts, the balloons and ribbon decorations, and especially the large number of first communion envelopes stuffed with cash.

My typically disorganized mother was still scrambling to buy me a black suit and white tie three days before my coveted religious event. The required formalwear was the mandatory fashion of all the little boys making their First Communion at St. Angela's. On those last few days before my Communion, my mother was still scrambling to find me a black suit and a white tie to wear. At the last minute, she decided to take me to my grandparent's house after school so that she would be free to go shopping to find what we needed.

For the last few years, my mother dropped me off at my paternal grandparents' house in Jefferson Park on Fridays after school. I would spend the weekends alone there with them, away from my brothers and my friends. I believed later on that my mother thought that my being around my grandparents at such a young age would keep them from fighting and arguing, which in reality, wasn't the case.

My paternal grandfather, Salvatore Mazzara, and his wife, Costanza, immigrated from Atina, Italy (in Frosinone, near Rome) in 1955. Although they both came to the United States to seek a better life, my 'Nonna Costanza' was never sold on the American Dream. She thought that Chicago was a disgusting, filthy city. She never appreciated the cultural diversity of her adapted home. She disliked the American way of life, didn't want to learn English, and especially hated minorities. I remember going grocery shopping with her as a young child and watching her refusing to enter a grocery aisle if an African American person was shopping in the same aisle. Being around my grandparents at a young age, I learned the Italian language and the culture of being a first-generation American.

After being in America for more than twelve years at the time, Nonna had made up her mind that she had enough. She wanted more than anything to return to her tiny little town of Atina and finish out her final years with my grandfather, my 'Nonno Toto.'

But Salvatore Mazzara, or 'Nonno Toto' as he wanted us to call him, wanted nothing to do with returning to Italy. He worked as a forklift operator in a tool and die factory in the city and made great money with benefits. He was in the operators union Local 150, with a great pension and retirement benefits. He had assimilated well with his new homeland, spoke English reasonably well, and got along with everyone at work and at the local Italian Club on Diversey Avenue, where he would meet his friends and play cards for a few hours every day.

To make matters worse, Nonna Costanza had a violent, vicious temper. I had watched her throw a scalding pot of pasta with boiling water at my Nonno during one of their frequent arguments. She would scream and yell at him from the minute he came home from work until the last minute that he retired to his bedroom practically every evening. He would escape to the Italian Club almost every night just to escape the wrath of my Nonna Costanza, who would look for any excuse to pick a fight with him. They were two very miserable, unhappy people, and I hated going over there as a young child. My mother thought my being there would be a distraction for my grandmother from initiating another brutal argument with my grandfather.

On that Thursday evening, I was sitting at the table eating a pasta dish of some kind that my Nonna had especially prepared for me. I immediately noticed several empty bottles of beer near the sink, which immediately told me that my grandmother had been drinking, which wasn't unusual. When my Nonno came home late that night around eight o'clock, my Nonna immediately went after him verbally, screaming and cussing at him in Italian for more than an hour. There was a small room in the basement downstairs with a couch and a television, so I escaped downstairs to avoid all of the verbal commotions.

What seemed to be different on that day was that Nonna Costanza looked especially angry, and her eyes were bulging out of her head the very minute that Nonno Toto arrived at home. She was probably drunk, which accentuated her brutal, vicious temper even more. As I sat downstairs and tried watching whatever afterschool cartoons were on at the time, I overheard the breaking of some furniture, which sounded like wooden chairs. Apparently, my Nonno escaped into his bedroom

41

and locked his door, trying to avoid his very violent, hot-tempered wife. After several more minutes of screaming and yelling by the two of them, I heard a loud screaming noise that sounded so ghastly, so eerie, that it sounded as though it was coming from a horror film. Now being afraid, I sat downstairs frozen on the couch, unable to move. After several long minutes, I heard a loud gurgling noise, which sounded like it was coming from my Nonna.

The arguments and the loud noises had suddenly stopped, and it was now silent upstairs. The silence was so horribly scarry; I was deathly afraid to go upstairs. I didn't want to see what exactly had happened. There was a black, rotary telephone in the basement hanging on the wall, and I called my mother to come over immediately. I knew there was something wrong, and I sat downstairs alone for several long minutes.

I was afraid to go upstairs.

My mother had instructed me to stay downstairs until she had gotten there with the door closed. But after twenty minutes or so, I called out my Nonno and Nonna's name.

There was no answer.

I finally opened the door and creeped out of the basement in search of my grandparents. I went in every room looking for them to no avail. I finally walked upstairs to the bedroom where my Nonno Toto slept.

There was the most horrible sight that had shaken me to my core, every single day for the rest of my life.

Laying on the bed was the bloody sight of my Nonno Toto, his eyes and mouth open, wearing a white tee-shirt that was soaked in blood. It looked as though he had been stabbed in the chest several times, and there was blood gushing everywhere. The comforter of the bed was drenched in blood and was dripping onto the light beige carpeting.

I started screaming out of control, and I went looking for my Nonna Costanza in the other room, who was obviously in her room with the door closed. As the door was unlocked, I was crying uncontrollably, looking for her and calling her name. When I pushed the door open, I found my Nonna Costanza lying on the floor, her neck and her blouse was drenched in blood. She was still holding a huge knife in her hand, and she was lying face up in a vast pool of blood.

At that moment, I remember being so scared that I ran out of the house, screaming and crying down the sidewalk.

"My Nonno and Nonna have been killed!" I kept screaming and crying out loud.

The next-door neighbor, Albert Francisco, was watering his garden outside. He noticed me loudly crying uncontrollably, looking for someone to help my grandparents. I kept crying and yelling, telling the neighbor that my grandparents were now dead and full of blood. The kind neighbor, noticing that something was immediately wrong, brought me into his house with his wife next door and tried to calm me with a glass of milk and some chocolate chip cookies. He then immediately called the Chicago Police.

Several minutes later, the Chicago Police had arrived, and now all of the neighbors were gathering in front of the house. I later came to find out that in a fit of rage, my Nonna had stabbed my Nonno to death in his locked bedroom. She had a key made without his knowledge and entered his room, stabbing him repeatedly. The coroner's report stated that there were twenty-four stab wounds on his torso. Nonna Costanza then went into her own room and stabbed herself in the neck with the butcher knife.

It was a grizzly, horrible death scene that no seven-year-old boy should ever have to see or witness. When my mother and father finally arrived at my grandparents' house, my mother broke down and was inconsolable for several hours. I remember going over to my aunt and uncle's house with my two little brothers, staying there for a few days.

But my father, at the sight of losing his parents, was emotionless and didn't say a word. There always seemed to be some intense animosity between my father and his parents that I never understood. They had suffered as a family during World War Two, hiding and living in mountain caves, discovering dead soldiers' bodies in the fields, watching others activate and killed by planted land mines. At one point, my father watched my Nonno distract a soldier transporting a truck filled with dead soldiers while my Nonna stole the shoes off of their dead bodies.

My father was unusually stoic, and it always bothered me that he never displayed any emotion at their death. Instead of making my first communion on that Saturday morning in May, I was with my parents as they buried Nonno Toto and Nonna Costanza that Saturday afternoon at their funeral at St. Angela's Church. I never made my first communion along with the other boys and girls in my class. I never had a big first communion party like all of the other kids in my class.

The events of that horrible day remained embedded in my mind for the rest of my life. I can still feel the horror of finding my Nonno and Nonna stabbed to death in their separate bedrooms. I was traumatized to the point that whenever I would see a large kitchen knife, I would break into a cold

44

sweat and have sudden flashbacks of that horrific day in May 1967, two days before my First Communion.

"Quando arrivano i demoni, la morte segue sempre," I overheard one of my aunts tell my mother during my grandparent's funeral.

When the demons come, death always follows.

They say that a child's first encounter with death has a long-term effect on their psychological state of mind for the rest of their lives. Back then, there was no grief counseling or psychological therapy for children. There was no one to lean on in my family to discuss the losses and grief that I felt as a young boy, and my mother and father did nothing to console me. Perhaps they were embarrassed by the murder-suicide of my grandparents that they refused to acknowledge and talk about.

Looking back, I believe that their traumatic deaths had a long-term effect on all of us. The subject of death was a horrific experience for me that I was always fearful of. The demons in my future life played on the ghastly images of that terrible experience. My grandparents' death made my mother even more cold and stoic than she had been towards myself and my brothers during our childhood. She had married my father at a very young age and had us soon after that. She was a young wife and mother, and she regretted every minute of it. Her lack of love and understanding, her coldness toward us when she should have been more supportive and loving, had long-term effects on our attitudes towards ourselves and others.

With my paternal grandparents' sudden murder-suicide came a long series of tragic events that instinctively shaped my childhood. It was the beginning of a very long, dreadful march of abusive incidents and horrific experiences that no child should ever endure. I was a child of the sixties, and the harsh environment brought upon me at a very young age became the backdrop of the tragic incidents of my life.

As a young boy growing up in that turbulent decade, it wasn't unusual to turn on the television and hear about a president, a politician, or a civil rights leader being senselessly gunned down and assassinated for absolutely no reason. It was not unusual to watch the nightly news and see images of dying soldiers in Vietnam. It wasn't unrealistic to hear about the tragedies of people killed in city riots, backstreet murders, or gang-related homicides.

That horrible spring day of 1967 became a catalyst of several tragic, personal, and current events that shaped my morbid psyche for the rest of my life. The assassinations of both Martin Luther King Jr. in April 1968 and then the tragic death of Robert F. Kennedy two months later made me realize how fragile life truly was. Those heartbreaking, catastrophic events of watching national funerals on television and reading about beloved public figures' sudden death cast a melancholy, cynical attitude on my young childhood.

Fifteen months after my grandparents' tragic death, my uncle, who was only forty-one years old, was murdered. He was an arrogant, egotistical narcissist with movie star good looks who drove around town in a red and white 1959 Oldsmobile convertible and lived a double life. He pretended to be a happily married family man during the day while cheating and fooling around with several other women at his factory job at night. My uncle was hunted down and murdered on

Halloween night after working his night job at an auto factory, killed for having an illicit affair with a married woman.

My aunt and my three young cousins were forever traumatized, and they never got over his abrupt loss. His sudden death, along with the unexpected fatal heart attack of my aunt five years later, created a vacuum of grief and heartache that forever affected my extended family. My uncle's tragic, unnecessary murder was another example of how little control we all had of our young lives. His unexpected demise had again reinforced the demons of death that began to play out in my very young mind.

As a young boy, I became eerily fascinated with death. I began building caskets with Lego blocks and burying them in the sandbox in my backyard. I started reenacting suicides by tying a rope around my GI Joe action dolls and hanging them from trees in the backyard. I drew detailed illustrations of men being shot down and killed; their blood was colored vividly with red Crayola crayons. I began reading books about death and suicide, searching out death pictures at the public library and our school. It had gotten to the point where my school teacher became greatly concerned about my mental development and mentioned her concerns to my mother. I became entranced, yet haunted by sudden death, and how quickly a bullet from any gun or the pointed end of a butcher knife could suddenly and forever impact the lives of so many.

At a very young age, sudden, tragic death became the norm. At a very early age, death became a very realistic, dreaded enemy that everyone in my family especially feared. But no one more than my father. I understood very early that my paternal grandparents' tragic murder-suicide had a long-

47

term psychological effect on my father. His mean, abusive attitude towards his wife and children made him even more violent and cruel. Their tragic deaths opened the door to the sordid demons that came to dance in my mind freely.

During that Spring of 1967, there were no big parties in the garage.

No expensive gifts from relatives. No first communion envelopes.

CHAPTER SIX

Undrinkable Garbage - 1969

It was a beautiful Saturday afternoon in August as Robby Mazzara arrived at St. Angela Church for altar boy duty. His bicycle was making a squeaking noise, and the chain needed some oil as he pulled out the kickstand of his almost new, second-hand Schwinn ride, with the shiny chrome monkey bars and a white banana seat. Robby's mother had purchased the bicycle for him that previous Christmas. He locked the front wheel onto the bike rack and then entered the church sacristy from the side entrance door.

His friend, Marco Pezza, had already arrived early to serve Saturday afternoon mass that warm summer day. They had just met earlier that summer as the Pezza's moved into the house next door to the Mazzara's home on Cortland Avenue. The two of them got acquainted while meeting as altar boys at church, and when they both realized that they lived next door to one another, they got along famously.

Marco had brought along his transistor radio, and Robby could hear the new Beatles song "Hey Jude" playing loudly in the background. He was putting his black cassock on when Robby walked in the door.

"What's up, Robby?" as Marco shut off his radio.

"Hey, Marco. What's up with the gym shoes?" Robby asked his best friend right away.

They both knew Fr. Ghelfi's strict rules about the altar boy dress code and wearing gym shoes while serving mass was strictly forbidden. Fr. Ghelfi was the church pastor, and he ran a tight ship when it came to the rules and regulations regarding the altar boys and serving mass.

"I was at baseball practice, and I forgot to bring my other shoes," Marco explained.

"He's gonna send you home!" Robby said right away as he fumbled through the closet, looking for a black cassock that would fit him.

"He can't. He's not gonna find another altar boy ten minutes before mass. Besides, these are new gym shoes. And they're cool!" Marco answered.

Marco was wearing the new Converse, high-top basketball shoes that his mother had purchased for him the week before. He started preparing the water and wine cruets and went into the sacristy cupboard to get the red wine used for mass.

Robby noticed Marco grabbing a different bottle of wine, loosely corked in a dark, green wine bottle.

"Where did you get that bottle of wine? It looks different," Robby asked.

"It's my Nonno's. I told him we needed some wine for mass today, so he sent me over here with a bottle of his homemade wine. He figured Fr. Ghelfi would enjoy it," Marco casually answered, now knowing that he was breaking all of the pastor's rules that Saturday afternoon.

"Fr. Ghelfi won't even notice the difference," he sarcastically reasoned.

"Yeah, right!" Robby answered.

They both started laughing loudly and giggling at the thought of the priest saying mass using his grandfather's Italian, homemade wine. They both figured the pastor would enjoy the change in mass wine and might even ask Marco's grandfather for more.

The boys were both fully dressed and ready when Fr. Ghelfi arrived from the rectory, as the five o'clock Saturday mass was about to start in ten minutes. As he entered the church sacristy, his eyes were immediately fixated on Marco Pezza's shoes.

"Are those shoes appropriate for Holy Mass, Mr. Pezza?" the pastor asked.

"I'm sorry, Father, but I was at baseball practice today, and I forgot my black Sunday shoes," Marco apologized.

Fr. Ghelfi began putting on his holy vestments, including a purple chasuble, as people were starting to enter inside the church.

"You will need to remember this when you come to confession this week," he reprimanded. The two boys were in the fourth grade together at the grade school and more than familiar with Fr. Ghelfi's strict rules and regulations. Fr. Ghelfi was the parish pastor and ran St. Angela Parish with an iron fist. The deacon and the others had also arrived, and within several minutes, the mass was about to start. The entrance hymn started playing as the altar boys lined up with the others to begin Saturday afternoon mass.

St. Angela was a beautiful, old Catholic church in Elmwood Park, with high domed ceilings, gold-painted trim, and old-fashioned, stained glass windows. The white, Carrera marble altar looked majestic beneath the magnificently large, life-like crucifix suspended high above the wooden rafters. The old church was located a few blocks away from Harlem Avenue. Although most parishioners were Italian families, there were Irish Catholics, Polish and Latinos from the neighborhood who came to worship at the parish.

The church was the center of the Italian, Latino, and Polish communities back in the 1960s. Most of the neighborhood children went to St. Angela grade school to receive a "better" education. Back in those days, the neighborhood families dutifully trusted the nuns and the diocesan priests who ran and operated the local, community Catholic school. No questions were ever asked about how or why their children were being taught and, at times, severely disciplined. Many Italian and Polish families wished to stay in the local Catholic school's good graces, as there was a waiting list for the neighborhood children to be enrolled.

The nearby public grade school, located several blocks away, was beginning to become integrated. Many of the neighborhood parents resented the compulsory integration that the local school district was enforcing upon them at the time. Almost everyone in the neighborhood had 'racist' views regarding the public-school education of the Negro children with the neighborhood white kids. Nearly all of the parents didn't want their children going to school with them.

The Saturday mass continued uneventfully, as Fr. Ghelfi preached to his flock about faithfully following "God's Holy Commandments" and not be dissuaded by the 'modern, adulterous evils' that lurked rabidly within the community. Robby and Marco stood side-by-side next to the mass celebrant as he received bread and wine. The Saturday mass was more than halfway through when Fr. Ghelfi grasped the cruet filled with wine. He poured the wine into the gold chalice, looked up to the church rafters and the large crucifix hanging above, and gave thanks. Fr. Ghelfi then took a drink of the homemade wine from the gold chalice.

Robby and Marco looked at each other, both trying hard to keep from laughing, as Fr. Ghelfi had a cringing, distorted look on his face after gulping the red wine. Robby was biting his lip so hard to keep from laughing out loud; he could taste the blood in his mouth. The celebrating priest angrily looked over to the deviant altar boys, trying very hard to keep a straight face and look in another direction.

Fr. Ghelfi calmly finished blessing the bread and wine and gave communion to each of the worshippers, with Robby holding the gold platted paten. When the dispensing of communion was completed, the closing blessings were made, and the priest declared that the mass had ended. Fr. Ghelfi then darted a dirty look of revenge to both of his altar boys. As the closing hymn was played, Robby and Marco followed Fr. Ghelfi as they processioned out of the church and into the sacristy. The priest then stood outside and greeted all of the parishioners as Robby and Marco hurriedly disrobed their cassocks and tried to bolt out of the church's front door.

"We're in so much trouble!" Robby nervously said.

As the boys were trying to leave, Fr. Ghelfi grabbed them both by the arm and ordered them both back into the sacristy. When the church had emptied, Fr. Ghelfi angrily entered the back room, ready to do war with his two belligerent altar boys. He was foaming at the mouth.

"Which one of you two decided to switch the mass wine with that undrinkable garbage?" he demanded.

Both the boys stood there with their heads down, not willing to 'spill the beans.' Robby and Marco quickly became close friends that summer, and they were now loyal friends who had each other's backs. They had previously made a pact that summer, vowing to never 'rat' on each other, no matter what the consequence was.

"Would any of you two care to talk?" the pastor demanded.

Both boys stood there in the middle of the sacristy, in silence. Fr. Ghelfi then went into his cabinet drawer and pulled out a long, two-foot paddle with several drilled holes. Holding the paddle in his hand, he demanded an answer.

"If neither one of you talks, I promise that the punishment that you'll both receive will be far more painful together than the agony you'll receive alone," Ghelfi demanded. He was trying hard to coax an answer out of the boys. They both continued to stand there in silence.

"The mass is a very holy ritual, and you two boys have disrespected the Lord," he lectured. Both the boys stood in silence, staring at the floor for several long minutes.

Suddenly, Marco Pezza spoke up. "It was me, Father. It was me. I'm sorry. It was my grandfather's wine. I'm sorry," as Marco started crying profusely, confessing to the harmless prank.

More long minutes of silence as Fr. Nicholas Ghelfi stared at the two young boys, holding the paddle in his hand. Ghelfi was a smaller man, balding, and in his late thirties. He had an intimidating presence about him and wore his black cassock and dangling gold cross as if they were sacred vestments directly from Rome. He was the typical Catholic school disciplinarian who believed that children should be only seen and never heard.

He often wore his reading glasses on the tip of his noise, and he had this piercing look of anger that he made with his icy cold blue eyes, often instilling fear into any young boy or girl who had broken any one his many school rules. The total disrespect that the two young altar boys had demonstrated was far more insulting to the pastor than the actual innocent trick during the mass itself. It was an 'unholy' deed that the young altar boy participated in, and he needed to be severely punished.

Next to the church sacristy was a tiny office with a desk and a rotary telephone. Instead of physically punishing both of the boys with a paddle, he asked the boys to come into the small room.

"Okay, I would like you to call your parents and let them know that you both will be suspended from serving mass for the next two weeks. Robert, you will go first."

Robby Mazzara called his parents from the telephone and explained to his mother what he had done. Before he finished the phone call, Fr. Ghelfi asked him to pass the phone over to him.

"Hello, Mrs. Mazzara?"

"Yes, Fr. Ghelfi, I am so sorry for what my son has done with his friend. I promise you that it will not happen again," Mrs. Mazzara apologetically said to the pastor.

"Well, Mrs. Mazzara, I am a little annoyed about this incident. However, if your son wishes to do some penance for his mischievous actions, I would be willing to..."

"Oh, yes, Fr. Ghelfi. Whatever you think is appropriate. Robby is more than willing to do whatever penance you feel is suitable."

"Ok, Mrs. Mazzara. Please have Robert report to my rectory office after school this

Wednesday. He will be cutting the grass around the rectory and the church grounds. I will provide the sandwiches and the lemonade."

"Oh, thank you, Father. Thank you for being so forgiving," Mrs. Mazzara said to the pastor over the phone.

Then Fr. Ghelfi passed the telephone to Marco.

"Now Marco, I can assure you that your penance will not be so nice," as Marco was dialing the telephone.

Unfortunately, Papa Enzo answered the telephone. As Marco explained to his father what he had done, Fr. Ghelfi could hear the abusive screaming that Papa Enzo said in Italian over the phone to his son. Understanding the Italian language, he asked the young boy to pass the telephone over to him at that moment.

Then Fr. Ghelfi said to Papa Enzo in Italian,

"Mi scusi, Signor Pezza, ma non c'è bisogno di capire suo figlio. Stavo per suggerire come penitenza che è venuto in canonica dopo la scuola questo mercoledì e tagliare i cespugli intorno alla chiesa mentre il suo amico taglia l'erba. Fornirò la limonata e panini," he said to him, trying in vain to calm him down.

The pastor had nicely told him as penance that he would have Marco come to the rectory after school this Wednesday and trim the bushes around the church while his friend Robert cut the grass and that he would be willing to provide the lemonade and sandwiches.

Papa Enzo was silent on the telephone for several moments until he consented to the pastor's suggestion. Fr. Ghelfi then smiled and hung up the phone.

While still holding the paddle in his hand, the pastor admonished the two young boys.

"You're both fortunate that our landscaper quit last week, and the grass and bushes need to be badly trimmed," he smiled, still holding the paddle in his hand as though he was still about the spank the two of them. Robby and Marco both smiled at the pastor as they grabbed their personal belongings and began to proceed out of the sacristy.

As they were both leaving, Fr. Ghelfi made one last directive:

"Marco, did you say that your Nonno made that wine?"

"Yes, Father."

"Have your Nonno drop off a few bottles of his wine at the rectory. We can use some enjoyable 'homemade vino' for dinner," the pastor said to the boys with a smile.

Fr. Ghelfi had just admonished the boys several minutes earlier that the wine was 'undrinkable garbage.'

Robby and Marco then quickly walked back to their bicycles rode away to their houses several blocks away. They had both figured out that God was on their side on that Saturday afternoon when the pastor allowed the two of them to do landscaping instead of being severely punished. As Marco said goodbye to his friend, he threw his bike down on the neatly trimmed lawn in front of the house and ran up the stairs to the front entrance. As Robby was peddling his bicycle away to his house next door, he stopped and stood still. He was only less than a hundred feet away from the Pezza's household next door. He suddenly heard some thunderous noises coming from Pezza's front living room. The clamors were loud and apparent, as the front door was still open. They were loud, deafening sounds of Marco screaming and crying, reverberating across the neighborhood, as his father was severely beating up the young boy as soon as he had walked in the door.

They were thunderous screams of terror that Robby Mazzara would never forget.

CHAPTER SEVEN
Grade School Fight - 1970

The school bell had rung loudly as Sister Mary Fran let our fifth-grade class out for lunchtime. I quickly ran for my locker as the smell of hot tomato soup, and grilled cheese sandwiches filled the hallway. I grabbed my snacks and my lunch money and walked quickly to get in line. It was a warm October day when some of us could take our black ties off and stuff them in our pockets as we walked single file into the St. Angela School cafeteria.

By that time in my childhood, I was a very arrogant little punk and took my share of cootie shots and bruises from the tougher kids in class. I was smaller than most boys, but my temper tended to make up for my lack of size and common sense. Of course, having a hot temper didn't mean much in the fifth grade. It only reinforced that you were either crazy enough or stupid enough to get into a lot of ridiculous, very foolish fights. Back in the fifth grade, every little boy had something to prove; who was tougher, who was cooler, and of course, who had the most comic books and the best baseball cards.

I was always aware enough of my surroundings to know when I was or wasn't being threatened, and getting into the school lunch line was one of those times. The older kids from the sixth, seventh and eighth grades got into the school cafeteria later than we did, so we had to hurry in line and get first dibs on the chocolate milk before the older kids showed up. On this day, my routine wasn't any different. Hurry up and get your hot lunch and chocolate milk before the older kids showed up and took "cuts" in line ahead of you.

I was four kids away from the doorway and grabbing my tray when Jimmy Jakubowski pushed his way in front of me. Jimmy was a big seventh-grader who was a good head and shoulders taller than I was and had no problem pushing his size around.

"Cuts, Mazzara!" he exclaimed. All I could see was a massive white, smelly shirt push its way in front of me.

"Hey!" I shouted out. I didn't have a chance to say anything else before he turned around and stared down at me. Damn, he was ugly. His brown hair was all messy, his reddish-colored skin was covered with oily, white head pimples, and tiny blemish scars protruded from his neck. His black tie was half off of his shirt, and he looked as though he were ready to remove it from his neck and tie it tightly around mine.

"You got a problem, Mazzara?" The wind of his breath smelled so bad that it took all of my strength to keep from coughing in his face. The shadows of his teeth were discolored and yellow as if they hadn't seen a toothbrush in months. His beady green eyes were staring down at me, and he seemed to be looking for an excuse to pound me, hard enough to taste the green linoleum floor.

I was too intimidated at that moment to say anything. He just stared down at me, then snickered something to the effect of '*what a little shithead*' and turned around to grab his tray, his hot grilled cheese sandwich, his tomato soup, and of course.... the very last carton of chocolate milk.

I was pissed. By the time I was holding my tray with my food, my hands were shaking. My silverware was clattering as I tried to calmly find a place to sit and eat my lunch.

There was a long table near the window at the cafeteria's corner, where most of my friends and I sat down to eat and trade our baseball cards. I was a little excited to show off the Chicago Cubs Ron Santo baseball card I had just gotten last night at Mike's Deli. Billy Kozar was waiting for me with his lunch at the end of the table.

"Hey Robby...what's up?" he said as I placed my tray down.

"Jakubowski is an asshole," I exclaimed, looking around to make sure that Sister Jean, the lunchroom monitor, didn't hear me swear.

"You didn't get any chocolate milk?" he asked.

"No...that jerk cut ahead of me and grabbed the last one."

"They just put out another crate of chocolate milk, and there is still some left now," Billy said.

"Really?" I looked behind me and noticed the other kids smiling with chocolate milk cartons on their trays.

"I'm going back to get some."

I ran back into the lunch line, grabbed a chocolate milk, and walked back quickly to my place at the cafeteria table. As I was about to sit, I felt myself fall rapidly to the floor.

The chair had been pulled out from under me.

As I looked up from the ground, that ugly, gross, disgusting Jakubowski was staring down at me, laughing as I was struggling to get up and catch my balance. He grabbed my white shirt, crinkling the buttons between his fingers as he pulled me off balance.

"Who are you calling an asshole, Mazzara?" He was starting to pull me closer to that polluted, smelly wind that came from his mouth. Suddenly, the crack of a ruler crossed the back of Jakubowski's head. It was Sister Jean, standing right behind him.

"Put him down, young man." She yelled out as he released me back up against the wall.

"Back to your seat and finish your lunch!"

His beady green eyes were glaring at me as he began to slowly turn away, towards his table, to his lunch and his ugly, rude seventh-grade friends. I finished my lunch in silence, too embarrassed and

61

too scared at the moment to look up at my friend, Billy.

"Are you going to take that shit from that ugly bastard?" Billy finally said.

I looked at him intently. Was he serious? Did he think I could stand up that ugly, disgusting piece of dogshit?

"You can take him, Robby! Don't let him make you look like a chicken shit."

Billy was right. What kind of tough fifth-grader was I if I let this ugly seventh-grade bastard push me around? My face starting turning red, and my blood started to boil as I replayed the chair and lunchroom line incidents in my head, over and over again.

I picked up my tray, threw away the garbage, and walked quickly over to Jakubowski's table.

"Hey, asshole!" I exclaimed after noticing Sister Jean was on the other side of the lunchroom.

The green-eyed monster suddenly noticed me as he gazed up from his dog dish with complete and total anger.

"Four o'clock...after school; at the football field."

I was challenging Godzilla to a fight.

He slowly stood up. He was ready to cock his fist back and pound me to the floor, right then and there. But by some miracle, he controlled this violent urge.

"I can't wait to kick the living shit out of you, Mazzara!"

He said it so loudly, even Sister Jean turned to hear him from the other side of the room.

Great.

I now had a date at the football field with the toughest, meanest bastard at St. Angela's School.

I was going to get destroyed.

I was sitting that whole afternoon impatiently in class, nervously watching the red second hand of the classroom clock, then the big black hand, go around and around in circles…1:30…2:00…2:30…3:00. I must have looked at that clock a thousand times. My best friend, Petey Rodriguez, sat behind me in class, and I could feel his eyes drilling holes into the back of my head.

He finally broke his silence while Sister Mary Fran was facing the chalkboard.

"Now I KNOW you're fucking stupid!" he whispered from behind. I turned around and looked at him, pretending not to know what he was talking about.

"Are you nuts? Are you whacked? A fight on the football field with Jakubowski? Are you ass-bent, fucking crazy?"

"Stop swearing before you get us busted again," I quickly said, hoping Sister Mary Fran didn't hear our conversation.

She was looking for an excuse to prosecute the both of us again with another after-school detention.

Petey's dad was now driving as a Teamsters truck driver, and he learned all the latest and greatest swear words from his father. His gutter-style street language could be performed like Shakespeare, but I didn't have the courage or the nerve to recite the descriptive, colorful poetry that came out of Petey Rodriguez's mouth.

"He pulled the chair out from under me. Even Billy says he's got it coming."

"Oh! I see! And you're going to be the one to give it to him?"

"Just shut up, alright?" I tried to quiet him down. I was nervous enough about my four o'clock date with destiny without Petey reminding me about what an awful mistake I had made at lunchtime.

I was starting to play it out in my mind. If I just walked home quickly after school, maybe no one will notice. Perhaps everyone will soon forget my stupid, foolish fight date at the football field. I needed an excuse not to show up. What would be a good one? I had to run home and babysit my little brothers? I had to rush home and clean out the garage? I was playing all the excuses in my head, over and over and over again.

Finally, Petey hands me a blank sheet of paper and a sharpened No. 2 pencil from behind.

"What's this for?" I innocently asked.

"Write up your 'Last Will and Testament.' I get your baseball cards. Marco wants your comic books. Billy can have your orange Schwinn bike with the monkey bars and the white banana seat." I looked at him and knew he was serious.

"Don't worry. I'll make sure your Mom gets it."

By then, the three-thirty school bells started to ring. I felt the back of my neck turn red, and my white, wrinkled shirt was beginning to absorb all the perspiration. I grabbed my books and started to walk out quickly towards the classroom door. I was thinking that, maybe, I had way too much homework to be thinking about all of this after-school foolishness. But Petey, Billy, Marco Pezza, and another friend, Johnny Orozco, were standing by the doorway, making sure that I didn't walk too far away.

Marco Pezza and his family had just moved into the house next door to ours on Cortland Avenue, and although he was in another class, he hung out with us during recess and after school.

"Robby," cried out Marco.

"The football field is that way," pointing to the opposite doorway on the other side of the school.

I slowly turned around and walked back towards my friends, wondering which one of them I should say 'good-bye' to first.

"Robby, what are you nervous about?" Billy sarcastically said.

"This is all your fault, you rat! You know damned well I can't take this guy. What was I thinking listening to you?"

"He only said it because he wants your baseball cards!" chimed in Petey.

"But I called them first."

What a swell bunch of friends I have, I thought to myself. These guys were all fighting over my stuff, and I wasn't even dead yet.

"How am I going to take this guy?" I asked my so-called pallies, thinking I was going to get an intelligent answer.

"Just kick him in the balls and run like hell!" said Petey, with that half-cocked smile on his face.

I could tell he was salivating over my baseball cards, the heartless bastard that he was. They were all starting to giggle and smirk at Petey's comment when our friend Johnny looked as though he had a divine intervention. We all had a lot of those in Catholic school.

Johnny Orozco lived a few blocks away from us, and we didn't always play together like the other boys. He was the more intelligent, quieter one of my friends. He was looking at me very intently from behind his dark, thick, horn-rimmed glasses.

He was the class nerd, but we kept him around because he got us through a lot of our homework papers. Johnny would also help us cheat on the classroom tests, and he let us look at his answers when Sister Mary Fran wasn't looking.

He finally blurted out something that I will never forget for as long as I live.

"Give him the Suzie-Q," he said quite directly as if we all knew what he was talking about.

"What? A Suzie-Q? What the hell is that?" asked Marco, knowing that his answer was probably going to be a waste of our precious time.

"I've been doing this book report on Rocky Marciano. He was the only heavyweight boxer to ever go undefeated. He was always a little smaller than most of his opponents, but he could always duck inside and then give them the most vicious, most powerful right hook there ever was. He called it the Suzie-Q. His right-hand punches were awesome."

"And your point is?" I asked.

"Stay under his reach, Mazzara." Johnny strategically said.

"Stay with him from the inside, then throw him the Suzie-Q with everything you got."

This was all coming from the class nerd, who just learned about boxing from a Rocky Marciano book report. But the tone of his voice was so out of the ordinary, so wrapped in confidence; I couldn't tell if this was really coming from him or Angelo Dundee.

I was starting to find some slight quiver of confidence with Johnny Orozco's suggestion when Billy went into his pocket and pulled out a small, metal object.

"Here, Robby...this is what I was trying to tell you about."

The small metal object was gold brass in color, with four attached rings for each finger, welded to a three-inch bar.

"What is this?" I asked, as my ignorance was starting to become embarrassing.

"They're brass knuckles, you moron. Keep these in your pocket, and don't let anyone know you have them, especially Jakubowski. As soon as he's not looking, put them on and hit him as hard you can. If you nail him right, you'll knock him out!"

The three of us looked at Billy in silence as if we had all witnessed an unexplained miracle.

This was a gift from heaven, sent by the Patron Saint of After-School Fights.

"That's not fair fighting," exclaimed Johnny, who was starting to show his boxing ignorance.

"Fighting is never fair," Billy calmly said.

"Mazzara is a fifth-grader going against a seventh-grader twice his size. Does that sound fair to you?"

"Take the brass knuckles with you, Robby. It will even the score. Just don't get caught, or you'll be doing detentions until you're thirty!" I grabbed the brass knuckles from Billy, and I hid them away.

I suddenly felt the weight of a hundred pounds transfer from my small shoulders into my right hip, pants pocket. The fear of this fight was starting to subside, as I felt the faith and confidence of my friends pumping me up, keeping me focused on this historical date with destiny,

If I could pull this off, I thought to myself, I was going to be the most famous kid to ever come out of St. Angela's School. This fight would be more famous than Frazier and Ali, Tunney and Dempsey, Baer and Braddock. This was going to be the biggest fight of the century.

The five of us began to proudly walk, maybe, a little too confidently, towards the back door of the school... in the direction of the St. Angela football field.

CHAPTER EIGHT
The Suzie-Q

I could feel the bright afternoon sunlight blind my eyes as I walked toward the football field with my friends. I was trying to walk as closely as I could to Billy, hoping that some of his courage and confidence would rub off on my blue windbreaker jacket and brass knuckles. My new friend, Marco Pezza, who was in another class, also came to join us after school.

Petey, Marco, Johnny, and Billy were all making small talk together, and neither of us was paying any attention to the noise coming from the football field. As we walked alongside the gated pathway towards the field, the crowd's sounds and the noise started to get louder and louder, as if the commotion of an open-air carnival was waiting ahead.

As we opened the gated fence entrance door into the football field, I could not believe my eyes. Petey and Billy started to gasp as I heard Marco exclaim very slowly:

"Oh......My......God."

The football stands were packed with Saint Angela students, the bleachers filled with kids starting from the first row all the way up to the top. They were all noisily awaiting my arrival, as some of them began to clap their hands and scream out my name as my friends and I strolled onto the field, directly across to the fifty-yard line.

"Maz-zar-a, Maz-zar-a, Maz-zar-a!"

The chants from the cheering crowds were all coming from boys and girls in the bleachers that I had never seen before, yelling out my name as if they were witnessing the arrival of a rock star.

"I don't believe this!" exclaimed Marco. "You've got all of Elmwood Park cheering you on, Robby!"

A cold chill started to overcome my body as the sweat began to soak the back of my white shirt.

"You can't let them down, Mazzara. Everyone is here rooting for you." Billy said.

The claps, the cheering, and the yelling from everyone in the stands made it almost impossible to hear what my friends were saying next to me. We stood there as lone figures on the fifty-yard line, standing proudly in the middle of the football field. Suddenly, jeers and boos starting coming from both sides of the stands as my opponent began to appear on the football field.

Jimmy Jakubowski and his crew of hoodlums were walking into the football field as if they were the reigning heavyweight champs, beaming proudly at the jeers and obscene chants coming from the crowd. As hisses and boos continued to get louder and louder, Jakubowski ignored the bad vibes coming from the crowded bleachers. At one point, he even flipped his middle finger and waved it around as if it were an American flag.

As they all approached the fifty-yard line, Tommy Shields, who was a popular eighth-grader, pushed himself into the middle of both me and Jakubowski. He started smiling and thrust his arms out as if to pretend he was a Las Vegas fight referee.

"Okay now, boys!" he started saying, as I could see Jakubowski's beady, green Godzilla eyes fixated on my face.

"I want a clean, fair fight. No kicking, no biting, no hitting below the belt. I'm going to call you both into your corners, and you'll both come out fighting."

Marco started to laugh out loud as he heard Tommy's instructions, but I began to panic and went into shock.

How in the hell did a minor lunchroom incident turn into a full-blown, scorecard, light-heavyweight championship boxing match? How did we end up on the school football field, with two hundred plus spectators lining the bleachers and football stands, chanting and screaming for the taste of blood?

"Any questions?" asked Tommy, as he looked directly at me.

My eyes started to well up with tears, and it took every ounce of my emotional strength to keep from bawling my eyes out. At that moment, I had never experienced fear the way I was feeling it at that instance. I felt like crying. I felt like screaming. I felt like throwing up. I wanted so badly to just throw my jacket over my head and run away from that football field as fast as I could. Billy must have been noticing my reaction and was relating to the actual fear which was starting to overcome me. He put his arm around my shoulder and started to walk me back about ten yards away from the middle of the field.

"We're ready to do this!" Petey said in his cocky tone of voice. But Billy ignored the other guys as he slowly walked me away from where he could talk to me alone.

"You know, Robby...you don't have to go through with this."

"And what am I supposed to do? Run with my tail between my legs? I will be the biggest coward this school has ever seen." I exclaimed.

"Where did all these people come from? I'm going to get my ass kicked in front of the whole damned school!" I started getting emotional.

"I'm scared, Billy. I'm scared! He's going to fucking kill me! I'm going to die!"

My eyes were filling with tears, and they began dripping down my cheeks uncontrollably. All of the fear and the agony of what was about to happen come out of my mouth in a voiceless gasp of air.

"Robby!" screamed out Billy. "Look at me!"

70

I tried to control myself as the urge to bellow out my fears and scream for God's mercy momentarily subsided.

"Nobody is going to die! Do you hear me?" Billy loudly said.

"Nobody is going to die! He's not going to destroy you. Put your arms over your head when he starts punching. Crouch down, let him tire himself out." "He's going to get tired of wailing on you. Just take his punches across your body!"

Billy started to sound like an actual boxing coach.

"When he's not looking, put those brass knuckles on, and then keep your eyes on me. When I tell you, you hit him as hard as you can. Got it?"

I started to gasp for air as my whimpering cries for God's intervention began to subside.

"I'm not going to let you get hurt. We'll jump in and stop it if we have to."

I felt the roll of steel in my pants pocket as I looked over to the other side of the fifty-yard line. Jakubowski was already high-fiving his hoodlum friends as if the fight were already over, glancing and laughing at me in between his victorious gestures. They mocked me as if they had already beaten me up and defeated me before the fight even started.

High-fives? Victorious chants? Already? Are you kidding me?

Something inside of me ignited. My stomach started to burn with anger as my teeth began to gnaw and grind with rage. I began to realize that this worthless piece of dogshit was going to do his very best to destroy me, to embarrass me, to emotionally cripple me in front of the whole damn school. I could hear my father's voice in my head.

"Never let another man knock you down." he used to tell me.

"And when he does, you get up...again and again, and again."

71

At that second, my anger, grade school stupidity, and raw emotion combined together as I summed up the courage to walk up to that fifty-yard line.

"If anything, Jakubowski, you're going to get very tired of hitting me!" I said to myself.

Tommy Shields, the referee, put both of our hands together in fist touch.

"Come out fighting, boys."

Petey started chanting out the "ding, ding, ding" noise.

How annoying, I thought to myself. I needed to remind myself to hit Petey, my so-called friend when this fight was over.

At that second, a sudden burst of pain came across the top of my head. I was totally unprepared for the first volley of punches Jakubowski started to deliver. He must have hit me directly in my face three or four times before I could put my arms over my head. I could immediately taste the blood dripping from my nose as the pain from the thrust of his punches began to expand from my head and arms and directly onto my shoulders. I tried to crouch down and took two or three steps back to try to get up to my fighting stance.

As I looked up, Jakubowski was glaring at me with his fists cocked, looking as though he wanted to play with me for a while before going in for the kill. He took another wide swing at my head, which I could duck away from, but then caught me with his left hook. I managed to stay on my feet as another volley of three or four punches continued to land on my shoulders and my arms.

I stepped back again, but this time I lunged at him with my uncoordinated right hook.

I missed him.

"Come on, Robby! Give him the Suzie-Q!" Marco Pezza kept yelling.

The rest of the guys that were standing around starting laughing, ridiculing me and my new nickname.

"Yeah, Susie! Way to fight like a girl." I heard one of Godzilla's friends say as I was trying to collect my balance.

Jakubowski started to laugh as he hit me across the side of my face. I could feel the stinging pain travel across my skull as he hit me on the other side of my face two or three more times. I lost my balance and fell to the ground. Tommy came over to break away from Jakubowski and began counting to ten. I looked over at Billy as he started nodding his head, which I figured was the signal to pull out my secret weapon. I stayed on my knees and discretely put my right hand into my pocket, grasping the metal brass knuckles I hoped would save me that afternoon. Tommy was still counting, and maybe he was up to eight or nine when I finally got up from the ground.

Jakubowski came at me again, and I crotched myself into a ball as he kept hitting my shoulders and the top of my skull, over and over and over. The whole time, I kept glancing at Billy, who was standing twenty feet away with Petey, Marco, and Johnny, his arms crossed. He was motionless as the punches and hits from the monster's clinched fists were starting to feel like concrete boulders being thrown against my body.

I started to say the "Our Father" prayer very slowly to myself, trying to keep my mind away from the pain grueling me further and further into the ground.

I kept gripping the brass knuckles in my right hand, waiting for the right moment.

I suddenly heard Billy yell out my name as I looked towards his direction:

"Now, Robby, NOW!"

At that second, Jakubowski was within arms-length of my right-hand swing. I lunged forward with my right hook, tightly gripping the brass knuckles in my clenched fist as I hit him squarely across the side of his mouth. I could feel his mouth crack open, and blood was spewing out of his face as his jaw began to dislodge from the rest of his green-eyed, ugly Godzilla head. It was the perfect right hook.

The perfect "Suzie-Q."

Jakubowski, as if to lose his balance, as if in slow motion, fell backward, hitting the ground headfirst. Billy quickly ran up to me and grabbed the brass knuckles from my clenched fist before Tommy, the referee, would notice. Everyone in the crowd and on the sidelines was fixated on Jakubowski, wondering what had happened and how the green-eyed monster ended up on his back. There seemed to be a dead silence of almost ten seconds or more before everyone realized the outcome. He was out cold.

I had knocked out Jimmy Jakubowski.

The crowds from the stands started cheering and rushing onto the fifty-yard line as if everyone had witnessed a miracle. The noise and the chants became deafening as Billy, Petey, Marco, and Johnny tried to pull me away from the crowd.

"We need to get out of here before they figure out what happened," said Billy, as he grabbed my arm pulled me towards his direction.

At that instance, the noise of police sirens started to ring out loudly along the back of the St. Angela football field, as everyone in the bleachers and football stands started to scatter. My friends and I started walking quickly towards the entrance gate, trying to blend in with the rest of the crowd. Two policemen were waiting alongside the entrance way and stopped the four of us as we were trying to escape all of the commotion.

"Where are you boys going?" said one of the officers.

At that moment, I could taste the blood dripping profusely from my nose and into my mouth as I was trying to look like an innocent bystander.

"You look like you've been in quite a fight there, young man."

Before I could even respond, I heard one of the officers from the middle of the football field call for an ambulance as another policeman ran towards the fifty-yard line where Jakubowski was lying flat on his back. Several of the kids were standing around Jakubowski as one of the officers started kneeling next to the green-eyed monster, assessing his wounds.

"Is he dead?" I heard one of the spectators ask.

"No." said the officer.

"He's just pretty battered up."

At that moment, Jakubowski started groaning and moving his arms, cradling his jaw as he was regaining his consciousness. By then, several squad cars and an ambulance began arriving at the football field. A crowd of people, including Fr. Filippon, the new school principal, began ascending the grounds, trying to assess what had happened that afternoon.

Fr. Filippon was an older, slightly balding man who wore his collar and draped cassock as if it were a sacred Vatican vestment. He was not very tall, but he seemed to carry an intimating aura of authority that no one ever questioned. Fr. Filippon was one of those disciplinarians who only needed to clear his throat and stare at you with his callous blue eyes, gazing from behind his reading spectacles perched at the bottom of his nose. His silent but stern demeanor was infamous and managed to bring many Elmwood Park hoodlums down to their knees over the years. Several paramedics arrived and started tending to Godzilla's war wounds, while another came over towards me.

"Let me take a look at you, kid." as he sat me down on one of the football bleachers and applied gauze to my bleeding mouth and nose.

"You must be quite a fighter. That kid lying down on the ground is twice your size." commented the paramedic.

I didn't say a word as Fr. Filippon slowly walked over towards my direction after talking to one of the police officers.

"Mr. Mazzara...." he started to speak slowly.

I stared up at Fr. Filippon, trying to look more like a victim than a gladiator.

"We will need to get you into my office so that we can call your parents and discuss your suspension."

I tried to plead the "Honest Father, none of this was my fault." speech, but I could tell he didn't believe a word of it. I knew even then that it was a mortal sin to lie to a priest, and especially, Fr. Filippon.

"What I would like to know, Mr. Mazzara, is how you managed to knock out Jimmy Jakubowski with one punch?"

He had obviously obtained some blow-by-blow information from the crowd of kids gathered around the makeshift boxing ring on the fifty-yard line.

I shrugged my shoulders and tried to look stupid. Fr. Filippon gazed at me silently for what seemed to be the longest ten seconds of my life.

"Divine intervention, Mr. Mazzara?"

Another moment of silence, as I tried to keep myself from smiling at his question.

"Maybe St. Michael the Archangel was looking out for you today."

St. Michael? Was he the Patron Saint of After-School Fights? I didn't want to ask.

He started to gaze at me with his famous, intimidating stare silently. After another minute of silence, he slowly spoke:

"Perhaps, Mr. Mazzara, the great sword of St. Michael was firmly clenched in your fist as you landed that incredible right hook into Jimmy Jakubowski, wouldn't you agree?"

Oh shit. He knows about the brass knuckles. Now I'm fucked. But I wasn't going to admit to anything.

"Would you please care to tell me how you managed to knock him out?"

I thought for a moment and then gave him one of my classic answers.

"I said an 'Our Father' before I hit him."

The Principal studied my response and then started laughing out loud.

"The Lord definitely works in mysterious ways." as he shook his head.

I could tell Filippon wasn't buying any of this. I then gathered my jacket and held the gauze up against my nose to stop the bleeding. I slowly got up from the bleachers and dutifully escorted Fr. Filippon towards his office.

As I was entering the building, Billy, Marco, Petey, and Johnny were already standing next to the entrance doors waiting for me. Billy Kozar gave me one of his confident smiles, letting me know that he was proud of how I had handled myself and fought my battles that day. Marco Pezza looked scared, and Petey Rodriguez was disappointed. It was apparent that he would have to wait for another opportunity to snatch away my baseball cards.

Johnny Orozco just looked at me proudly and made a clenched fist with his right hand.

"Suzie-Q.," he said softly.

I looked back at him and smiled, making sure the Principal wasn't looking.

"Suzie-Q," I whispered back.

Rocky Marciano would have been proud.

CHAPTER NINE
Marco's Childhood - 1971

Marco Pezza lived next door to the Mazzara's on Cortland Avenue in Elmwood Park. He was somewhat of a shy sixth-grader at St. Angela's, and he wasn't very outgoing until he felt comfortable, and it took him a long time to outgrow this awkward stage in his childhood. He was the oldest of three children, with a younger brother and sister in the third and first grades that he often looked after at home.

Besides playing sports with his friends, his mother, Cira, signed him up for piano lessons a few years earlier, and he spent a half-hour every day after school practicing, playing on their old, upright piano in their living room. His usual routine was to rush home after school at three o'clock and get his schoolwork done. He would then spend a half-hour or so banging on the piano until one of his friends would come knocking on the door.

"Marco, Marco," one of the boys would often call out in a sing-song tone of voice instead of ringing the doorbell. No kids were allowed to ring the doorbell when calling out one of their friends to come out and play in those days. Another reason also was that some of us were too little to even reach the doorbell. One of those friends was usually either Robby or Petey, as Billy lived down the street seldom came over to get them. He usually waited for the three other boys to show up at his house before playing baseball, street hockey, or football down the street. Johnny wouldn't come out and play as often as the others, as he was either locked up in his room doing homework or reading a book.

When the four or five boys got together to play, they owned the neighborhood. Cortland

Avenue was usually the homecourt for their baseball, football, or hockey games that usually went on until dark. The other boys in the neighborhood would be invited to play as well, and it was not unusual to see nine or ten little boys throwing a football or baseball in the middle of the street. Sometimes, the smaller children and their mothers would come over act as spectators once in a while. Some of the parents even acted as referees in watching their intense, pick-up street games. They would usually continue to play for several hours until the streetlights either came on, or one of their mothers would come outside in the middle of the street and call them home for dinner.

During a couple of those intensely cold Chicago winters, Billy, Marco, Robby, Petey, and some other boys constructed a backyard hockey rink, using water from the backyard hose and a few long two-by-fours laying around. That small pond of ice became the local neighborhood hockey rink, with as many as thirty or more children playing hockey or learning how to 'break their necks' on single-blade hockey skates.

Those innocent, outdoor games that those neighborhood boys would play during their years growing up were the mainstay of most neighborhoods in those days, occurring either on the streets, the nearby playgrounds or in their backyards. The children playing together did an excellent job of hiding the domestic strife that was going on in many of those little kid's homes. The children of those days spent very little time indoors unless they were forced to. Back then, almost every little boy's childhood was spent outside playing with the neighborhood kids.

Playing outside was a form of escape for every little boy who had domestic, abusive issues at home with their families, and Marco Pezza's house was no different.

His father, Vincenzo Pezza, had immigrated to the United States from Sicily after the war, coming from an impoverished family. He worked as a laborer for many years before becoming a heavy equipment operator for a Chicago-based construction company. 'Papa Enzo,' as the other boys referred to, was a psychologically unbalanced, miserable man.

He had a violent temper and usually unleashed his anger and rage towards his wife and children. His mother, Cira, was also Sicilian and had married her husband when she was only eighteen years old. They had three children immediately together and stayed at home while her husband worked to support the family.

Vincenzo Pezza was considered a 'neighborhood monster' by the other children and their parents in the neighborhood, and everyone steered clear away from him. Most of the neighborhood boys called him a 'fucking prick' behind his back, including his son.

On many occasions, he had threatened several boys for trampling across his tomato garden while playing ball in the neighborhood. He had gone ballistic on a few neighbors for parking in front of his house after clearing off a parking space for his pickup truck after a snowstorm. He kept his front lawn immaculate during the spring and summer months and would often yell at anyone naïve enough to walk their dogs across his slovenly tailored grass.

To say that Papa Enzo was abusive, offensive, and cruel were understatements. He cracked around his wife and kids with his belt buckle regularly. His wife Cira, being very shy and fearful, didn't know a whole lot of English. She was very old school, having been born and raised in Sicily.

Cira Calzante Pezza never called the Elmwood Park police whenever she was beaten up for not having dinner ready on the table on time. With Papa Enzo being extremely jealous, he would often beat her whenever another man even looked at her and often did so in front of their children.

It had also been revealed many years later that Papa Enzo habitually molested his children at a very young age. The three of them grew up believing that it was natural for their fathers to undress and fondle them when they were barely in grade school. Their mother, Cira, would look the other way, deathly afraid of the intense beating she would receive if she ever spoke up and said anything to her abusive, vicious husband.

With all of the beatings and household abuse that Marco's mother experienced, she became manic-depressive. Her dark, deep depression started after they were married and continued to worsen as the years went on. Her sad, melancholy moods greatly affected her abilities to keep up with the Pezza household, for which her demonic husband took no understanding or remorse.

Papa Enzo expected his house to be neat and immaculately clean, his dinner promptly ready and on the table, and his clothes clean and pressed. He demanded his children to eat in silence during dinner, as he was a deep believer of his kids 'being only seen and not heard'.

After dinner, little Marco, along with his brother Anthony and his sister Rosaria, if they couldn't go outside to play, went to hide in their bedrooms afterward. Since Marco's bedroom window on the second floor was right across Robby's bedroom, they would often exchange notes in the form of paper airplanes that they would fly across each other's windows. One time, one of those paper airplanes missed their target and fell onto the sidewalk, falling right in front of Papa Enzo. Realizing what his son was doing upstairs, he went up and beat little Marco incessantly, putting deep welts and bruise marks on his legs and across his back.

One afternoon, in the Spring of 1970, little Marco had walked home from school, arriving at the usual time of 3:15 pm. He entered his house through the side kitchen door, which was always unlocked. As Marco took off his jacket, he noticed his mother slumped on the kitchen table. At first, he thought that she was sleeping, with her head buried in her arms. He called her name and tried to shake her awake several times. But her body was cold and stiff, and she wasn't moving. It took several minutes for little Marco to realize what had happened.

He ran next door to Robby's house, frantically banging on the front door until little Robby answered.

"Something is wrong with my Mom. Call an ambulance!" little Marco exclaimed to his friend as he let Marco in through the front door and grabbed the telephone.

Within five minutes, several Elmwood Park patrol cars, along with a firetruck and an ambulance, arrived in front of the Pezza home on Cortland Avenue. Robby's mom kept Marco going back over to the house, as his father was contacted and eventually arrived home. By that time, Marco's little brother and sister had arrived home from school shortly after, and they all stayed at Robby's house while the paramedics tried in vain to revive their mother. She still had a very faint heartbeat at the time, and she was quickly loaded into the ambulance and taken to the hospital.

Marco's mother had overdosed on some sleeping pills after sending her children off to school that morning. There was an empty bottle of sleeping pills, stored nicely in the medicine cabinet, deposited back in place on its glass shelve where it belonged.

Marco's father, Enzo, was in shock initially and couldn't tell his children what had happened to their mother. It was left to Robby's mother to explain to them later on that night that their mother, Cira, had been taken to the hospital and wasn't going to be coming back home.

She had died at the hospital that evening, unable to be resuscitated from a cocktail of two dozen Ambien sleeping pills, along with a large pitcher of red Kool-Aid to help her swallow them down. Cira Calzante Pezza was a victim of suicide, capitulated by the physical abuse that she had been consistently experiencing at home.

Marco's mother was manic depressive, untreated and unattended to let the demons of her unhappy marriage destroy her to the point of self-destruction. She was abused to the point of no return, and it seemed as though the neighborhood monster, Vincenzo Pezza, was unrepentant after her death.

He refused to believe that he had caused or was responsible for her intensely miserable and depressive state of mind. He openly cursed her in front of his children for leaving him alone to take care of them with no help from anyone. He eventually sent for his sister living in Italy to come over and live with them for several years until the kids were old enough to take care of themselves.

Eventually, Marco, his sister, Rosaria, and his little brother, Anthony, figured one man instigated all of the horrific tragedies that occurred for many years in their household. With all of the tormented physical, emotional, and sexual molestation they had all experienced as young children, they rightfully placed the blame of their mother's death squarely where it belonged: On the shoulders of their abusive father.

Marco enlisted in the Army after high school and then enrolled in the police academy, eventually becoming a detective for the Chicago Police Department. His sister became a hairdresser, while his younger brother joined the operator's union as a heavy equipment operator. They all eventually isolated their father in their later years, pushing him as far away as possible from their lives. They all refused to talk or acknowledge him as he retired and lived alone in his small, red-bricked bungalow on Cortland Avenue.

The authorities never caught up with Vincenzo Pezza with all of the terrible abuses he inflicted on his late wife and children. He was never charged with any crimes. But the physical battery, molestation, and abuse accusations became well known within the village in later years, as his three children continued to testify to anyone in Elmwood Park who would listen. By the time the Pezza children had become adults, they venomously hated their father with an intense passion.

Marco's youngest brother, Anthony, became an intense alcoholic, just like him. He was killed in 1996 when the car he was driving with two others rear-ended another vehicle in a drunk driving accident on the Kennedy Expressway. His alcohol level was three times the legal limit.

His sister Rosaria, who was married and divorced twice, was hospitalized several times for nervous breakdowns and several suicide attempts. She tried to bring up past childhood abuse charges against her father years later by suing him in court, but the civil lawsuit was eventually dropped for some unknown reason.

And of course, after becoming a Chicago P.D. detective, Marco, after years of hard drinking and drug use, eventually hit rock bottom. Without a doubt, one can safely say that Marco Pezza was a mistreated victim of his abusive father.

But Papa Enzo never felt responsible, living the rest of his life unscathed. He never admitted to anything, calling his children ungrateful liars. He was never repentant. He continued to play cards with his few friends at the social club on Diversey Avenue when he wasn't playing bocce at the club. He never felt any remorse or guilt for how he had raised his children and the sadistic manner in which he treated his family.

His wife was a 'crazy lady' he would tell others, and his children were all lazy and entitled. They were always asking him for money whenever they contacted him, he would say. He was never convicted, and he never stood trial for the terrible, horrific acts that he inflicted on his family all those many years ago.

That all changed one night in front of the Dante Alighieri Club.

CHAPTER TEN
The Baseball Team-1972

Little Johnny Orozco had just finished playing a baseball ball game with his friends on that warm summer day during the Summer of 1972. They all played baseball just a few blocks away from his house on 76th Avenue and Bloomingdale. He was on the sixth-grade baseball team, and they practiced at the baseball diamond behind Elm Middle School three afternoons a week and played games every Thursday night and Saturday afternoons.

Johnny was the nerdy one of the five boys. He spends two to three hours a day doing homework and received straight A's. His mother signed him up for baseball that summer because she wanted him to get out and make more friends. She was worried about him spending too much time at home and encouraged him to spend more time with his few friends. Billy and Robby played on the baseball team, the 'Elmwood Tigers', and even though Johnny was playing outfield, he enjoyed being with his neighborhood pallies.

Elena felt terrible about the unstable life she has managed to provide for her only son. Her husband, Elisar, had left her alone with a two-year-old baby ten years ago. She was forced to fend for herself, have to wait tables, clean houses, and do other 'miscellaneous activities' to make money and keep a roof over their heads in the place they were renting.

Those 'miscellaneous activities' included Elena bringing home various men to spend the night at her house late when her son was supposedly sleeping. Elena Orozco was a low-level prostitute in her spare time, going to bars late at night when she wasn't waiting tables and hustling men to pay her money for sex. Rather than hiring a babysitter when Johnny was a toddler, she would leave the little boy home alone and asleep while she got all dressed up and went to the bars, bringing home different men throughout all hours of the night.

With some of the men Elena brought home, she had brief relationships with, and they would move in as boarders. They paid rent in exchange for other benefits, shared her bedroom, and hung out around the house. Some of Elena's 'boarders' were very nice. Some of them were not so nice.

Johnny remembered one evening when he was five years old. His mother was working that night waiting tables while her boarder-boyfriend at the time, George, was hanging out at the house, drinking beer and watching TV. Johnny wasn't feeling well and began to miss his mother. At that point, after asking for her several times and not finding her around, he started crying uncontrollably. Johnny cried for several hours until George, who was now drunk, went into Johnny's bedroom and beat him incessantly. By the time Elena had arrived home from work, Johnny was bloody and bruised, while George was passed out on the couch.

A few years ago, there was another incident when Johnny was asleep in the other room while her mother was arguing with one of her new lovers. The screaming and arguments got louder and louder until Johnny could hear chairs and tables being broken, with Elena yelling even louder. The police were eventually called, and her lover was taken away in handcuffs. But not without Elena suffering from a broken jaw, a busted nose, and several stitches on her head.

To say that Elena Orozco was an unfit mother was an understatement. Trying to raise Johnny without a father and very little money was extremely difficult and a daily challenge.

A year prior, Elena got remarried to an older man named Joe LaFatta. He was fifteen years older than she was but seemed to provide the stability and financial security that she was looking for. Within six months, Johnny's 'stepfather' proved to be the worst of all the men she had ever brought home.

Joe LaFatta had a mean, angry, jealous streak and was incredibly resentful of all of Elena's boyfriends, both past and present. Because she had a temper, they spend a lot of time having verbal and physical altercations, usually resulting in Elena or Joe going to the hospital for their injuries. The police were called many times to the house, and Joe would eventually get arrested, spending several nights in jail.

Besides his jealous, angry temper and the physical abuse he had often inflicted on his mother, he was also a pedophile. Johnny remembered waking up in the middle of the night with Joe sitting on the edge of his bed, his hand inside of his pajamas. When Johnny tried to push him away, he forcefully pushed his left hand over his mouth while fondling him with his right. He then threatened him to keep the incident quiet and not tell his mother or anyone else, or he would otherwise inflict a beating on both of them.

He promised that when he was through, they would both wish that they were never born. Johnny remembered being scared to death, afraid to mention anything to anyone.

On that Thursday summer evening, Johnny, Billy, and Robby had finished playing a baseball game. Everyone piled into the coach's cars to go to the local Dairy Queen for ice cream on Grand Avenue, as Johnny seemed to be enjoying himself with his two friends and the rest of his teammates. Petey and Marco came over on their bikes to meet them at the Dairy Queen, and the baseball coach decided to include them in their post-game celebrations.

It was after nine o'clock and time to go home when Johnny started crying uncontrollably. He couldn't stop crying, and the other boys had no idea why he was so upset in front of the Dairy Queen on Grand Avenue.

"I don't want to go home," Johnny continued to say.

"Why?" the other boys kept asking.

"I can't tell you. I just can't. Can I spend the night at your house, Robby?"

The other four boys looked at each other, initially not understanding why Johnny had a problem with going home for the evening.

"But why, Johnny? What's the matter?" Robby asked.

"It's that asshole that's living with us..." he managed to say.

After several long minutes of silence, Billy Kozar, being the most street smart of all five boys, put 'two and two' together. Realizing why Johnny didn't want to go home, Billy convinced the others to escort Johnny home and spend some time with him at his house, hopefully watching TV.

"We'll go home with you, Johnny. Nothing's going to happen."

Because of the many fights that Billy had gotten into in the neighborhood, he carried around a switchblade and a set of brass knuckles with him at all times.

As the five boys walked into Johnny's house, Joe LaFatta was in the family room, watching TV and drinking a beer. They all sat on the couch and adjoining chair, pretending to be interested in the 'Dragnet' program he was watching. Suddenly, Billy got up to change the television channel.

"Hey, you little bastard? What are you doing?"

"I'm changing the TV. Nobody wants to watch this shit," Billy responded.

Joe LaFatta looked at the five boys and then gave a loud directive to Johnny.

"Your friends need to go home," he loudly ordered his stepson.

At that point, Johnny started to get scared and looked over at Billy. He could see the terror in Johnny's eyes.

Billy coldly smiled at LaFatta.

"We're not fucking going anywhere!" he defiantly said.

At that point, Joe LaFatta, being that he was now drunk and had too many beers, displayed his angry temper at the five boys.

"Get the fuck out of my house!" he loudly demanded as he stood up from his easy chair, still holding a beer in his hand.

At that point, Johnny, feeling empowered by his four friends, stood up to LaFatta.

"My friends are not going anywhere. This is MY house," Johnny stood up in front of his stepfather.

All five boys got up from the couch and stood up in front of LaFatta as if to defiantly stand up to his unreasonable demands. LaFatta, now feeling threatened, raised his hand and punched Johnny in the face with his clenched fist. Johnny went flying off his feet and initially landed back on the couch before rolling onto the floor.

The other four boys jumped in and began pummeling LaFatta with violent punches and kicks to his body and his head as he fell onto the carpet. LaFatta, trying desperately to defend himself, grabbed the vase on the table and began to raise it, attempting to throw it at one of the boys.

Billy, seeing this object coming, pulled out his switchblade and stabbed LaFatta in the arm. LaFatta immediately fell onto the floor, tried to hold his bleeding arm while the other boys continued to brutally attack him. All of the boys started taking turns kicking and punching his face and body until Joe LaFatta was lying on the floor, completely unconscious.

At that point, Elena walked into the house and saw that altercation that was going on in her family room.

"What the hell is happening?" she demanded.

Johnny, crying profusely, ran to his mother's arms and explained to her what had happened in their family room that evening. She then looked at Billy, knowing that he was the oldest and the boys' leader.

"I think your husband has been having his way with your son," he quietly said.

91

She looked at Johnny, and she then started crying uncontrollably.

"Why didn't you tell me?" Elena demanded to know.

"He said he would beat us both up if I ever said anything. He said that he would make us wish we were never born."

Now understanding what was going on, Elena continued sobbing as she picked up the telephone and called the police. The five boys were in the Elmwood Park police station for almost four hours, as they each separately recited the events of that evening to the detectives. It didn't take long to figure out what was happening in the Orozco household. Each of the boy's parents was called, and each boy was picked up one by one.

As Billy stood there at the police station waiting for his father, one of the detectives approached him.

"I'm supposed to take that switchblade away from you, Billy. That's a weapon that you're not allowed to have," Detective Roselli said.

Billy obediently took out his switchblade and tendered it over to the detective.

"If I take this knife away from you, how long will it take you to get another one?" he poignantly asked Billy.

"A few days," Billy said with a slight smirk on his face.

Detective Roselli smiled. "Well then, what's the point of my taking this away from you if you're only going to have another one to replace it?" the detective asked.

They both stood there in silence.

"I'll make you a deal, young man. I will let you keep this blade, with the understanding that you will only use it to defend yourself and your friends, as you did for them tonight."

Billy smiled and nodded his head.

"Joe LaFatta has always been a piece of shit. I've been hoping that someone would finally give it to him for a long time. I just didn't expect it to come from five sixth-graders."

Billy smiled as his father came to the front door to pick him up. The detective winked at Billy and his father.

"We'll keep this between us," he said as he shook Billy and Casimir's hand.

They both smiled back at the Elmwood Park detective and walked out of the police station.

Joe LaFatta spent that night in the emergency room, with five stitches to his arm and several more stitches applied to his head wounds. He also had two broken teeth and suffered from an intense concussion from the head pounding he had received from the boys.

When he was released from the hospital, he returned to the Orozco house, to only find his clothes and belongings sitting in boxes at the driveway's edge. An Elmwood Park patrolman immediately arrived, informing him that he was no longer living there. Elena had gotten a court order of protection and had filed for divorce.

The boys never spoke about that night again. But the five of them realized at the time that, as long as they stuck together and had each other's backs, that no one would ever 'mess with them' again. They were twelve and thirteen years old now, and they were growing up to be men.

93

They were a team, an indestructible unit of five young men who would never allow anyone else to violently have their way with them. No one was ever going to abuse them again, they thought. They all wanted to believe that no one was ever going to 'fuck' with the five of them ever again. Unfortunately, there were more beatings to come.

Ten years later, Joe LaFatta's body washed up on the beach one morning near Rogers Park. His partially decomposed body was covered with multiple stab wounds. The Chicago P.D. had no suspects or clues about what had happened to him or who had committed the murder.

It was right about the same time when Billy Kozar started fishing on Lake Michigan. Billy had gotten his father to go fishing with him after he graduated high school, and they both enjoyed fishing on weekends, going on many fishing trips together.

LaFatta' s washed-up body on that beach also coincided with another interesting fact: Three days earlier, Billy Kozar had just purchased a brand-new fishing boat.

CHAPTER ELEVEN

Praying For Karma - 1973

I was in the eighth grade at St. Angela's School, and I was looking forward to going to high school in the next year. The last year of grade school at St. Angela's was when we thought we could rule the world. We could take over the cafeteria, fool around at the library, crack jokes in the back of the classroom, and blow off our homework as often as possible.

For all intents and purposes, Johnny Orozco was carrying the four of us through our final grade school year. We were copying off of him while taking our tests in Sister Katherine's class, changing some of our answers to ensure that we didn't all get the same score. We were huddling up at my house twice a week and pooling our homework together, ensuring that our assignments were completed on time.

Johnny didn't seem to mind pulling us through the eighth grade at first. But by the middle of the school year, we all realized that we had to do some deed or offer something to make it worth his while. This was when I came up with a 'homework fee.' We all had decided that if we all pitched in and paid him ten bucks a week, that he would collect a total of forty bucks, which was a significant dividend for any thirteen-year-old kid in grade school.

I had an agreement with my parents that they would give me some money each week as an allowance of sorts. For some odd reason, my parents didn't feel that they should have to give me any money at all for doing anything, so I always had to scrounge around, looking for odds and end jobs around the house to earn some cash. Sometimes I would collect five or ten bucks here and there working around the house, with either my mother or my grandmother giving me a few bucks.

Unfortunately, most of my money would pay the 'homework fees' to Johnny each week, which pretty much left me penniless. It finally came to the point where I was constantly looking for money anywhere I could, and I was always two or three weeks behind on the homework fees. I was still too young to get a job working somewhere, and even the local paper route in Elmwood Park wasn't available. I realized that I needed to desperately earn some money.

I finally realized that my valuable baseball card collection and my treasured comic books had some value. On Saturdays, I would take my bicycle and go to the local hobby store on Harlem Avenue to sell off some of my baseball cards and comic books.

It got to be a pretty good gig. After several trips to the hobby store, I had managed to catch up with my 'marker' to Johnny, and I still had another fifty bucks to spare. For a few months that spring, I felt as though I was flush with cash. I didn't want to tell my parents what I was doing, as they would have significantly disapproved of my hustling off my collection for money.

For a few months, this went on until one night; I had made the mistake of leaving my wallet on top of the counter in the kitchen. My father had just arrived home from work, and he happened to grab my wallet by mistake, being that they were both black leather billfolds and looked very similar. When he looked in my wallet, he immediately noticed that I had sixty dollars in cash.

For some stupid reason that I can't understand to this day, my father immediately assumed that I had stolen that money from my mother's purse. She was always asking my father for money, and she never had a good explanation as to where all of our household money was going.

That spring morning, I had gotten a notice while I was in class that my mother was waiting for me to pick me up. It was only ten o'clock in the morning, and we didn't usually break for lunch in the cafeteria until after noon, and it was still too early. When I went down to the school office, my mother didn't say a word. She managed to convince the school secretary that I had to rush home in an emergency.

Whether my father was troubled or upset that day, I'll never know. He confronted me and immediately assumed that I had stolen that money from my mother. I tried to explain that the cash was from my selling off my comic book and baseball card collection, but to no avail.

He grabbed a wooden two by four that he had hidden in the bathroom and began beating me incessantly with it over my body and my head, hitting me with his fist using his other hand. He beat me so hard that there was blood gushing out the side of my head, and I felt like my left arm was broken from trying to shield off his violent strikes against my body. When I finally fell to the floor, my father began kicking me while I was curled up in a ball, trying to protect myself.

The most heartbreaking thing about that whole violent beating at home was that my mother idly stood by and watched my father beat me to a pulp. I remember her standing there, almost smiling, while I was getting beat up for 'supposedly stealing money out of her purse.' She was so fiscally and financially irresponsible, and she had no idea where her money was going every week, so she truly believed that I was stealing money from her.

I still remember all of the blood gushing out of the side of my head from that two by four, and I was crying uncontrollably. After about an hour or so, my mother cleaned up my blood off of the kitchen floor and put on several band-aides on my head to stop the bleeding. I probably should have gone to the hospital for stitches, but my mother seemed to believe that the bleeding would stop if she put on enough fresh band-aids. My father then demanded my mother to take me back to school that same afternoon.

I remember sitting in the back of Sister Katherine's class, holding a cloth up against my head to stop the bleeding. When she finally noticed all of the blood, she asked me what had happened, of which I told her that 'I had an accident and hit my head on the coffee table at home. I was afraid to mention the truth to them because I knew enough at that age if the authorities would have confronted my father, that he would have eventually taken out his violent temper on me even more.

I stupidly covered up for him, and I lied to the school nurse when I was finally sent back down to the office to treat my head wound. At that time, I had some large, black and blue marks on my left arm and shoulder from my father's wooden weapon that morning, and I tried to cover it up with the red sweater that I was wearing.

I think the school nurse eventually figured out what had happened because she immediately left me alone in the office to talk to the principal of our school at the time, Fr. Anthony Weir. But for some reason, the principal and the school nurse decided to do nothing. The nurse came back and applied first aid ointment on my head wound and sent me back to class for the rest of that day.

Marco and Petey, who were sitting two rows away from my desk, eventually noticed my injuries and mentioned something to Billy and Johnny about it after school. I remember walking home from school with them, as they all tried to comfort me with promises of revenge against my abusive father. As young teenagers, we all fantasized about what we were going to eventually do to our physically abusive parents when the time came. That time, we all figured, would be when we were old enough to own a firearm and drive a getaway car that would take us far away from Elmwood Park.

I remember mentioning something to my mother about the beating incident many years later, to which her response was, 'well, you never stole money again.'

There were a few more incidents during that school year when my Buzz Boy friends would show up to school with various injuries and bruises on their faces and bodies. Petey got beat up for talking back to his father one time, while Marco got cracked several times for not doing his weekly chores. We were all enduring some kind of physical abuse at home during that time, and we really couldn't do anything about it.

We couldn't call the authorities, knowing that there would be dire consequences for all of us if we had done so. And as was the usual case, the local authorities in town would never initiate taking us away from our abusive families, as that sort of thing at that time was never done.

During our last year of grade school at St. Angela's, we all managed to comfort each other, making sure that we all knew that we had each other's back during that time, even if it was only psychologically or emotionally.

Growing up in fear of our abusive family life at home took a tremendous psychological toll on all of us. We never shared the love and closeness that we found out was essential in close-knit families. We all grew up only as objects of anger, and we were constantly demeaned for our very existence within our own homes and families. We all grew up feeling that we were conceived accidents that our fathers and mothers had to put up with and endure.

Johnny, Petey, Billy, Marco, and I all had the same psychological issues growing up in that Chicago suburb; we never felt safe. We all grew up waiting for the other shoe to drop in the form of a physical beating, violent molestation, or a verbal beratement that demeaned our psychological state of mind. We were always being put down, humiliated, and degraded for one illogical reason or another. We all grew up not feeling very good about ourselves, and we all struggled to find our self-worth and personal securities that were so important to find at that time in our lives. All of the significant abuse at home took a tremendous toll on the five of us and had a long-range effect on our personal psyche.

None of us had good relationships with our parents and especially our abusive fathers. We all spent our time together during lunch, latently harboring all of the hatred and manifesting the disgust and animosity we had for our parents. It all took a tremendous toll that the five of us never recovered.

At that time in our lives, we only hoped that all of the bad karma would eventually come back around one day.

CHAPTER TWELVE
Marco's Little Sister- 1973

Marco Pezza had just celebrated his fourteenth birthday that year, and he had immediately found a job working at a grocery store as a box boy and bagging groceries. Frank's Fresh Market was located on Grand Avenue in Elmwood Park, which was several blocks away from Courtland Avenue. The owner, Frank Ingraffia, seemed to be always looking for help, and he was always happy to hire neighborhood boys at minimum wage.

As Marco got a job working at the store, he was able to get his friends, Petey and Billy, a job there too. At minimum wage of $1.60 an hour, the three boys could bring home fifteen to twenty dollars a week working part-time at Frank's after school.

They all seemed to enjoy working together, as they took their bicycles to their jobs at three o'clock after classes at Holy Cross High School. They would have fun doing buggy-cart races in the grocery store's parking lot, flinging containers of cottage cheese into the garbage incinerator, or having broomstick fights in the back room. Their boss had reprimanded them a few times when they were caught horsing around, but he seemed always to take it all in stride.

"Boys will be boys," he would always say to the older cashiers and stockroom employees whenever they were bothered by their antics. Their boss seemed to have a very easy-going personality and seldom got angry with his store employees or personnel.

When they weren't fooling around, the three of them worked hard four days a week until ten o'clock every night. They would take their bicycles home together in the dark to Cortland Avenue, or one of their parents would pick them up after work if the weather became too inclement for them to ride their usual modes of transportation.

One early evening, Marco was sent home early from the grocery store after only a few hours of work. He took his bicycle home, which was never more than a fifteen-minute ride, and laid his bike next to the side of the garage like he normally did. When he entered his house from the back door, he immediately heard some loud crying upstairs in his sister's bedroom.

Rosaria was no more than twelve years old, but she was started to develop earlier than more of the other girls her age. She had already fully developed breasts and had been getting her menstrual period for over a year. As Marco had run upstairs to see what was wrong, he heard his father's footsteps, Papa Enzo, run into the master bedroom and lock the door.

At that moment, Marco saw something that had physically and emotionally shaken him for the rest of his life.

Laying on her right side, Rosaria was practically naked, crying profusely as her clothing had been strewn across her bedroom. She had not heard Marco enter her bedroom. Her buttocks were wet with bodily fluids, and there was blood on the sheets and covers.

"Rosa, what happened?" Marco immediately asked in a loud voice, almost gasping with horror.

Upon discovering that her older brother had entered the room, his sister covered herself immediately and buried her face into her pillow, crying even louder.

At that moment, Marco realized what had happened. His sister had been molested and raped by their father.

Marco had then recalled a similar incident when he was a very young child in the first grade. He remembered waking up in his bed with his clothing removed in the middle of the night and intense pain and blood coming from his buttocks. He didn't understand at the time what had happened, but he did recall his father coming into his bedroom in the middle of the night.

At that moment, Marco became extremely angry. He then walked over to the closed, locked door of his father's master bedroom where he had been hiding and continued to bang on the loudly, demanding his father to come out.

As he was knocking loudly on the door, he heard loud sounds of something breaking, as if it were broken furniture.

Suddenly, Papa Enzo opened the bedroom door and immediately hit Marco over the head with the wooden leg of a broken chair. As Marco fell back, Papa Enzo had hit his son several more times with the wooden leg across his shoulders, back and arms as he tried to defend himself.

"What did you do to Rosa?" Marco kept screaming as the father continued to hit him. As Marco continued to lay on the floor, Papa Enzo immediately ran downstairs and out of the house. He then jumped into his car and left as if to try to escape the violent and perverted crimes that he had committed to his children.

Marco ran next door to Robby Mazzara's house. With blood spilling from the gash he had received from his father's weapon, Robby's mother attended to Marco's wounds. He didn't mention anything at that moment as to how or why he had been beaten so severely by his father or what had happened to his sister. Although Mrs. Mazzara realized that his father had probably beaten Marco, she refused to get involved, having violent family and marital problems of her own.

Marco and his brother, Anthony, who was playing at a friend's house at the time, ended up spending the night at the Mazzara house. When Mrs. Mazzara went next door to check on their sister Rosaria, she had locked herself in her room and refused to let anyone in.

She stayed locked up in her bedroom for almost two days, refusing to go to school. She only came out to use the bathroom when no one was home. Papa Enzo didn't return to his house until the next morning, in a drunken state. He had been at the bar drinking most of that evening, and he entered his house expecting his other children to be home.

When he realized that his two sons were staying next door with the Mazzara's, he walked upstairs to check on his daughter. Rosaria refused to allow her father back into her bedroom after he knocked on the door several times. He continued to bang on his daughter's bedroom door, demanding that she open up the door and allow him inside. After a few hours had passed, Papa Enzo passed out on his bed, next to the broken chair that he had used to inflict damage onto his oldest son.

It was several weeks until life at the Pezza household returned to normal from that autumn day. Marco, Anthony, and Rosaria would have dinner at the Mazzara household. At the same time, Papa Enzo initially stayed far away, hiding himself from facing his children at the Cloverleaf Lounge on Diversey Avenue. Afterward, as if to try to make amends, he would have a few pizzas and fast food waiting for his kids when they came home from school, trying desperately to make amends for the brutal sins he had committed against them.

It was a tragic time in their young lives. Back in those days, people looked the other way when they saw physical child abuse or family violence within other households in their neighborhood. Everyone always presumed that their naughty kids 'had it coming, and they were always allowed to play together outside until the streetlights came on. None of the young children in the neighborhood ever talked about anything that was ever going on behind the closed doors of their tragic households.

In the 1960s, physical child abuse and child neglect were never recognized as significant problems that required identification and intervention. It wasn't until the 1980s and later when child neglect and sexual abuse started gaining attention. Each type of family violence developed its own set of definitions, research, and interventions, but very few incidents were ever reported, especially within the suburbs of the big cities.

In recent years, psychologists, family doctors, sociologists, and medical researchers had begun to examine family violence, seeking commonalities among various forms of child maltreatment, domestic violence, and even elder abuse. Although these close family relationships' very nature made it reasonable to look for common risk and protective factors, these unspeakable, violent interactions continued in the forms of family violence.

But as the debate continued about what determined 'family violence' in a close-knit family, the children in the suburbs were only 'disciplined.' According to the ignorance of so many suburban attitudes, that sort of thing just didn't exist. That kind of violence only took place in the black neighborhoods and inner cities, where drunken boyfriends and husbands beat up their girlfriends and wives, often abusing or even killing their unwanted children. Discussing family violence regarding molested children and physically abused spouses just didn't happen back then.

According to those who lived in the suburbs, individuals who perpetrated these violent acts on their victims were either black drug addicts or immigrant alcoholics who lived in the inner city's tenement neighborhoods. The suburban victims of such violent family behavior were conveniently hidden away from the community, and family violence was never a prevailing issue within the boundaries of accepted social-cultural norms.

Back then, society turned a blind eye to the closed doors of family violence. The nature of family cruelty and brutality was never conceptualized back then, and it was never an important issue of modern culture. The country in that period was too busy protesting the Vietnam war, racial inequality, or inner-city poverty to take on the violent occurrences that were going on within the closed doors of suburbia.

Like all the suburbs back then, its occupants made themselves believe they lived in Pleasant Valley neighborhoods, with their well-maintained, manicured green lawns and their white picket fences. There were no family interventions by either the medical authorities, family welfare services, or police in those days. Unless someone was found dead in their garage or hanging from their basement rafters, these issues or occurrences never made the nightly news and were not important. Domestic violence and child abuse was never a prevailing issue, and it was never discussed.

Like any suburb during that period, people often assembled at the end of their driveways, always cheerful, always smiling. The residents of Cortland Avenue were no different. Only on rare occasions were they ever seen walking together to mass on Sundays. They intermittently borrowed cups of sugar or milk from each other when the convenience stores were closed. The neighbors leaned against their backyard wooden fences and discussed politics, religion, and especially the Chicago Cubs. Other than the occasional summer block parties, the suburbs' residents barely knew each other's names, let alone whatever was occurring in each of their private households.

On Cortland Avenue during the sixties, all of the husbands and fathers were too busy working and struggling to make their mortgage payments to be actively involved with their children's lives.

One seldom saw a father playing baseball with his son or kicking a soccer ball to his daughter. Most of the fathers had immigrated from the old country and experienced the hardships of war. They came to start a new life, and being a good father or husband wasn't high on their priority list. They believed that their wives should be subservient and that children should only be seen and not heard. They worked exceedingly hard and never bothered with their children, allowing them to play on the streets and finding their source of entertainment or trouble until the streetlights came on. There were no Boy Scout meetings or Indian Princess weekends for the fathers of Cortland Avenue back then.

Overworked dads came home to their families and beat up their wives and children for almost any reason or excuse. They took out their tempers and frustrations on their families after sometimes drinking down their problems at the neighborhood bar.

Behind their locked wooden doors, wives were getting thrashed by their abusive or alcoholic husbands. Children were being beaten and whipped, with some being privately molested by their violent fathers.

The families of Cortland Avenue had their own hidden skeletons, concealed way on top of their musty, vacant attics.

And nobody was saying a damn word.

CHAPTER THIRTEEN
Shop Class - 1975

It was barely eight o'clock in the morning as we were gathering in the classroom of our high school shop class. It was the first day of school at the all-boys Holy Cross High School on Belmont Avenue in River Grove. Billy and I were happy to share a sophomore class together. We were sitting together on the high-top wooden tables and benches set up along the adjoining industrial classroom.

"What's up, Robby?" I heard Petey Rodriguez's voice sitting behind Billy Kozar and me as we were all patiently waiting for our shop teacher to show up.

"Where's Marco and Johnny?" Petey asked.

"Are they in this class too?" I asked.

"That's what they told me," he replied.

I had not seen a whole lot of Petey, Marco, and Johnny that past summer. I had gotten a summer job working cement construction as a laborer with my Uncle Ernie to save money to buy a car that year. Being that we were all 15 years old at the time, we were all looking forward to getting our driver's licenses and driving when we all turned sixteen. Billy, being that he was going to be sixteen in December of that year, had already taken driver's education classes that summer. We were all looking forward to Billy getting his license first, and we were starting to make plans of all the partying and cruising we were all going to do when Billy started driving.

As Fr. Parenti was beginning to start class, Marco and Johnny walked in together.

"So glad you could join us, gentlemen," the shop class teacher duly noted the late-arriving students. "We start the first period promptly at 8:00 am."

"Sorry, Father," Johnny apologetically replied, as they both sat at the two open benches chairs next to Billy and me.

Fr. Parenti was the industrial shop teacher at Holy Cross, and he ran a tight ship. He had structured the class methodically to where we would need to study all of the industrial machines and tools, lathes, table saws, and stamping machines that were needed to create whatever special projects we all decided to endeavor that school year.

We all had been together in either the same class or the same school since the third grade at St. Angela's grade school in Elmwood Park, and we were all pretty fortunate that we were able to be in the same first-period class at Holy Cross High School.

Being the class nerd, Johnny wasn't thrilled about wasting his intellectual talents making wooden containers and shop plaques. He wasn't excited about being pulled away from the biology and chemistry labs that he so much more thoroughly enjoyed. Johnny was more interested in science experiments and mixing chemicals that go 'BOOM.'

On the other hand, Petey was more mechanically inclined and looked forward to this shop class as his favorite and hoped he could get into the small engine repair class offered that spring.

We were all looking forward to taking driver's education classes and getting our driver's licenses that school year. The topics of our conversations and the beginning of our sentences always started with "when I start driving," and we all had our plans on when, where, and what kind of cool rides we all would be cruising around in.

We had all gotten to know one another pretty well at that time in our lives, and our conversations, thoughts, and desires were pretty simple: Who was driving, who was going out with which girl, who was drinking and going where to what concert and of course, who was having sex and getting laid. We had the habit of gathering for lunch after the fourth period and sat at the same long table in the back of the school cafeteria. Back then, it was okay to smoke in school, so our table was in the Holy Cross cafeteria's smoking section. All of us were smoking then, and we all found different ways and sources to get our cigarettes.

I was particularly attached to Newport Lights, as these were the same brand of cigarettes that my Uncle Ernie was smoking over the summer. I kept a carton in my locker, far away from the knowledge of my parents and, particularly, my over-bearing, asshole father. Billy, Marco, and Petey were smoking the standard Marlboro Lights, so they seemed to interchange and bum cigarettes off each other, especially at lunchtime. Johnny, the class nerd who was supposed to know better, vowed off cigarettes and nicotine altogether, as he knew of the unhealthy hazards of smoking. But when we were all out or were at the high school dances, Johnny always bummed one of my Newport Lights. He would usually cough and hack for the first two drags but then got used to it and managed to finish his cigarette without embarrassing himself.

During that time in our lives, we all very good friends, away from all of the complications of our personal family lives that seemed to influence us as we got older effectively. Either four or five of us were always together, going to the high school dances every Friday night at either Notre Dame in Niles, Trinity in River Forest, or Fenwick High School in Oak Park. We would often "skip" sixth-period class and walk over to Mister C's Coffee Shop on West Belmont Avenue for a late lunch, coffee, and cigarettes. Since our school was very close to Elmwood Park, we could take the CTA bus to our home destinations after classed finished at 3:15 pm. If one of us weren't either on the football, basketball, track, or wrestling teams, we would take the 3:45 bus home and sit in the back of the bus where we could sneak in one last cigarette drag before going home to our respective home lives.

The four of us, except Johnny, decided to try out for the football team that sophomore year. Practice started at 3:30 pm, where we met and suited up and did drills for an hour and a half. During the last hour in the weight room, we then worked out doing lifts, squats, and bench presses. That fall, we were all competing to get into the "220 Club". That was the bench-pressing maximum of the gladiator weight machine, the full rack of total weights needed to bench press 220 pounds. We were all trying to get our names listed in that elusive weight room and be a part of that exclusive fraternity.

That fall was the only year the four of us played football together, and Petey and I decided to join the wrestling team later that year. Marco played defensive tight end, and Billy was the team's quarterback, and they both got a considerable amount of playing time in their high school football careers.

Petey and I became wrestlers, and that year had respectable winning records for our weight classes, at the 132 and 140-pound weight groups,

111

respectively. But my high school sports career was marred by one situation that I had to deal with while growing up.

My father was adamant about my playing high school football and demanded that I quit the team that year. It was only after a tremendous amount of begging and coaxing by myself and my mother that I was able to join the Holy Cross wrestling team.

I always practiced hard after school and spent a considerable amount of time in the weight room after practice. But the wrestling coach, Mr. Gordan, became aware of my situation at home early on that he tried to help prepare for. The night before every wrestling match, he tried to send me home two or three pounds underweight.

My father didn't believe in my fasting and going without dinner the night before each wrestling match and forced me to eat at dinner time. This always put me two or three pounds over on the day of the meet, and I would have to spend a considerable amount of time running laps around the school's indoor track or in the locker room sauna to try to make weight. This procedure of making weight before each wrestling match made me quite tired and exhausted. I had difficulty wrestling three, two-minute wrestling matches without getting fatigued and then finally losing the match. After several wrestling matches and the same weight dilemma, I decided to defy my father's demands of eating dinner one evening.

"Robby...eat!" he would demand me to do, as I would only move my food from one side of my plate to the other.

"Eat your dinner, goddammit," he continued to yell that cold winter evening as I kept procrastinating eating my meal.

He finally lost his temper one evening as he grabbed my hair and pushed my face into my food. He then began banging my head against the table several times until I started crying, begging him to stop.

My mother only stood there helplessly as my father unloaded his temper on me. He disapproved of my desire to make weight that following day and further advance in my wrestling career. That next day, I showed up at Coach Gordan's office, with two black eyes and three pounds over-weight. Because he didn't have another wrestler to fill in the 132-pound weight class, I was forced to again run indoor laps on the track and an hour in the locker room sauna. The only good thing that came out of that incident was that I was matched up against a lesser quality opponent from Brother Rice High School, and I could easily pin him in the first period.

Coach Gordan was more than aware of the physical and emotional abuse I was experiencing at home, and at one point, tried to talk to my father after practice. My dad only hung up the phone on him, telling him to 'mind his own damn business and to be thankful that I was still on the team.' For those reasons, Coach Gordan made sure I was two or three pounds under before sending me home the night before a wrestling meet.

We all gathered each first period in shop class at 8:00 every morning that semester, discussing, laughing, and plotting our daily lives as high school sophomores every day. There was always something to be planned. There were the Friday night dances at different high schools, the fall football games, basketball games, and the Wednesday night wrestling matches that we needed to discuss and plan our fun together. Those moments in high school were the most carefree periods of our lives.

On one winter morning in December, Fr. Parenti instructed us to plan and plot out our shop projects. We all had different ideas of whatever it was that we wanted to make. Billy wanted to make an adjustable wooden lamp. Marco wanted to make a wooden jewelry box for his mother, while Petey decided to make a plaque. But not just any plaque. A plaque with the centerfold of Miss January from the new Playboy magazine that had just come out. I was almost certain Fr. Parenti was going to send him down to the office for detention. But he only laughed, betting that he couldn't properly finish the project and make it look like it was professionally done.

Johnny and I were both stumped. He wanted to make a wooden ashtray until I reminded him that a wooden ashtray would only burn and catch on fire after enough cigarette butts were deposited. I had no idea what I wanted to make until Fr. Parenti suggested that I stamp something on the industrial lathe and stamping machine that would commemorate our getting our drivers' licenses.

We all had become the best of friends together since grade school at St. Angela's, and I wanted to stamp something that would commemorate our friendship. We all had last names with either one or two 'Z's in them, and I wanted to stamp a sort of key ring that would reveal the common consonant in our names...Mazzara, Orozco, Pezza, Kozar, and Rodriguez.

'The 'Z' Gang' was my original choice, but while trying to stamp it out on the brass material that I was using, the name came out crooked and didn't look right. I asked Johnny for his opinion, and he could only come up with our initials 'MOPKR-Z,' which looked more like an Illinois license plate than an official keyring. I asked Billy, who came up with the 'Five Z's,' which sounded more like a singing group. I finally broke down and asked Fr. Parenti for his thoughts.

He mentioned that we were always talking together during class, gossiping, and plotting our activities each day in his shop class. Our continuous talking seemed to create a loud 'buzzing' noise while the industrial shop machines were going during shop class. He made a good suggestion, and I planned and stamped it out on the large sheet of brass metal that he provided for me. I then stamped out five brass medallions, which I proudly polished and drilled a hole into each one. I then acquired steel rings and attached them to brass medallions that I had just polished and completed.

At lunch, we talked together and were excited about Billy taking his driver's test that Saturday morning. I then pulled out the brass keyrings that I had made in shop class and presented them to each one of my friends. I explained to Billy, Johnny, Marco, and Petey the moniker concept, based on the common letter 'Z' in all of our last names.

They were all delighted to have key rings and medallions that they could now use for their car keys, and we promised each other that we would always and forever keep our keyring medallions.

The brass medallions proudly displayed our gang's name that we would always refer to ourselves from that day forward.

They simply said: BUZZ BOYS

CHAPTER FOURTEEN
The Junior Prom - 1976

I had just returned home from the do-it-yourself car wash on Grand Avenue that day for the second time, making sure that my car was fully cleaned and polished. I had purchased my used 1974 Chevrolet Vega from my Uncle Paul that spring for the discount price of eight hundred dollars, and I was happy to have a set of wheels.

During my junior year, I was dating a girl from another school named Michelle Trembley from Mother Guerin High School. She was a pretty brunette with a great figure. Michelle was my first love (not counting the second grade), and she knew of some great places where we could go parking at the end of our dates. She had found a remote, dirt road in Lombard near the running path where we often went, and she wasn't bashful about going off and parking there.

I had asked her to accompany me to my junior prom, and she was all excited to go. She had saved her hard-earned money working as a waitress at Mister C's Restaurant on Grand Avenue and spent hours shopping with her mother to find the perfect prom dress.

I vacuumed my car upholstery twice and spent nearly two hours polishing and waxing my car for that special night. Earlier, I picked up my white, long-tailed tuxedo from Picardi Tuxedo shop on Harlem Avenue and had already acquired the corsage of flowers for that evening.

I was getting ready for my junior prom at Holy Cross High School. I had asked my girlfriend at the time, Michelle Trembley, to escort me on that evening, and I wanted to make sure that everything was perfect for our anticipated night at my prom. I only needed to shower and put on my formal evening wear and pick up my date, who lived in Melrose Park.

As a high school junior, my young experiences with dating, girlfriends, and relationships were quite limited. As an immature sixteen-year-old, I was a teenager with very raw emotions. I felt everything very intensely. I was extremely sensitive, quick-tempered, and like most other teenagers my age, wanted to be accepted by all those around me. Although I had my close 'Buzz Boy' friends in high school, I felt I was the most sensitive and the most vulnerable of the five of us. I didn't react well to jokes made at my expense and had difficulty dealing with failure. I was a teenage age 'perfectionist' and expected things in my life to always go perfectly. When they didn't, it bothered me to no end.

At sixteen years old, I consistently wore my heart on my sleeve. And like any young teenager who often does, my heart was constantly getting beat up and bruised. With the physical abuse that I often experienced from my father, trying to fit in with the rest of the world seemed difficult. Any positive feelings of self-esteem and dignity seemed like an impossible task. For that reason, I was looking so forward to a perfect evening with my prom date, and I planned every last detail to go without a hitch.

I originally asked my father to loan me his new 1977 Lincoln Continental Mark V several days before to drive for that evening. I swore to him that I would take special care of his new, black beauty. I had even promised my father that I would come home at an early hour, hoping that I could make a good impression on my 'Buzz Boy' friends and my prom date.

But of course, as I expected, his answer was 'No.' He was not about to let a newly trained, sixteen-year-old driver, who only had his driver's license less than six months, take out his brand-new Lincoln Continental to the junior prom. I figured that if I had brought that car back home in anything other than showroom condition, I would have probably bought myself another beating.

So, I made the best of it. I spent hours polishing and immaculately cleaning my 1974 red Chevrolet Vega. I had never had any mechanical problems before, and it seemed to be a pretty reliable vehicle going back and forth to school and home. I had little choice but to take my car as my chariot of choice for that evening.

I slowly got dressed, putting on my newly acquired white tuxedo, with the specially ordered shiny white shoes, white bow tie, and long tails. I looked like a pure white glass of milk. After all of the 'ooh's and ahh's from my mother, with me posing by myself for pictures in the living room, I got into my extra clean, red Chevy Vega and drove over to Michelle's house.

Michelle was wearing a light blue, satin gown with sequins and long sleeves that flowed elegantly to the floor, with low-cut features that barely covered her 'Double D's.' That was an acronym us boys used in our school for 'deli display,' or a girl with very large breasts. Her mother was all excited to take our pictures, and we posed in front of her red rose garden in the backyard for almost thirty minutes.

I then opened the door for her as my car was parked on her driveway and climbed in to start the car, eagerly inserting the key into the ignition.

It wouldn't start.

I felt a sinking feeling come over me, and I continued to turn the key, not knowing why the car wasn't starting. At that point, her father came outside, and we both opened up the hood. Knowing very little about engines at the time, Mr. Trembley helped me figure out that the battery cable was loose and had a hard time connecting with the starter. He helped me tighten the battery cable and lent me a set of jumper cables to keep in the trunk of my car if I had any more car trouble that evening.

That was the beginning of many bad omens that were in store for us on that special night.

We drove to the Aqua Viva Banquet Hall on Harlem Avenue, where our junior prom was held. I walked into the hall arm in arm with my date and found the table where Billy, Petey, and Marco were sitting with their prom dates, all dressed up and ready to enjoy the evening.

Billy was dressed in a black tuxedo, complete with a black, ruffled shirt and black bow tie. He had his hair combed completely slick back, and with his newly grown sideburns, looked like he could have been getting ready to do an on-stage Elvis Presley show. By then, Billy Kozar's normal attire was usually a black leather jacket, a black shirt and a pack of Marlboro cigarettes in his front pocket, so his wearing a tuxedo was completely out of character. His girlfriend at the time, Barbara, a very pretty brunette who lived two blocks over and was his steady 'go-to' girl whenever no one else was available.

Petey was dressed more conservatively, wearing a standard black tuxedo he had borrowed from his older cousin, Manuel. His cousin was required to wear a tuxedo to work as a theater usher at the Portage Cinema on Irving Park Road. His date was a girl he started seeing from Regina High School not too far away, named Jeanine. She was a

119

plain, unassuming blonde with a large overbite and protruding silver braces. His date seemed rather quiet, as if she was embarrassed to be with Petey in his cousin's movie house costume.

Marco was dressed in a velvet, green tuxedo jacket, with a green ruffled shirt, bow tie, and shiny black, high-heeled shoes. He was dressed sharp and looked as though he was ready to go to a dinner show at the Villa Venice on North Milwaukee Avenue. His date, Marianne, who was a sophomore from Dominican High School, had never gone out with Marco before that evening. She had no idea what to expect from either Marco or his 'Buzz Boy' friends sitting at the table.

Johnny had gone to Picardi Tuxedo with me and rented a white tuxedo-like mine, minus the long tails. His date was a young girl named Amanda, whom he had never been out with before. She lived three blocks away and was also a junior at Mother Guerin High School. Johnny's mother and Amanda's mother were good friends, so they both decided to fix their children to attend the Holy Cross Junior Prom. Amanda was in the same grade and same school as Michelle. But because she was a class nerd like Johnny, my date had very little in common with her, and they didn't know each other very well.

We both arrived at the table, and I sat next to Marco and his date, across from the others on that large, well-decorated table. There was a floral centerpiece of white gardenias, and I had a hard time seeing Billy and Barbara sitting directly across from me.

After making small talk with everyone, I looked over at my prom date, Michelle, making sure that she was ready to have a good time. But by looking at her face, I could tell that something was wrong. I asked her a few times if everything was okay, and she insisted that she was fine.

Then suddenly, Michelle got up and yelled out 'YOU BITCH' to Johnny's date, Amanda, and walked out to the bathroom in tears. Johnny and I looked at each other in complete shock, not understanding what the problem was. Marco didn't immediately say anything, but Billy seemed completely amused.

"What just happened?" I said as Johnny and I were completely stumped at what had just occurred.

"They're wearing the same dress," Billy observed.

"Huh?" Johnny exclaimed.

"Your date and Robby's date are both wearing the same dress."

I looked at Johnny's date, Amanda, and sure enough, she was wearing the same light blue satin gown with long sleeves that Michelle was wearing. If it wasn't for Amanda's protruding braces and Michelle's 'deli display' breasts, they could have probably passed for twins. After several minutes of sitting there in silence, Billy and Marco's date decided to go into the women's bathroom and console my date, trying in vain to convince her that their wearing the same prom dress was only a coincidence. It shouldn't affect the outcome of the evening.

As our fried chicken, green beans, and mash potato dinners were being served, Michelle finally came out of the bathroom and sat back down next to me at the table. But she had a dirty look on her face and barely said two words to me.

Being only sixteen years old and having difficulty controlling my own raw emotions, I became upset as well. I was finding it difficult to enjoy myself and finish my chicken dinner. Everyone else at the table seemed to be eating and enjoying themselves, making small talk, laughing, and joking. But my prom date, Michelle, only sat there in silence, still brooding over the fact that someone else at the table was wearing the same prom dress that she was.

At that point, Billy, Marco, and Petey decided to get up and go outside for a cigarette, and they asked me to come along.

"Hey, Robby, don't let this bother you, man," Billy advised, as we all took out our Marlboro Light cigarette packs and lit each other's cigarettes.

"Girls get all hot and bothered about stupid shit like that," he exclaimed, as I was taking a long, well-needed drag from my cigarette.

"Don't let this ruin your evening," Marco said. "Let's all just have a great time, fuck the prom dresses!"

After several minutes of joking outside with my friends and finishing my smoke, I decided to let myself get past this minor crisis and make the best of the evening. As the rock and roll band "Comstock Lode" started playing, everyone else got up and started dancing. After several songs, the band began to play Chicago's "Colour My World." At that moment, Michelle grasped my hand from under the table.

"I'm sorry, Robby. I didn't mean to over-react. It's just that I went through a lot of trouble to buy and get fitted for this prom dress. The lady at the dress shop told me that no one else had this blue satin dress, and I wanted so much to look good for you. I didn't expect Johnny's date to have the same dress on."

She smiled and passionately kissed me at the table. At that moment, I decided to accept her apology, and we got up and danced for several songs, most of them being slow dances.

The rest of our evening went without a problem as we continued to dance and drink sodas at the Junior Prom. Marco and Billy went outside and snuck in a flask filled with Jack Daniels, so we were all spiking our drinks while the dance monitors (several of them were priests) were keeping a keen eye on all of us.

"Make room for the Holy Spirit" was a popular reprimand from the dance monitors when they saw us dancing too closely.

But after several spiked Diet Cokes, we were nonetheless dancing very, very close together. The band finished playing at midnight, and that was our cue to end the evening and go home.

But Billy Kozar suddenly got the bright idea to go to the Lincoln Hotel in Lincoln Park in Chicago. His excuse for his date was a pizzeria restaurant located there and that we were all hungry for pizzas after eating our very limited chicken cuisine. I had heard from Marco that Billy had a hotel room reserved for all of us to go there and party afterward. But I had promised my parents that I would be home at a decent hour, which meant before two o'clock in the morning.

We all gathered ourselves and walked out to the parking lot of the Aqua Viva Hall and into our cars. As I started my car and began to put it in gear, I could feel the rear tire on the driver's side going 'clump, clump, clump, clump.' I exited my vehicle and looked at the rear tire.

It was flat.

"Oh my God," were my initial words, followed by several descriptive swear words after that. I now had no choice but to change the tire of my car in my very white tuxedo. Several of my friends had already exited the banquet hall's parking lot except Marco, who saw that I was having car problems. He got out of his car and, together, spent the next twenty minutes changing the tire of my Chevy Vega. By then, my white tuxedo was no longer sparkling white. I had dirt and grease on my hands, and my tuxedo pants were covered in dirt.

"Robby, do you still want to go to the Lincoln Hotel?" Marco asked.

I looked over at Michelle. She smiled and nodded her head, looking as though she still wanted to party. At that moment, I fantasized about her 'DD's as my young, inexperienced eyes were too busy undressing her from the driver's side of my car.

"Okay," I agreed, and I followed Marco over to the hotel located in Lincoln Park on North Clark Street.

I followed Marco in his blue Pontiac Grand Prix. Within twenty minutes, we were all standing outside waiting to enter the posh, elegant hotel on Clark and Lincoln Avenues. There was a revolving door entrance into the hotel, so each of us had to stand in line to enter the small revolving door one by one. For some reason, I was at the end of the line, so after Michelle had entered and gone through the revolving door, it was my turn to enter. As I had entered the revolving door, the door suddenly stopped, and I felt myself being tugged from the entrance.

The tails of my tuxedo had gotten caught in between the revolving doors.

Several of my friends were standing in the lobby, laughing and watching this whole Marx Brothers comedic scene unfold. I continued to push the revolving door as hard as I could. But I was genuinely stuck. Michelle, noticing that I couldn't get out, ran over to one of the hotel attendants and, within minutes, brought over a maintenance man with a small step stool and some tools. Within several minutes, the revolving door was released, and I could escape my front door adventure.

Not only was the white tuxedo now dirty and full of grease, but I was hot and sweaty from trying to free myself from that defective revolving door. While everyone enjoyed a good laugh, we all walked over to the Luigino's Pizzeria, located in the hotel lobby. As Billy approached the hostess, we were all told that the kitchen was closed for the evening and no longer accepting any more customers.

At that moment, it was past one o'clock in the morning, and Marco, Johnny, and Petey had all decided that it was probably a good idea to call it a night, much to Billy's disappointment. So, we all said goodnight to each other and walked over to the parking lot across the street where our respective cars were all parked.

Michelle and I sat inside my Chevy Vega, and my prom date immediately pulled my dirty white tuxedo jacket off, and we started mashing and grabbing in the car. As things between us were starting to heat up, I decided that it would be a good idea to turn the radio on while we slowly moved towards the back seat of my car.

But when I turned the radio on, it was dead. I turned the ignition on and tried to start the car. Nothing.

At that moment, I got a very sickly feeling in my stomach as Michelle was starting to lose her patience with my unreliable Chevy Vega and me. As I tried to get the car to turn over, she started chastising me, wondering why I didn't have another more reliable set of wheels to take to the junior prom.

I opened the hood and continued to fidget with the battery cables, realizing that they continued to get loose. All of my other friends had left the parking lot, and we were the only ones left in the parking lot trying to get my car to start. After futile attempts to start it, an older man in a Chevy Nova pulled into the parking lot to park his car. He must have immediately seen me struggling to get the car started as he pulled his car up next to mine, and we continued to work on my car together. After several attempts at jumping the battery, and motor finally turned over.

I decided that it would be a good idea to race my car to Melrose Park and get back home as soon as possible. Michelle, by then, was being a little bitch. She complained about what a rotten time she had with me at our junior prom and how stupid I was, believing that I could use my car to show her a good time that night. When I pulled onto her driveway, she jumped out of my car and slammed the door without even saying goodbye.

It was almost a quarter to three in the morning when I finally showed up back home, wearing my dirty tuxedo and my hands still full of dirt and grease. My father was sitting on the couch, waiting for me to arrive. I think he was ready to physically hit me for coming in so late that evening until he turned the light on and saw all of the dirt and soot on my white tuxedo.

"What the hell happened?" he asked.

At that moment, I laid into him. I accused him of ruining my junior prom, telling him that none of the night's misadventures would have ever happened if I had access to his new Lincoln. I was angry. I was despondent. And I was ready to come to blows with my father.

For the first time, my father only smiled, amused by my nights' chaotic events. He then brought me outside, where my car was parked on the driveway. Holding a flashlight and a long screwdriver, he opened the hood and showed me a technique that probably would have saved me a tremendous amount of disappointment and heartache that evening.

"Robby," he said, "you gotta put a screwdriver onto the bolt near the coil and across to the starter. This car has a bad habit of shorting out the starter."

I came to find out later that this was a factory defect of Chevrolet Vegas. Several factory recalls were made on that General Motors engine to fix the consistent electrical short on those starters.

At that point, my father laid a long screwdriver against the top of the coil and the engine starter, and my car immediately started right up. Smiling, he handed me the long screwdriver and the flashlight.

"Keep these in your car," he patiently said. Still barefoot, my father walked back into the house and retired to bed.

I only stood there on our driveway, holding the flashlight and the long screwdriver in my hands with tears in my eyes. I stood over that car for several long minutes, wishing I could throw a match into the gas tank and watch it burn in flames. That

Chevy Vega was the source of all of my evenings' problems, and I had never felt so angry.

Looking back at my junior prom, I slowly realized that some life events happen for a very good reason. As I was in this hot and heavy relationship with Michelle Trembley during my junior year in high school, I got to see another side of her that I probably would never have seen. I also saw a calm and patient side of my father, which he seldom ever revealed, as he tried to explain to me how to circumvent that engine problem should it ever happen again.

And finally, I realized that some things in life don't always go as planned and that you have to be ready to expect the unexpected. I learned that night that when life hands you an unexpected bowl of lemons, that you do your best to turn it into a large pitcher of lemonade. Some things in life all boil down to attitude. I think that had I reacted more favorably that evening with that night's unforeseen events, that we would have both made the best of it and had a good time, regardless of the outcome.

I reached over into the open window of my Chevy Vega and turned off the ignition.

That car never stalled again.

CHAPTER FIFTEEN
Senior Year -1977

I was driving my car into the parking lot of Holy Cross High School, listening to a good song on the radio while looking around for a parking space. On that particular morning, the Eagles song 'Lyin' Eyes' was on, and as usual, I always kept driving my car around the parking lot until the song was over. I was late to my first-period morning English class, but I didn't care. I had just gotten accepted into college after busting my butt trying to keep up my grade point average for the last three- and one-half years. As a final semester senior in high school, I figured that I had all the perfect excuses to slack off.

I had a dishwashing job at Gottlieb Hospital after school, which I worked from 6:00 pm to 11:00 pm five nights a week. I usually stopped by my grandmother's house every day after school, where she usually had a homemade dinner of butt steak and French fries every night waiting for me, along with a large bottle of ketchup.

It was the Spring of 1977, and I had just gotten accepted into Michigan State University. I was looking forward to getting into their pre-law program, as I always intended to be an attorney. I watched many reruns of 'Perry Mason' on television and had just read the book 'To Kill A Mockingbird' several times after reading it in my first period English class with Fr. Saunders. I had met and admired my father's attorney, Joseph Russo, who had an office downtown and practiced corporate law. He used to come over to the house to do business and visit with my father, who had his tool and die shop in Melrose Park. Mr. Russo became my role model, sitting down with me on several occasions and enthusiastically talking about a difference he had made practicing law within the community.

"Good Morning, Mr. Mazzara," Fr. Saunders enthusiastically said as he greeted me walking into first-period English class ten minutes after eight o'clock.

"It's such an honor to have you join our class this morning," the other boys in the class began laughing.

"Sorry, Father...the traffic on Grand Avenue was bad," as I took my seat next to Petey and Johnny.

Fr. Ronald Saunders was a popular English teacher who was one of the 'cooler' priests. He was part of the religious congregational order that was in charge of running the high school. He had more than enough reason to send me down to the principal's office for another after-school detention. Still, he preferred not to punish many of the seniors enjoying their final semester at the all-boys high school.

Fr. Saunders was one of those extraordinary father figures who made an unforgettable impact on the lives of all the students he encountered. He was one of those teacher-priests who tried not only to enlighten you on the subject he was teaching but made an impact on your life as well. He was a tall, portly man with red hair and a hearty laugh who was very proud of his Boston Irish roots. He was a devout Boston Red Sox fan and would often be seen walking around the hallways wearing his black, long cassock, gold crucifix, and red, 'Bo-Sox' baseball cap.

Fr. Saunders was also our guidance counselor. He had a small office in the back of the school, past the library, where his comfortable office digs had a cozy leather couch and some black leather chairs. He always left his office unlocked and open to his students. His office was usually filled with students hanging out, reading, or doing their homework on his couch. He loved his high school students and especially the seniors.

To say that Father Saunders was truly a 'Man of God' would be an understatement. In the four years we were at Holy Cross, and I never saw him get mad at any student or ever lose his temper.

I remember walking into Fr. Saunders's office once and finding Petey sitting in the priest's chair behind his desk, smoking his pipe. I had thought for sure he would get thrown out and get suspended that day. When Fr. Saunders finally arrived back at his office, he found Petey enjoying his pipe and relaxing behind his desk. Fr. Saunders laughed that hearty laugh of his. He then loudly reprimanded Petey for trying to take up pipe smoking and advised him to stick to menthol cigarettes instead.

"If you're going to kill yourself, Mr. Rodriguez, do it with cigarettes. It's a much better way to die," he joked.

He was always smiling, always joking, and his patience with his students and especially the seniors in our class were endless. I had seen him as my counselor a few times every semester, along with the rest of my 'Buzz Boy' friends.

He was more than aware of our abused, violent lives at home. Saunders paid extra attention to the five of us, checking on our welfare almost daily.

In the late seventies, no one ever talked about the child abuse allegations that have become more prevalent recently with some of the Catholic

131

clergy and young children. With all of the negative problems that the five of us experienced at home, we all looked to the church and our Catholic high school as our refuge places.

Fortunately, while we were students going to parochial schools during the seventies, we didn't see any of this in our childhoods. Speaking for myself and the rest of the 'Buzz Boys,' we looked to many of the priests in our school for personal and emotional support, and Fr. Saunders was one of our favorites. Whatever physical, emotional, or moral abuse in our lives, it never came from any of the Catholic priests we knew.

That morning in English class, we were in the process of memorizing a poem by Robert Frost titled 'Stopping by Woods on Snowy Evening.' Fr. Saunders made all of us commit to that poem to our memories, and we were graded on how many mistakes we had made reciting back that poem.

For Fr. Saunders, that poem encircled many deep lessons in life. Lessons of patience, living in the present moment, and appreciating the wonderful world around us. The woods symbolized the wildness, the external madness in a looming irrational universe. It implies the significance of finding peace in a conflicted society within a dark, wicked world. The poem's sleep portion signified death and the distance to that ultimate destination we all eventually encounter within our own lives. He wanted all of us to use that poem as a means of finding inner peace, a peace that we were all struggling to find amid our own stressful, violent young lives.

That Robert Frost poem became a life mantra for the five of us. That popular poem became a blueprint of life's lessons that we all took comfort with whenever we were inclined to recite it. The verses of every stanza posed a particular meaning, a specific lesson that we all carried with us for the rest of our lives.

Stopping by Woods on Snowy Evening

Whose woods these are, I think I know.
His house is in the village, though;
He will not see me stopping here
To watch his woods fill up with snow.

My little horse must think it queer
To stop without a farmhouse near
Between the woods and frozen lake
The darkest evening of the year.

He gives his harness bells a shake
To ask if there is some mistake.
The only other sound's the sweep
Of easy wind and downy flake.

The woods are lovely, dark and deep,
But I have promises to keep,
And miles to go before I sleep,
And miles to go before I sleep.

-Robert Frost-

I remembered sitting at the bar years later with Marco and Petey, reciting that poem by heart. We would penalize each other by doing hard whiskey shots for every stanza we screwed up reciting. Throughout my whole life, I've probably recited that poem to myself a million times.

When my daughters were teenagers in high school, I recall making them memorize this Robert Frost poem as well. I would add an extra ten dollars to their twenty-dollar allowance if they could recite the whole poem from memory, hoping that they would learn the importance of that poem and how it related to rigorous daily life lessons.

During my senior year, I was dating a girl from another school named Linda Rice from Dominican High School. She was a beautiful, vivacious brunette with a great figure and a bubbly personality. I met her around the fall of my senior year in high school, and I ended up taking her to homecoming. She knew of some great places where we could go parking at the end of our dates. She had found a remote, dirt road in Lombard near the running path where we often went, and she wasn't bashful about going off and parking there.

We would often double date with Johnny, Billy, Marco, and Petey with their girlfriends regularly, some of us piling into Marco's brand-new Pontiac Grand Prix or Billy's Trans Am. We started out going to movies and late-night dinners or coffee at Mister C's Restaurant on Grand Avenue. We would all go to the Portage Park Theater on Irving Park to see 'Rocky,' 'A Star Is Born' and then later, 'Saturday Night Fever.'

By the late spring, we had all gotten bored with the Friday night high school dances and started going to the 'La Notte' discotheque at Belmont Avenue on Saturday nights. We would all dress up in our brand new, three-piece suits, open-collar shirts, and platform shoes. We learned all of the newest dance moves under the glittering disco ball on the lighted dance floor.

We could usually count on at least three of us being available to go out 'clubbing' on Saturday nights. On most nights, we would meet at Billy's house, pile into his car at eight o'clock, and start hitting the bars and discos until midnight. Back then, most of us had either fake ID's or we knew some of the bouncers at the door.

We all had curfews, and we tried to push our time limits to one o'clock, sometimes two o'clock or later. We would all get into trouble now and again for blowing our curfews. Some of us would show up with bruises or black eyes from the beatings we got from our fathers for underage drinking at the bars and coming home at two o'clock in the morning.

One occasion was when we were all going out together on Good Friday to the La Notte disco. It was almost nine o'clock, and Billy was starting to feel guilty.

"Guys, do you know what day this is?" he said while driving.

"Yeah, it's Good Friday...so what?" Petey said.

"Yeah, well, did anybody go to church today?"

"What? Are fucking kidding? Who the hell has time to go to church?" Marco replied.

"How we gonna go out and drink and pick up broads without going to church and kissing the feet of Jesus on Good Friday?"

"I think you're out of your fucking mind," Johnny said.

"No, no...we can't," Billy insisted. "We can't go out to the bar until we go to church and kiss the feet of Jesus."

At that point, Billy turned the car around, and within ten minutes, we were all at St. Angela's Church. The five of us were standing in line with our three-piece suits on, our hands folded, ready to kiss the feet of Jesus on Good Friday before we all went out drinking and partying at the La Notte disco.

There was another instance when I had told my parents I would be home by midnight. Instead of going straight home after hitting the bar, Billy had met some girls at the disco and wanted to meet them for coffee afterward, dragging Marco and me along.

I didn't end up coming home until after two o'clock in the morning. My father was waiting for me in the dark with the broken leg of a wooden chair. When I walked in the door, he hit me on the head so hard, and he must have knocked me out unconscious. I woke up on the kitchen floor several

135

hours later, with my mother putting ice on my head injury and trying to stop the intense bleeding. When my mother finally took me to the hospital for stitches, she had told the emergency room doctor that I had come home drunk and hit my head on the corner of the wall. Unfortunately, the doctor didn't question it, and I got five stitches on the corner of my forehead.

On another occasion, Billy had a minor fender bender with his new Grand Am while we were out that Saturday night. He had damaged the front bumper of the driver's side of the car, and we knew that Billy would be in trouble with his dad. He dropped us off at home that night, but then we didn't see Billy for several days, and he missed a week of school.

When he finally came back, his facial bruises had healed from the intense beating he received from his father that night for getting into an accident with *his* car, purchased with money that *he had earned*.

There were other instances with Marco and Petey, where they were kicked around and beaten up from time to time. Marco got caught smoking by his dad while Petey smashed up his father's new Lincoln Town Car. As we started turning eighteen years old, we all started realizing that we were of the age that we didn't have to stay home and deal with our regular beatings and abusive behavior anymore.

We all swore that we would move away from our homes when we graduated from high school. Marco and Petey roomed together in a small apartment in Franklin Park after high school, while Billy went to live with his aunt in Chicago, not very far away. Marco later enlisted in the Army in 1979. When he was honorably discharged, he signed up for the police academy and was later hired into the Chicago Police Department.

Billy signed up with the union and became a pipefitter, working with a plumbing contractor in Chicago, earning enough money to buy himself a house in the city.

Johnny and I went away to college. Johnny got a full scholarship to the University of Illinois in their pre-med program. I went to study pre-law at Michigan State in East Lansing. I had saved and earned enough money, finding part-time work after school delivering pizzas, then later, working for United Parcel Service. In every case, we all managed to move away from home when we were done with high school and pulled as far away as possible from our parents, especially our embattled fathers.

By the time we had put on our graduation caps and gowns on that sunny day in May 1977, we all knew that we had more than a few reasons to celebrate. We had all made plans to move as far away as possible from the physical and emotional abuse we had experienced at home our whole lives. Whether we were going away to school or getting our own places to live, we knew that there was nothing they could do about it at the age of eighteen.

We were now, in our own minds, at the age of majority. We were old enough to vote. We were old enough to be drafted. We were old enough to work and hold jobs, get our own places, and formally tell our asshole fathers to go 'fuck themselves.'

We were now independent. We were now free. Nobody was ever going to hit us or beat us up ever again.

CHAPTER SIXTEEN

Loss of A Brother - 1978

I had just finished my first year of college at Michigan State University and was home for the summer. Against my better judgment, I was hoping for a quiet, peaceful summer away from all of the pressures of studying and trying to keep up with my classes and my grades. Of course, needing a well-deserved break from all of the partying that I was doing with my new batch of friends was also a well-needed reprieve.

Joining my fraternity, Sigma Phi Epsilon, during that spring while still trying to keep up with my studies only added even more pressure for me at school. That probably wasn't one of my smartest moves in college, as Greek life on campus was a huge distraction from my studies. I found myself holed up in the library every Sunday, from early in the morning until very late at night, trying to cram in four days' worth of studying into one full day. Since our weekends always started on Thursday nights, with a fraternity party at the frat house, then continuing on Fridays and Saturdays made for an exhaustive social schedule, which put more pressure on my trying to keep up with my grades. Miraculously, I had managed to tweak out a 3.40-grade point average after my first year at college, and I was still in their very competitive Pre-Law program.

I was also anxious to come back home to Elmwood Park to see my Buzz Boy friends again. Besides socializing with Petey and Billy during the Christmas break, I had not seen or heard from my childhood friends during my first year at college. Billy had gotten into a pipefitter apprenticeship program in the city, and Petey had gotten his CDL license and was driving a truck for a cartage company downtown. Billy and Petey were rooming together with a small two-bedroom apartment off Irving Park in the Jefferson Park neighborhood.

Johnny had a full academic scholarship to the University of Illinois in Champaign and was in their pre-med program. I had heard from his mother that he was fairly occupied with the biology program and seldom came up for air from studies. He was living on campus and was a resident assistant for his dormitory there, along with a part-time job assisting in one of the campus biology labs.

Marco had joined the Army that spring after having difficulty finding a job after high school and wanted to get as far away from his father as possible. I had heard that he was stationed at an Army base in Hamburg, Germany, and there were no plans for him being state side for another year. Other than an occasional postcard which he sent to my mother a few times, no one had heard from him.

Coming home that summer was a little difficult because of what was going on with my two little brothers, Michael and Jimmy. My father was verbally and physically abusing them, especially after I had gone away to school. My brother Michael was a year younger than I was and had just finished his senior year at Holy Cross High School. He had gotten his driver's license, purchased a car, a 1975 Chevy Nova, and planned working construction with my Uncle Ernie that summer. My father was dead against buying a new car and getting his independence away from him and the family. Michael had no plans of going to college, as he struggled with his studies in school and everyone realized early on that Michael had a better future going into the trades rather than college.

My little brother Jimmy had just finished his freshman year at Elmwood Park High School. He convinced my parents that going to a Catholic high school would be a waste of money for him, and they seemed to be a little more lenient in his upbringing than they were with Michael and me. Although Jimmy's grades were a little better than Michael's, he seemed to be in no hurry to get serious about his future.

During the last few years, my brother Michael had become rather rebellious. Michael was a big boy. He spent a lot of time in the weight room, and he grew up to be six feet, two inches tall, and 215 pounds of bulk and muscle. He overshadowed my five-foot, ten-inch frame and had an incredible amount of strength. He could bench press over three hundred pounds and regularly did arm curls with one-hundred-pound barbell weights. Unlike myself, who grew up with the fear of God for our father, my brother Michael decided he would outgrow and bulk up himself, hoping he could intimidate my father with brute fear rather than with reason. Being that my father was only five feet seven inches tall and one hundred and seventy pounds, one would think that my father would think twice before going after Michael.

But whatever my father lacked in size, he made up for with his sheer craziness and violent temper. It seemed like no matter how big my brother was, my father always made it known that he had brought him into the world and that he was happy to take him out. My brother Michael's increased strength and brutal size did little to deter my father and his brutal temper. He and my father went at it a few times and had some very heated arguments over his joining the Holy Cross football team in high school, against my father's wishes. Dad and Michael got into some very physical altercations several times, and Michael wasn't afraid to defend himself and hit him back whenever my father tried to hit him. By the time he graduated from high school, Michael had been thrown out of the house and lived with one of his friends.

There had been some rumors that my brother Michael was taking steroids, which probably contributed to his physical bulk and mental rage. We were both working construction jobs with my Uncle Ernie (my father's little brother), and we were making a decent wage for the summer. Michael had plans to get his heavy equipment operator's license and join the Union Local 150, working for my uncle's construction company. That summer, I wanted to get close to my brother and my Uncle Ernie, and we spent a lot of time drinking beers and doing shots after work. I had seemed to lose touch with both of them during the last few years, and I wanted to reinstate and strengthen my relationship with them.

Diamond Lil's Bar and Grill on North Milwaukee Avenue was a great meeting place for all of us to get together. Since Billy and Petey lived nearby, we would all get together on Friday nights, have a few drinks, shoot pool, and enjoy each other's company. That summer was such a carefree time for all of us. Little did I know that within a short period that I would lose them both.

Michael had been taking a cocktail of drugs during that time, besides all of the steroids. He was doing 'eight balls' of cocaine regularly, smoking weed with my Uncle Ernie after work, and was partying pretty hard that summer. In August of that summer, I was supposed to return to East Lansing back to Michigan State to start my sophomore year. One evening, my brother Michael came over to the house in a fit of rage and picked a violent fight with my father. Michael was pulled over by the police the night before and did not have a valid insurance card. Michael had gotten the insurance for his car through my father that previous spring, but for whatever reason, my father let the insurance expire without informing Michael about it. As it had turned out, my brother was driving his car for several months without insurance, and my father knew it and didn't say anything to him about it.

When Michael came over to the house, he was already dopped up on drugs and was pretty wound up and angry. He went after my Dad, slamming him up against the wall and drilling him several times before my mother, Jimmy, and I got in the middle to break it up.

"I will take you out of this world, you son of a bitch," my Dad continued to tell Michael.

"Not if I take you out first," my brother continued to respond.

After several angrier words, my brother stormed out of the house. He got into his Chevy Nova, igniting his wide wheel tires and slamming on the accelerator, pulling out of the driveway in a violent rage. My father knew that Michael was high, and he could have taken away his car keys and made sure that he didn't drive. But Dad was so angry, and he just didn't care. He was still seeing red and was in a rage, wishing every terrible nightmare on my brother.

Unfortunately, my Dad's terrible wishes against my brother came true that Thursday night. We got a phone call from the Illinois State Police at 12:30 in the morning.

Michael had gotten into a horrific automobile accident, rear-ending a tractor-trailer truck on the Eisenhower I-290 expressway going eastbound towards the city. The car was completely totaled, and my brother Michael was pronounced dead on the scene.

We had to all go to the Cook County Coroner's office on Twenty-Sixth and California early that morning to identify the body of my brother. Part of my brother's face was missing, and the rest of his body was so mangled up due to the crash, and part of his legs had to be amputated and severed and get him out of the wrangled pile of steel. My brother, my mother, and I were completely broken up, and for several hours, we were inconsolable.

Except for my father. He was stoic, almost emotionless as the Cook County coroner took off the white sheet covering my brother's mangled, severed body. It was as though he was looking at my dead brother's body out of spite, as though that car accident was his well-deserved penance for physically going after him that night.

I blamed my father for my brother's death that night. I couldn't look at his face anymore, as every time that I made eye contact with him, I wanted to grab a violent weapon, a knife, a hammer, a gun perhaps, and finish up what my brother Michael started. My father's stupid, unreasonable ways of trying to control everyone in our family had come back to haunt him in my brother's death. Had he not let Michael's car insurance expire, or had he taken the responsibility of making sure my brother had important insurance on his vehicle, then perhaps, that tragic accident and my brother's violent death would have never happened.

After my brother's solemn funeral at St. Angela's the following Monday morning, I packed my things and loaded up my car without saying another word to my father. I immediately drove back to East Lansing to deal with my grief, tragic loss, and uncontrollable anger against my father. I had lost my brother because of my father's spite, and his lifelong physical abuse and violent anger

143

against all of us had not only destroyed our family but pushed my brother into an early death.

He didn't have to delve into steroids and drugs, had my father learned the meaning of what he needed to be as a loving father to his children. My dad spent his whole life filled with anger, spite, fury, and resentment. We were all the byproducts of his violent episodes, and according to him, it was by the grace of God that he had allowed to grow up in his house.

Three months later, my Uncle Ernie was coming home from work in his Ford F150 pick-up truck. As he traveled down a two-lane highway, the two laborers traveling with him began joking around. Ernie started joking back with them and soon laughed so uncontrollably that he didn't notice the road's bend. A six-wheeler tractor-trailer came at him from the other side, and Ernie didn't see the truck approaching him. The tractor-trailer slammed into Ernie's pickup truck, cutting the truck cab in half and instantly killing Ernie, while the other two laborers he was traveling with survived.

With the death of my brother and my uncle's death shortly afterward, there was nothing left for me in Elmwood Park.

CHAPTER SEVENTEEN
A Fishing Trip - 1983

The early sun was glistening on quiet Lake Geneva that Saturday morning as Billy Kozar pulled his fishing boat up to the launching dock. His father, Casimir, was with him in his Ford F-150 pickup truck and had jumped out of the truck to guide him on the boat launch.

Billy's dad had just turned 70 years old and had recently retired from his tool and die job in Wheeling. Billy enjoyed taking his father fishing with him on Saturdays, as it allowed them to bond together and began the long process of healing their long-standing differences. Now 24 years old, Billy worked as a pipefitter for a construction company in Melrose Park for the last five years and enjoyed his time off on weekends for fishing.

His eighteen-foot Crestliner Kodiak with a 55-HP Mercury engine had just been purchased last summer, and Billy was trying to get more time enjoying his favorite pastime on weekends. It was the middle of July, and the weather was perfect for enjoying a relaxing day on the lake. Billy relished bringing his father to Lake Geneva, as the fishing there was ideal for catfish, perch, and largemouth bass.

It had taken a long time to convince his father to come fishing with him. The elder Kozar had always been deathly afraid of water and never wanted to ever be on a small boat of any kind. Billy slowly got his father interested in fishing by starting him off with an "ugly stick" fishing pole that he had purchased for Father's Day. He then brought him fishing a few times off of Lake Geneva's peer and several other small lakes in the area until Billy was able to buy a small fishing boat. For the last year, 'Papa Kozar' has been accompanying his son on his Saturday fishing expeditions, and it has allowed the two of them to heal the tremendous scars that Billy has struggled to overcome his whole life.

Casimir Kozar had mellowed out over the years and had attempted to make peace with his oldest son and his family. He had stopped drinking and attempted to preoccupy himself with woodworking, landscaping around the house, gardening, and playing cards with his friends on Friday nights. Billy's parents were trying to bring peace into their lives after struggling with Casimir's alcoholism, his infidelities, and his gambling issues, for which his mother and family had severely suffered.

In his older years, Casimir has learned to control his anger and his temper. At the age of 70, he had slowly realized that he was no longer a young man and that his time on earth was, perhaps, limited. The older man has learned to think first before illogically losing his violent temper, although his family had suffered greatly during this learning process. Casimir had always violently beaten his wife and children incessantly, and his mother Bozena had come to the brink of having her husband arrested on many occasions.

The weekend fishing outings had become an endeavor of healing for both father and son, offering an activity that the two of them could enjoy together on the lake, doing what they both loved.

Billy and Casimir had launched the boat from the platform and started the engine while the other parked the pick-up truck. Grabbing all of their fishing gear, Billy climbed into the boat while Casimir held the steering wheel, and then they both ventured off into the middle of Lake Geneva. Billy was quite familiar with the various types of fish available on the lake, and he took the boat out quite far from the shore, near the highway overpass. They shut off the boat engine and then baited and dropped their lines. They then sat on the opposite sides of the boat and relaxed, occasionally recasting their lines onto the water.

"How are you feeling, Pop?" Billy asked his father.

"My chest has been hurting lately. I went to the doctor with your mother the other day, but he keeps telling me it's heartburn."

Billy looked at his father with concern. "Did you go to the hospital and get some tests done?"

"No."

"Why not?"

"Dlaczego powinienem płacić za testy, skoro mój lekarz nic nie mówi?" Casimir angerly replied in Polish, questioning why he should pay for tests when his doctor said it was nothing.

"Pop...doctors make mistakes too. Don't you want to make sure that they're right? Wouldn't you rather have a second opinion?"

"No. I am not going to pay $2,000 to the hospital."

"Pop...it's covered under Medicare."

"No!" he stubbornly replied.

Billy decided to drop the subject, as he was well familiar with his father's intense stubbornness.

They continued to fish off the boat as the two of them caught several largemouth bass and some perch. Billy enjoyed bringing fish home to his mother, who thoroughly cleaned and fried the fresh fish for dinner in the evening. After an hour, his father was still sitting, holding his fishing pole, when he decided to try to make conversation with his son.

"Billy...you still hate me, don't you?" as he looked his son in the eyes.

"No, Pop.... you're my father. I don't hate you."

The old man smiled.

"You have hated me for a long time. I was not a good father to you."

147

Billy only sat there, looking at his father silently for several minutes.

"I was a terrible husband to your mother. I was a horrible father to you and your sister. I know that God will give me what I deserve when I go someday."

Billy tried to be empathetic, trying to understand the sudden confession from his hard-shelled father.

"You did what you had to do," Billy said.

"No, Billy...God will never, ever forgive me for what I have done my whole life and the way I mistreated my family. When I came to this country with your mother, we had nothing. I was always worried that we would have it taken away, like in the old country with the Communists. We were never allowed to have anything. And when we came to this country, we were able to buy a house and a car and put you and your sister through school. I had a hard time adjusting," Papa Casimir confessed.

"I always feared that someone would come and take everything away from us. I was always afraid."

A few silent moments.

"Is this why you drank."

"Yes."

"Is this why you beat us so badly? With scars that we suffered from our whole lives?" Billy finally confronted his father.

More silence.

"Billy...I am truly sorry," the old man said.

"I love you, Billy. You have made me very proud. I do not deserve to be your father," Casimir said, tears welling up in his eyes.

There were more silent moments as Billy was trying to put his head around this emotional conversation. He had never known his father to be remorseful about anything, and he had never apologized for anything that he ever did wrong.

Billy started to get tears in his eyes. Despite all of his father's lifetime beatings, all of the emotional, physical, and verbal abuse he endured from his dad, he had never heard him confess his sins.

The older man got up from his seated position to recast his fishing line, then looking over at Billy with a big smile on his face. He had suddenly felt relieved to have finally unloaded the emotional burden he had been carrying inside and was happy that he could finally tell his son how he felt.

Suddenly, Casimir dropped his fishing pole and grabbed his chest. He began loudly groaning as Billy was reeling his line, trying to bring in a fish. The older man grasped his chest hard while standing up.

"Urgh!" he loudly screamed.

He then suddenly passed out, falling off of the edge of the boat and into the lake. Seeing his father suddenly fall in, Billy went to the other side of the fishing boat, throwing him a lifejacket into the water.

The old man was having a heart attack and was in the water, trying hard to stay afloat. Grabbing a paddle, Billy extended it to his father, hoping that he would grab it while bringing the boat closer so that he could pull him back in. Casimir's head kept bobbing, drowning in the middle of the water, trying to fight for air as he temporarily grabbed the paddle.

Billy tried hard to pull his father out of the water but was unable to do so. Casimir, not knowing how to swim, kept fighting and panicking in the water while Billy tried to pull his father closer to the boat to bring him back inside. As Papa Casimir was holding the paddle, his son was bringing him closer to their fishing boat.

When he was less than five feet away, Billy suddenly released the paddle. He completely let go as the old man's whole body sank into the water for the third time.

Billy watched his father sink to the bottom of the lake. He stood there on the boat and watched his father helplessly drown there in the middle of Lake Geneva.

"I'm sorry, Pop," he managed to say in Polish.

He waited five minutes, making sure that his father's body didn't resurface before throwing another lifejacket at the drowning body.

Another fishing boat was nearby, approximately 500 yards away, and Billy began frantically calling for help. The other fishing boat started its engines and quickly came to Casimir's rescue. There were three men inside, and as the boat approached Billy's, one of them threw Casimir a rope and a lifesaver. Within five minutes, with the assistance of the other fishermen, Billy was able to pull his father from out of the water. At that point, one of the other fishermen called 911.

As they stretched his father in the other boat, one of the men began administering CPR. Frantically hitting his chest, he kept blowing air into his mouth, trying in vain to resuscitate him. After working on him for over ten minutes, one of the Coast Guard patrol boats had arrived. They administered CPR on Casimir as well but to no avail.

He wasn't breathing. He no longer had a heartbeat. Papa Casimir was dead.

A hundred or more people were beginning to gather inside of St. Angela's Church in Elmwood Park as Billy escorted his mother Bozena to church on that warm Wednesday morning. With the dark, wooden casket opened, Casimir Kozar's body was peacefully displayed while hundreds of people filed past his coffin.

150

I had gotten to the church around 9:45 and was asked by the family to be a pallbearer. I went over the casket where the family was standing and offered my condolences to Billy, his sister Monika and his mother, Bozena.

"I don't understand, Robby. He was holding the paddle, and I was about to pull him back into the boat. He suddenly let go and allowed himself to drown," Billy tearfully said, describing the final moments of his father's life.

It was all a lie.

Not knowing any better at the time, I hugged my best friend even harder as he tearfully cried on my shoulders. It was many years later when Billy finally told me the truth.

"You're a great friend, Robby. You've always been by my side, no matter what."

I only smiled. "We're Buzz Boys, remember?" I cheerfully reminded him.

At that moment, Petey, Johnny, and Marco arrived at the church and went through the receiving line, giving their condolences to the Kozar family.

The funeral mass, said in both English and Polish, was over in less than an hour, and we all followed the hearse to the cemetery. As we carried the coffin over the cemetery plot where Casimir was to be buried, the priest said a short prayer service. Everyone was given a red rose, as when the short service was over, all the funeral attendees placed their rose on top of the casket.

I had noticed that Bozena, Billy's mother, was without emotion throughout the whole funeral mass. She wasn't crying. She wasn't grieving. She only stoically stood there next to her husband's casket, watching everyone place their red roses on the coffin while each was saying a quick prayer.

As the last of us were about to place our roses on the casket, I stood behind Billy as he held his mother's hand. She finally went up to the casket. Kneeling on the grass, she said a quick prayer.

She then loudly exclaimed something in Polish.

"Nigdy ci nie wybaczę, kurwa drań". She then coldly walked away.

Everyone who was Polish that had heard her gasped as if to be shocked at what she had loudly said. Billy was also alarmed as he tried to grab his mother"s hand. She only pushed him away, as she was upset, and then walked back over to the waiting car.

Billy shook his head, and trying to fight the tears, placed his rose on the coffin.

'Goodbye, Pop, I'm sorry," as he wiped the tears from his eyes.

We all then walked away from Casimir"s grave. I was silent as the five of us, Billy, Petey, Johnny, Marco, and myself, walked arm in arm away from the cemetery and into our cars.

We were all standing at the bar ordering drinks at Ristorante Italia on Harlem Avenue, as the funeral luncheon was well attended with over one hundred guests. Billy was gracious, holding it together well while everyone continued to express their condolences while toasting to Casimir"s memory. I looked over at the table and noticed his mother, dressed in black, sitting alone, stoically staring off as if to be in a trance.

With Petey, Johnny, and Marco standing next to me, we all had our scotch or vodka drinks in our hands, and Johnny proposed a toast to our fellow best friend.

"To Papa Casimir...may he rest in peace. And may we all be there to support you as we help you remember your father," Johnny said. Johnny Orozco was always good with words and making toasts.

We then raised our glasses, as I could tell that Billy was more than appreciative of his childhood friends being there to support him in his time of need.

I looked again at Bozena Kozar, who was still stoically sitting there, alone.

"Billy," Johnny then asked him, in front of the rest of us, "What did your mother say to your father"s casket back there at the cemetery?"

Billy swallowed hard. "She cursed at my father and walked away."

Petey, finishing his drink, pressed Billy.

"But what did she say?"

Billy, with tears in his eyes, softly repeated his mother's cold words:

"I will never forgive you, you fucking bastard."

CHAPTER EIGHTEEN
Top of the Hancock - 1988

The thick, misty clouds of the Chicago skyline made it impossible to see all of the inhabitants down below on Michigan Avenue. The thirty-ninth floor of my office suite may as well have been located in heaven, as it was only on cloudless sunny days that I would be able to view the hustle and bustle of the city down below.

I had just finished another divorce deposition and was in my office to catch my breath until another client appointment. At the age of 29, I was a very successful divorce attorney indeed. I had just moved into my sky scrapper office at the top of the John Hancock Building, which encompassed a twelve-employee staff, including two law clerks. I was becoming well known at Cook County Court building as a high-power divorce attorney for my ruthless reputation, and I couldn't have been more delighted. I was not afraid to do whatever was necessary to acquire a satisfactory settlement for my clients. I once had the bedsheets of one of my clients' cheating spouses' girlfriends introduced in a divorce trial after having the stains tested for DNA. I had a long list of private detectives and former coppers who were all too happy to do my dirty work to get whatever was necessary to acquire a favorable settlement. My law reputation was fast becoming a bargaining chip for any scheming spouse wishing to play hardball with their former, significant others.

And yet, for all of my law career milestones and accomplishments, I felt empty. With my now successful career and growing reputation, I was not a content human being. I was hardened. I learned to protect myself emotionally, never letting many people near the high, stonewalled barriers of my heart. I had grown and toughened significantly from that abused, timid little boy in Catholic school from Elmwood Park.

I had graduated from Michigan State University and attended Notre Dame School of Law, graduating magna cum laude. Until that point, I was a confirmed bachelor, and my hardened approach to people and relationships made me a difficult person to get close to. Although I was never married or divorced at the time, I felt as though I had gone through the process thousands of times before with my clients. It all made me very skeptical of the marriage process, almost to the point where I had very little faith in the marital institution itself.

I was content to keep only a few close friends and my 'Buzz Boy' pallies. After several bad emotional relationships, I was all too happy to help my clients rescue them from the very institution I believed so little in. My employees called me the "Ice Man" around the water cooler behind my back, and they never dared ask me for anything that wasn't covered in their employment contract.

I was light years away from that timid little schoolboy at St. Angela School in Elmwood Park. Those memories of being abused and cracked around by my father were just a faded remembrance. My abusive childhood had practically been erased from my mind. I hadn't talked to my father for several years since going away to college, and it was probably better that way.

When I went away to school, I had a job and saved enough of my own money. Along with the needed student loans for law school, I put myself completely through college and law school without asking my abusive father for one fucking dime. I didn't want to be indebted to him for anything. He had robbed my childhood away from me, and at that point in my life, I had absolutely no use for him.

My memories of my 'Buzz Boy' friends were probably the only good thing coming out of my jaded childhood in Elmwood Park, and I spent most of my time blocking those awful memories out of my mind.

I had thought about my baseball card collection and my collection of 'Superman' comics for some odd reason. I remembered having stacks and stacks of them that somehow 'disappeared' from my childhood home on Cortland Avenue. I had a feeling that my father threw them all away, out of spite, when I moved out of the house without my blessing. I was light years away from Elmwood Park, and I liked it that way. I only talked to my mother over the telephone and stopped by there to visit when I knew my father wouldn't be around. I detested the man, and I refused to make peace with such a stubborn, selfish, sub-human being. The emotional pain, the psychological and physical suffering he had put my siblings and me through was enduring anguish that I didn't need to revisit.

By staying away from Elmwood Park, far away my childhood home, was just the way I preferred it. I worked and lived at my downtown office and Oak Street condominium, and I was perfectly content with that. I was literally the man of steel, able to leap tall buildings in a single bound, rescuing poor, rich damsels in distress from their evil, cruel husbands.

As that chilly October day had ended, I was sitting in my high-rise office at eight o'clock in the evening, watching the tiny specks of people and cars living their lives down below on Michigan Avenue.

I was alone at night in my office, again. This was becoming such a nightly ritual, day in and day out, and I was beginning to wonder why I even bothered buying that high-priced condominium on Oak Street.

I spent almost all of my time either in the office or in court and had spent very little time doing anything else.

Truth be told, I was feeling lonely. I tried those online dating services and only found them a great source for one-night stands. In all honesty, I had pushed away everyone who ever wanted a meaningful relationship with me. My loneliness and unfulfilled feelings inside had only amassed my outward cold reactions towards the world around me. And all of this was beginning to take a toll.

I was drinking more, spending weekends and evenings at whatever watering hole either myself or Marco and Petey had chosen to close until two in the morning. Of all the Buzz Boy pallies, Marco, Petey, and Jack Daniels were my most trusted drinking buddies. Johnny had graduated from medical school a few years ago and never had any time to get together outside of his residency at Chicago-Western Medical Hospital. Billy was always working overtime, having just gotten married and awaiting their newborn baby on the way. My life at that point didn't lack anything. I had more than my share of one-night stands and a black book full of phone numbers that I could call at almost any time for any potential 'booty call.' I didn't need a partner. I didn't need a romantic companion.

I was doing just fine, me and Jack, thank you very much.

But on that particular evening, I was lonely. I had nobody to go home to. Maybe it was time to rethink my approach to life, love, and marriage? Maybe it was time to learn how to love and trust another human being? Because certainly up to that point, my relationships were only the closest to my Buzz Boy friends and Jack Daniels.

Maybe I was ready for a life partner. The right partner. Someone interested in knowing and understanding me, who wouldn't judge me. Someone who wouldn't push me into marriage, children, and the house with the white picket fence in Northbrook.

I sat in front of my laptop computer at the end of the day, taking a meaningless sip from my cold coffee cup. It was past eight o'clock when my desk phone rang.

"Robert Mazzara," I answered.

"Robby...it's Billy."

"Hey Billy, how's married life? I haven't seen you in a few weeks."

"Doing great, if you call going to work from seven in the morning until seven at night six nights a week a great life. Doing fine, though. Julie is expecting any day."

"That's great, Billy. I'm happy for you."

A moment of silence.

"How are you doing, Rob?"

"Busy here at the office. There is no shortage of people looking to get divorced, that's for sure."

"I'll bet."

Another silent moment.

"Hey...Julie asked me to give you a call. One of her cousins from Milwaukee has moved back to Chicago, and she wanted to go out for dinner tomorrow night, perhaps the four of us. Would you be interested?"

I thought about it for about three seconds.

"Wait! Is this not another one of Julie's fix-ups again?"

"No, no, Rob, it's her cousin. She used to live in Chicago years ago and has moved back into town. They didn't want to go to the bar and thought going out for a quiet dinner somewhere would be nice, just the four of us."

"Just the four of us, huh?"

"Well yeah...no big deal. There is that new restaurant on North Clark Street that's supposed to be pretty good. I forget the name."

"Ristorante Puccinella?"

"Yeah, that's it."

Another silent moment.

"Billy, be straight with me. Is this another one of Julie's ugly girlfriends?"

Billy hesitated. "No, Rob, it's her cousin. She came to our wedding. I met her once, and I thought she was hot. They were close when they were kids, as she used to live in Elmwood Park. She's moved back into town, and she didn't want to do the bar scene."

I thought for a moment.

"What's her name?"

"Her name is Anna. She is a nice girl and very pretty. She got transferred over to a new job working for Abbott Laboratories up in Northbrook. Just got her MBA from Marquette University, and she got a good job working for them as a management and logistics consultant."

Not thinking in-depth about who it could be, I accepted Billy's explanation at face value.

"Okay...sure. I've got nothing else going on tomorrow night. I will meet you all there."

"Great, Robby. See you tomorrow night at eight o'clock."

As I hung up the phone, I realized that I just got hustled into another blind date, compliments of Mrs. Julie Kozar. She had probably watched reruns of the 1958 movie "Matchmaker" a dozen times or more and aspired to make all her single friends a wonderful match with one another.

I didn't think any more about it, figuring it would be another boring, dull Friday evening out with friends. I then packed up my briefcase, grabbed a Diet Coke from the small refrigerator in my office, and embarked on my short taxi ride home.

It was a Friday afternoon, and I had just arrived back in my office from a long day in court. I had spent most of the day filing motions and discovery requests for several of my clients, and the civil wars going on with my clients and the phone bickering back and forth with opposing counsel had left me with a terrific headache. I was having many migraine headaches lately, and I was attributing most of them to the stress associated with these high asset divorce estates and my very demanding clients.

After taking two aspirin, I motioned my secretary to hold my calls for the afternoon. I closed the shades to block off the October sunlight and lay back on my office chair with my feet up on my desk. I started taking deep breaths, deeply filling my lungs with air and slowly blowing out through my nose. I was trying to meditate and patiently waiting for my migraine headache to dissipate.

In, out, in, out. I breathed slowly.

My mind started to relax and wander, and I started thinking about my past, my school days, and childhood. For some odd reason, I started thinking about my early grade school days. It took me a long time to forgive my mother for throwing out all of those Superman comic books. They were probably worth a fortune now. How simple life was when I was at St. Angela School.

Then my desk phone buzzer rang.

"Mr. Mazzara, sorry to disturb you. You have a phone call from Mrs. Kozar. She says it's very important."

"Really?" I said to myself. Hopefully, they've decided to cancel, as my head was pounding so hard, I wasn't in the mood to go anywhere.

"Hello?"

"Robby, it's Julie. Hey, listen, Billy and I need to take a rain check tonight. I'm just not feeling well, and with this baby coming any day now, I'm just afraid I'll go into labor at the restaurant."

"Great. I have a pounding headache. We'll make it another night."

"Well, no Robby...that's the problem. My cousin was looking forward to going out tonight, and since she is alone and doesn't know anyone, I was hoping you could meet up with her at the restaurant?"

I immediately protested, "Come on, Julie! I'm not feeling well enough for another fix-up blind date! I've had a tough day, and..."

"Please, Robby? Pretty please? I just don't want her to be alone by herself tonight. She doesn't

161

know anyone. I was so hoping you could meet her, if only just for drinks...please?"

A long moment of silence. I decided to let her beg for a minute.

"Please, Robby? I'll be forever grateful."

'Okay," as I acquiesced. "But I'm doing this for you."

"Thank you, thank you, thank you, Robby! You're my favorite Buzz Boy! I love you!" as she was buttering it on thick.

"Knock it off, Julie."

"I will tell her to meet you there at the restaurant at eight o'clock. The reservations will be in your name. I will give her your name, and she'll be there to meet you."

"Thank you," she said again.

"Fine," as I hung up the phone. My headache was definitely not going away.

I took another Tylenol, knowing that I would need to take more after meeting another one Julie's ugly fixups.

Little did I know that this blind date on that Friday night would change my life.

CHAPTER NINETEEN
You're Superman

It was a little past eight o'clock as my taxicab was pulling up to 2025 North Clark Street on that unusually warm Friday night. It was a summer-like forecast for the rest of that autumn evening, and I was wearing my dress blue jeans, a stripped Tom Ford button-down shirt and a Hugo Boss dress jacket. My ability to dress well and meet the high standards of an urban, upscale, metrosexual was never a shortcoming, and making a good first impression was never an issue. After forgiving the cab driver for being almost twenty minutes late, I exited the taxicab and coolly walked into the restaurant.

"May I help you?" asked the hostess.

"Yes...reservations for two for Mazzara, please."

"Yes, Mr. Mazzara. Your party is waiting."

She graciously led me to the back of the quaint Italian restaurant, complete with the checkered tablecloths, piano bar, and Frank Sinatra music in the background. For some reason, as I was approaching the table, my heart started beating faster, as if I was a nervous schoolboy on his first blind date.

And then I saw her. My heart felt like it had immediately jumped out of my chest.

Anna was sitting, her legs crossed, wearing a blue dress, long, curly dark hair, light red lipstick, and her gorgeous brown eyes were fixated on me as I approached the table. She could have passed for a Hollywood movie star, as she was drop-dead gorgeous. Ava Gardner could not have looked any better as she stood up from the table to greet me with her hand extended. There was something about her eyes and her appearance that looked familiar.

"Are you Rob?" she innocently asked as we both shook hands.

"Yes, Anna. It's a pleasure to meet you."

We simultaneously sat down and absorbed each other's presence when she immediately asked.

"Do people call you Bob?"

"No. No one ever calls me Bob."

She started to stare at me, and there was a long, five-second silence.

"You look familiar to me," she said.

"Really? What gives you that impression?"

"I don't know. Just a silly thought, I guess."

A moment of silence.

"And what is your last name, Anna?"

"Sorrentino," she said. Although the name sounded familiar, it didn't ring any bells.

"I understand you're a lawyer?"

"Yes, I specialize in divorces and family law."

We ordered a bottle of the Belle Glos Pinot Noir wine and began to make ourselves comfortable as we made small talk about the restaurant's ambiance. After about the second glass, we started asking each other questions about our backgrounds and other personal questions, which she was a little hesitant at first to answer.

"Ever been married?" I asked her.

"Nope," she answered. "A few close calls, but no wedding bells. You?"

"Nope, no wedding bells."

Another long silent moment.

"So," I asked, "how long have you been in Milwaukee?"

"I've lived there most of my life. I moved there when I was eight years old. Used to live here in the Chicago area."

"Yes," I replied, "that's what your cousin Julie was saying. Where in Chicago did you live?"

"Elmwood Park," she replied.

"Really?" I said, not remembering her from being around the neighborhood.

"That's interesting. I grew up in Elmwood Park too. Where did you go to school?"

She took a sip of her wine and then replied, "St. Angela's. We used to live on Armitage Street."

Another moment of silence. I looked at her, but at that point, nothing was still registering.

"Where did you go to school?" she asked.

I smiled. "I also went to St. Angela's. We lived on Cortland." There was a long silence as Anna studied me intently. She was quiet for several long minutes.

Suddenly, she dropped her almost empty glass of wine on the floor. The glass broke, making a very loud noise, as Anna covered her mouth. Her eyes began to water excessively, and tears were streaming profusely from her face.

165

I was startled, not realizing yet what was happening. She was having some kind of reaction as if she was going into shock.

"Anna?" I curiously asked. "Are you okay?"

Anna continued to stare at me, and now she was copiously crying.

"Anna? Anna?" I reached for her hand.

"Are you okay?"

She quickly pulled her hand away.

"You're Superman!" she said in a soft voice.

"What?" I asked, completely confused. I was now starting to look at her as though she had three eyes.

"YOU'RE SUPERMAN!" she yelled out loud. Now her eyes were red and drenched with tears. She was sobbing as she viciously threw her napkin onto the table.

"I can't believe you don't remember me. You were my first love. You never showed up at the playground. You never came back!" She cried out even louder as customers from the adjacent tables were beginning to stare at the dramatic scene that was starting to unfold.

I was speechless as Anna grabbed her purse and her dress jacket and began to quickly walk out of the restaurant, crying, her face saturated with tears.

What the hell just happened? Superman? How the hell did she know I liked Superman as a kid?

Suddenly, a floodgate of memories from the second grade at St. Angela's School began to overpower me.

166

Was she the girl with whom I played Superman in the second grade? Was she the one with whom I walked to school every morning and played on the playground? Was she the one who scrapped her knee so badly on the way to school one morning that we walked arm in arm to the school's nurse? Was she the one with whom we played together in the sandbox?

Oh... My... God!

I bolted up from my chair at the table and chased after Anna, who had already dashed out the front door. As I was outside of the restaurant, I saw Anna fifty feet away, trying to hail a taxicab.

"Annie!" I yelled out. "Annie!"

I approached her and grasped her arm, for which she quickly pulled away.

"How could you forget, Robby?" she sobbed as I grasped her again and tried to pull her closer to me.

"I'm sorry, Annie! I'm sorry! That was over twenty years ago! It's been so long! I didn't make the connection!"

"How could you forget? You were *my* superhero. You were *my* Superman. We played together every day. You walked me to school every morning! We played in the sandbox together!" she cried.

I pulled her closer and began kissing her repeatedly on her cheek. I could taste her tears as I began to sob. It was so strange that I had felt so uninhibited, suddenly feeling so comfortable as to embrace her right there in the middle of North Clark Street.

"You never came back to our playground!"

167

"I'm sorry! I'm sorry!" I was pleading as the tears were streaming intensely down my face. I felt so terrible about the little girl in the school line, the little dark-haired girl in my class who once told me that she loved me and that she would never forget me.

"I waited for you. I came back for you every Valentine's Day like we promised. You never came. You never came!" she cried.

"I'm here now, Annie. I'm here now."

We began kissing each other and embracing in front of the restaurant in the middle of North Clark Street as a crowd of people began watching the drama.

"You're late, Superman!" she started to laugh and began hugging me tight, almost breaking my spinal cord.

We started chuckling, drying the tears off of each other's faces. Our giggles and our emotional tears became intertwined, and for several moments we couldn't figure out if we were both laughing or crying.

After all the years that had passed, all the personal tragedies and pains of growing up in Elmwood Park, and the intense hardships that I had endured over the last twenty years, the little girl who flew around the playground with me with her cape had come back into my life. My heart was still beating out of my chest, realizing that after all of these years, 'Supergirl' was back in my arms.

After several long minutes, I suggested, "I think we should go back inside and finish our dinner, Supergirl. Before they send the cops after us for flying away without paying!"

Annie laughed as she wiped the tears away from both our faces. We then carefully walked arm in arm together back into the restaurant. We wanted to make sure that our long, superhero capes didn't get tangled up and caught between the revolving doors.

Annie and I were engaged that Christmas. And on the following Valentine's Day weekend, in an old church in downtown Metropolis...

Superman married Supergirl.

CHAPTER TWENTY
A Grand Wedding - 1989

It was a mild February day when I woke from my couch early that morning. The sun was reflecting off Lake Michigan and was beaming brightly through my downtown condominium window. I had probably gotten no more than three hours of sleep that evening, but my body was already pumping adrenaline. I was filled with emotions of tension, nervousness, anxiety, apprehension, but most of all, excitement.

The second Saturday of the second month of the year, the closest day to what turned out to always be our favorite romantic holiday: Valentine's Day.

On that second Saturday, in the second month of 1989, it was our wedding day.

It was only six o'clock in the morning, but I was already wide awake. With all of the shots and drinking we had all done the night before, I should have had a hangover.

My Buzz Boy best friends had taken me out the prior night for my own special bachelor's party in my honor on downtown Rush Street. We were all out partying and drinking until almost three o'clock in the morning, and the five of us crashed at various places in my condominium for the night.

In putting our wedding day together, I had to choose a best man out of all of my Buzz Boy pallies. Petey, Marco, Johnny, and Billy were all my lifelong best friends, and the choice was difficult. They were all my childhood buddies, and having to choose one out of the others was a decision that I had neither the emotional strength nor the personal determination to make on my own.

They were all my best friends. We had over twenty-five years of friendship together at the time, from grade school at St. Angela's in Elmwood Park to Holy Cross High School in River Grove to going off to college and helping each other nurture our lives and our futures, apart from our abused childhoods.

We had all finally had gone out together on that previous New Year's Eve, and while the five of us sat at the bar at the Clover Leaf Lounge on Diversey, I had to make a diplomatic decision.

I gave four plastic straws cut at different lengths to the blonde bartender serving us, and she held them tightly in her fist while my four best friends drew them. The one who drew the shortest was my best man.

Petey Rodriguez drew the shortest straw.

The other Buzz Boys, Billy, Johnny, and Marco, were all very understanding, and I made them all acknowledge that they were all my best men. I wanted all of them to help me plan and participate in my wedding festivities.

Rather than having one very large bachelor's party, Billy, Johnny and Marco decided to throw separate bachelor's parties for me over the next month. Billy had taken several other buddies and me to a strip club on the Southside of Chicago the weekend after New Year's. We were doing shots while allowing ugly strippers to give us lap dances until two o'clock in the morning.

Marco threw a 'kegger' garage party at his house with over one hundred of our friends from Elmwood Park. Annie and her friends came as well, and it turned out to be a grade school reunion party of sorts.

Johnny kept it low-key and took all of us out for a prime rib dinner at Johnny Bistro's Steakhouse on West Hubbard Street two weeks before. He was quite busy at Chicago Western Medical Center, and having him participate in our pre-wedding activities was quite a stretch at that time.

Then last night was our rehearsal dinner at La Gondola Restaurant on North Dearborn Street. We had six couples standing up to our wedding, and we all giggled, laughed, and joked as we went through the motions at St. Peter's Church on West Monroe Street in the Chicago Loop before going out for dinner.

Annie was all excited about our wedding cake. She managed to find little statuettes of Superman and Supergirl holding hands together and got the baker to put them on top of the cake for our wedding day.

Afterward, Petey threw a large bar room party gathering at Butch Cassidy's Saloon with all of the stand-ups and thirty of our friends and wedding guests on Rush Street. We were all doing shots of whiskey, tequila, and grappa until we could barely even stand anymore.

Later that evening, Marco was sick and threw up in front of the restaurant's taxicab stand. Afterward, we all managed to crawl back home to my place, where we crashed on the floor, on different couches, and in my bedroom.

I let Johnny sleep on my bed since he was having continuous back trouble, while Petey crashed on the foot of my bed on the other side, drooling all over my bed sheets and pillow.

While Billy was loudly snoring in the other room, Marco talked loudly in his sleep, and Johnny was tossing and turning with back pain.

As I watched Petey drool his bodily fluids onto my new Marshall Field pillows, I stood in front of the window of my condo. I was staring at the bright sparkles of light from the sun rays dancing on each of the water's waves of Lake Michigan.

I thought about my future that day, knowing that I was about to marry the most beautiful woman in my life. It seemed so strange that the love of my life came to me while playing in a sandbox on the playground in the second grade. It was like an illusional dream of sorts.

This was the girl that I had known since the second grade. Even though she had not been in my life for the last twenty years, we quickly got to know each other over the last five months. It was as though she had never left Elmwood Park.

The little girl who wore a cape around the turnabout and played superheroes with me as a little boy was now going to be walking down the aisle to become my wife. The little girl who told me that she loved me at the age of seven years old in the attendance line at St. Angela's School would now be my life partner. The little brunette in the sandbox, playing with her bucket and shovel, who wondered if Superman would ever marry Supergirl, had never forgotten me.

I was her superhero. I was her Superman.

She must have known at a very young age that we were meant to be together, no matter what time or how far the distance displaced us and moved us so far away from each other, such a long time ago. She came back to find me, to rediscover our young, innocent love.

173

And on that afternoon, Superman and Supergirl were finally going to be together forever.

It was going to be a beautiful wedding day.

Had it not been for my father that afternoon, it probably would have been a perfect one.

I decided to wake up my Buzz Boy pallies by making them breakfast. It consisted of a dozen scrambled eggs, two packages of Jimmy Dean sausage, a large box of frozen hash browns sauteed with three large onions, two whole cartons of waffles, French toast from a whole loaf of wheat bread, a gallon of orange juice, and one large bottle of Stolichnaya vodka.

They all got up extremely hungry. By noon, everything, including the large bottle of vodka, was gone.

At that point, Billy went into his suitcoat pocket and pulled out two large envelopes which looked like airplane tickets, and announced to me in front of everyone:

"Now is your last chance, Robby. I'm holding two tickets for a flight to Las Vegas for tonight. We can catch the three o'clock flight to McCarren Airport and stay at Caesar's Palace for the rest of the weekend," he explained.

I found out later that he was bluffing, as the two airplane tickets he was holding were expired United Airlines ticket vouchers that he had used to travel to Detroit two weeks before.

"Just say the word, and we can ditch this wedding. If you've got any second thoughts, any apprehension, now is the time, Robby."

I smiled at Billy, trying to grab the tickets out of his hand. He pulled them away from my grasp and handed them over to Johnny, who then passed

174

them to Marco, then to Petey. They were all in on it, and for about ten seconds, I actually believed that those airline tickets were the real thing.

"Speak now, pallie, or forever hold your peace," Marco smiled.

"Thanks for your concern, guys. But I'm a family law attorney, and I'm immune from divorce," I arrogantly said.

"Okay, pallie. Whatever you say. You had your chance to bail out," Billy responded.

We all sat around laughing and drinking variant amounts of alcohol, ranging from champaign mimosas to Jack Daniels on the Rocks. One of the wedding photographers showed up at my condo at about one-thirty, and he photographed all of us dressing each other in our tuxedos. Marco kept drinking whiskey while a drunken Petey mooned the photographer a few times. I had only hoped that those pictures didn't end up in our wedding album.

A limousine came to pick us up at 2:30 from my condo downtown, and we made our way to St. Peter's Church in the Chicago Loop. The wedding ceremony was to begin at 3:30 pm.

When we all arrived there, my father and mother were already sitting there in the last pew waiting for us. Thinking that my parents were as excited as I was about this wedding, I took one look at them, and I could immediately tell something was wrong.

My father was extremely pissed off. My mother looked at me as I approached them as if she was trying to tell me to stay away from the both of them and not be confrontational.

But not knowing any better, I kissed my mother, and I tried to shake hands with my father.

175

"I need to talk to you," he only said.

"Sure, Dad."

We both walked toward the back of the church in the vestibule when my father suddenly grabbed me by my tuxedo jacket and shoved me hard, pinning me up against the wall.

"You fucking son-of-a-bitch! That rehearsal dinner last night cost me over three thousand dollars, and you and your goddamn buddies had a bar bill of over two thousand."

"Dad? What are you talking about?" I tried to plead with him.

I had come to find out later that my father had been drinking all morning and was extremely upset over the rehearsal dinner's cost the night before. He had unexpectedly pinned me up against the marble wall as I tried to push him away with my arms.

"I worked all my life to make a future for my family, and I don't need to watch you piss everything away," he started screaming in the vestibule of the church.

Billy, who was nearby, saw what was happening. Before I had a chance to defend myself, he grabbed my father by the collar and pushed him outside, practically throwing him down the church's steps and onto Monroe Street.

"You need to cool off, old man. You're not going to ruin your son's wedding day," he loudly said to him outside.

"You fucking guys are a bunch of goddamn alcoholics. You guys ruined my son!" my father was screaming in front of the church.

"You're an asshole, Mr. Mazzara. Of all of the fucking days, you decide to try to beat up your son on his wedding day!"

By then, Marco, Petey, and Johnny heard the commotion and saw what was going on. They then went outside to assist Billy.

"Stay the fuck away, old man!" Petey said loudly.

At that point, Marco was so angry he quickly approached my father and hit him hard with his fist, a right hook square across his jaw. My father went flying across Monroe Street as the afternoon traffic had suddenly stopped.

The Chicago police, who were probably in the area, immediately arrived. Marco was a Chicago patrolman, and he knew both of the officers who had shown up in front of the church. He was able to talk to them reasonably about what had happened.

"What do you want to do, Marco?" the officer asked.

"The old man is drunk. Lock him up for the night. Let's make sure he doesn't come back and try to ruin the wedding," Marco replied.

"Someone will be around to pick him up in the morning."

With that, my father was handcuffed and put in the back of the squad car. He was locked up in a jail cell at the Fourteenth District police station, where he remained until the next day.

That whole incident took no more than fifteen minutes. By then, my friends had realized that my father had been drinking earlier and was completely beside himself in total anger. I should have probably known that my father could not be trusted on that day. My father's anger was completely uncontrollable, and I knew I couldn't trust my father in all of his hysterical, violent rage. It was only logical that he would try to ruin our wedding day.

I was totally mortified. I didn't know if I should be angry and physically go after him at that point or just sit in the corner of the church and cry. I was only grateful that all of this happened before my future wife had arrived at the church. I would not have appreciated her realizing on our wedding day what a psycho, crazed, uncontrollable father I had.

What father would choose to ruin his son's wedding day?

I realized in therapy years later that my father displaying his temper at the church was his last attempt at trying to take control of my life. He had beaten me senselessly since I was a little boy. But out of respect, I never had the nerve to hit him back, no matter how out of line he was. As I got older, I had learned to stay away from him, which allowed me to go on with my own life without him trying to control mine.

Billy, Petey, Marco, and Johnny came back into the church and brought me into the men's room. They all then tried to console me as I attempted to pretend that the last fifteen-minute episode didn't happen. As he was smiling, Marco showed me his fist.

"I took out a nice piece of your old man before sending him to the shithouse. I know the coppers, and they're going to hold him there the rest of the night. That man will never terrorize you again," he proudly said.

"What an asshole," Billy said. "You would think he could at least control himself at your wedding."

Then Billy, Marco, Johnny, and Petey all hugged and kissed me. They each told me in their way how much they loved me and how they would always be in my life to watch over and protect me.

"We're the Buzz Boys," they all reminded me. "We've got each other's backs."

I then composed myself in the bathroom as the wedding guests were beginning to file in. As Petey and I stood in front of St. Peter's Church, a gleam of happiness appeared back on my face as I watched my bride walk down the aisle, escorted by her father. I looked at Marco, Billy, and Johnny standing together in the first pew, proudly smiling as I was about to be married.

Here we were, the five of us together, watching and witnessing a new chapter of my life. At that moment, we all looked like indestructible soldiers, standing proud and erect, knowing that whatever the future held for any one of us, that we would always be there for each other. We believed at that moment that there was nothing in our future that life could throw us that we couldn't defeat together. We really didn't have a clue. We had all underestimated our forthcoming lives and our bright futures going forward.

We were all proud warriors. We were five strong, indestructible men. We were the Buzz Boys.

Neither one of us had any idea how all of our demons from the years past, with all of the insurmountable, upcoming problems of our future years, would eventually defeat us.

CHAPTER TWENTY-ONE
Starting A Family - 1990

The bright sun of that summer Sunday morning was blinding as Annie and I walked out of St. Vincent Ferrar Catholic Church in River Forest. We had just attended nine o'clock mass that Sunday morning, as we had done every Sunday morning since our marriage that past February. My new wife, Anna Maria, was extremely religious and a very devout Catholic, so going to church with her every Sunday morning was a requirement.

I had drifted away from the Catholic church since graduating from Holy Cross High School. With my brother Michael and my Uncle Ernie's sudden deaths, blaming God for their early, tragic passing was easy for me. I had blamed my parents and especially my father, for all of the demons I had to battle while growing up, and I had decided at the time of their deaths that it was God's fault too. I couldn't understand how losing two of the closest people in my life could die such needless deaths at such a young age, and I never forgave God for both of their deaths.

It was Annie who helped me find the religious direction in my life. She helped me understand that what happened to my brother and my uncle was not God's fault. It was a destiny that no one could control, and I needed to accept and make peace with the fact that their souls were now in a much better place. It was difficult for me to grasp at first. Understanding and believing in a divine being in my life helped me control my childhood demons, and it helped bring more peace back into my life.

We had just purchased a three-bedroom Cape Cod home at 703 Ashland Avenue in River

Forest, near North and Harlem Avenues. We paid $397,000 for it, which was a considerable amount of money at the time for a starter home. It was a quaint, 2,100 square foot, red-bricked house built in 1918, with a fenced-in wooden yard and a two-car garage. We both liked being near the train station in Oak Park, and we both loved the area. Going to live in the Northshore was not an option, as the overpriced real estate and the snooty residents there didn't appeal to either one of us. We both wanted to live near the city, with the option of having public transportation to my office on Michigan Avenue. We had sold my Oak Street condominium downtown for $295,000 and had a significant amount of money for our down payment. But there was another reason why we both wanted to live in the suburbs and why we had chosen River Forest:

Annie was four months pregnant.

We were expecting our first child in December, and we both realized that living in my condominium on Oak Street just wasn't suitable for starting a family and living downtown.

We both wanted to start a family and raise our children away from downtown Chicago's busy lifestyle and living in River Forest was a good option. Since my parents were still alive at the time and living in Elmwood Park, and being that we had both grown up there, we thought that buying our first house together in River Forest was a good idea.

We both attended parochial schools when we were growing up in Elmwood Park, so we both decided that we wanted the same for our children.

We wanted our children to feel loved. We wanted our children to feel safe. We wanted them to know and understand on a daily basis that they were special and that they were loved. I didn't want to have my children feel as though their very existence was an afterthought and that they were in the way of our living our lives.

On December 13th, 1990, my oldest child was born. It was a cold, brutal day, with the windchill in the negative twenties. I had taken Annie to Resurrection Hospital on that early Saturday morning. I sat and paced around in the father's waiting room for several hours while my wife was in labor. Inside that waiting room, I remember perusing through some old magazines and playing with the television's remote control, trying to find something to watch that would interest me. I was the only expectant father in the room at the time, so there was no one else to talk to while Annie was in labor.

I noticed something on the wall of that room that was unusual and that I never forgot. Hanging on that wall was the painting of a little girl playing hopscotch on the sidewalk, while the other little girls in the picture were twirling the rope while she played. I then remembered the first day I had met Anna Maria in the second grade, playing hopscotch in the school playground.

The title of the painting was called 'Come Saturday Morning.' At that moment, I knew that God was about to give me a precious little girl who would adorn my life with smiles, laughter, and love for the rest of my living days. On that cold Saturday morning, I knew that I was going to receive a special little girl in my life, who would help me chase all the demons that had so stubbornly been planted in my brain by my abusive father when I was a little boy.

Diana Maria Mazzara came into the world at 2:15 pm that afternoon at six pounds, nine ounces. She was a beautiful little girl with a head full of black hair and a loud voice when she cried, letting the whole world know that she had finally arrived.

The next day, we took her home to our house in River Forest to a special children's nursery that we have painted and decorated, especially for her. I remember running to the store at the last minute before bringing my wife and daughter home, buying pink comforters and little girl accessories to put in my new daughter's bedroom to make them both feel welcome.

I remember those few days when little Diana was born as the most wonderful days of my adult life. Being a new father to a wonderful little girl was the most special experience that God could have ever blessed upon me, and I wanted to make this little girl the most special gift on earth.

Those next twelve months of raising little Diana and watching her grow up were the most amazing months of my life. I remember pacing around the house with her and singing soft lullabies to her at three o'clock in the morning when she couldn't sleep. I recall the very first days when she learned to walk, to talk, and to hold her little spoon while sitting in her highchair eating 'pastina' with tomato sauce. I remember my wife dressing her up in a blue velvet dress and talking her out to parties after she first started walking at eleven months old. I remember her running out to the dance floor and dancing as a toddler when she would hear the 'Chicken Dance' song.

Those were all wonderful memories of being a newlywed husband and father, memories that I knew I would forever cherish. It was incredibly glorious to have a little girl in my life. I remember her being almost two years old one summer, as she always wanted to go to work with me. I strapped her in the front seat of my convertible Corvette at the time and took her around to visit clients, bring her to my office downtown, and take her along.

During those early years of my daughter's life, I became distracted from my past. The miserable demons that had plagued me during the first thirty years of my existence seemed to be gone. Other than having an occasional drink on social occasions, I wasn't drinking that much. I would meet my Buzz Boy friends more often at my house or in my garage, watching football and hockey games at home rather than hanging out at Diamond Lil's Bar and Grill.

We were all becoming family men, with wives and children to distract us from the terrible demons of abuse, mistreatment, and violence that had plagued our young lives. We all went to work, put food on our tables, and dutifully paid our mortgages. We met and got together for each of our children's birthday parties and holidays. When the five of us got together, it was with our children and wives, bringing over food and desserts to each other's houses for all the occasions that made our young lives so special. There wasn't an occasion when one of us didn't bring along a VCR movie camera or a Minolta to take pictures of all of the special occasions that were so important in our lives.

We were so extremely grateful at the time, believing that we had finally chased all of those evil satanic experiences out of our lives. We were all responsible fathers with newborn children, taking care of our families, and being trustworthy husbands. We all ignorantly believed that our diabolical monsters had finally exited out of our lives for good. We believed at the time that all of those evil spirits that dominated our young lives in Elmwood Park would never come back to haunt us.

We were so wrong. After my second child Annette was born, I became very depressed and paranoid for some reason.

I truly could not find any peace with my present state of mind. I had a wonderful wife and a two-year-old daughter, a beautiful newborn baby, a nice house in the suburbs, and a thriving, successful family law practice in downtown Chicago. But for some reason, my inner demons were coming back to play in my mind.

I was very apprehensive. I was worried that I would lose my family. I was worried that I would lose my business and my assets. That paranoia played heavily on my mind, constantly wondering if I could possibly lose everything that I had worked too hard to keep.

As a result, I started drinking heavily again. I was meeting Marco and Billy for drinks at Diamond Lil's on Friday nights. It started off meeting them for one or two drinks before going home for dinner with my wife and kids. Then afterward, it turned into two, then three, then four-hour cocktail hours. I was making my way home from work at eleven o'clock at night, long after Annie had put the girls to bed and well after dinner.

She tried to be understanding at first. Annie knew that I was fighting inner demons that neither she nor anyone else could fight or control. But as my drinking became worse, so did my wife's lack of patience. We were now fighting more, as my drinking starting spiraling more and more out of control. I was keeping a bottle of Gentlemen Jack in the bottom drawer of my desk, snicking a swig between depositions and court appearances. Those were always followed by a quick trip to the bathroom for a gargle of Listerine and a breath mint.

The fights at home worsened, and so did my drinking. I was spending more time on the couch than I was sleeping with my wife, passed out in a drunken state after several hours at some downtown watering hole. I became more interested in going to the happy hours at any bar in the Chicago Loop than I was a husband and father to my wife and two daughters. My marriage to Annie became dangerously close to being dissolved, as she had considered filing for divorce during that time. She had threatened me a few times during our heated arguments, and it was probably a small miracle that she never filed.

And then one night, I was pulled over by a Chicago patrolman for swerving and driving my car recklessly on Harlem Avenue. I had dodged a bullet that night, only because the Chicago copper was a friend of Marco Pezza's, and they had graduated from the police academy together. He played 'catch and release' with a stern warning that there would be no get-out-of-jail-free card if he caught me drinking and driving again.

At that point, I realized that I was now a certified alcoholic.

CHAPTER TWENTY-TWO

I was in the Cook County Court House on Euclid Avenue in Rolling Meadows, waiting for my client to be released on a personal bond. It was the second DUI offense that he had been busted on, and I was hard-pressed to get him a respectable deal with the Cook County Prosecutor without any long-term jail time, license suspension, or exorbitant fines. He was a truck driver and a member of the Teamsters Union, and having his driver's license suspended wasn't going to work for him. My client needed his truck driving privileges for his livelihood. I practically had to have sex with the prosecutor to keep them from throwing him in jail downtown for a long period of time. I was annoyed at the number of times that I had to be called and assist him whenever he got into trouble.

I normally didn't do this crap. My family law practice didn't include traffic court and DUI cases. I only did this for friends. Good friends. Friends who seemed to take advantage of their best friend being an attorney.

I waited in front of the courthouse until my pro-bono client was escorted out by one of the Cook County Sheriff Deputies.

"Thanks, Robby."

"Fuck you," I quickly responded, letting him know of this incredible inconvenience of my having to practically sleep with the prosecutor to get him off without bail.

Petey Rodriguez put his arm around me, trying to suck up and demonstrate his deep appreciation. He knew it took a lot of effort to allow the authorities to let him walk out of that courthouse on that Monday morning.

"Boy, I am such a lucky guy to have Perry Mason as my best friend!"

"Are you kidding me? You know I don't do this shit. When are you going to fucking learn?"

Petey protested. "Is it my fault that the River Grove coppers busted me after having a few drinks? It was my thirty-second birthday, man; where am I supposed to go? To church?"

"You're a fucking truck driver, dammit! You know better. When you go out, have your wife pick you up or call a cab. Or better yet...call me! You have absolutely no idea what I had to do to get you released and from being prosecuted on another DUI charge."

With his arm still around me, Petey pulled my head closer to his, and he gave me a big, wet kiss on my cheek.

"You know I love you, pallie!"

"You need to brush your teeth. You've got prison breath!"

"I love you, Robby!"

"Again, fuck you!" I continued to grumble, only this time with a smile. Petey Rodriguez was very alluring and charismatic when he wanted to be. When Petey flipped on the charm switch, he could sway a cloistered nun into table dancing at a strip club.

Petey started laughing, not taking any of my verbal protests seriously.

"Did I teach you how to swear like that?" he innocently asked.

"Yes, in grade school. Don't you remember?" I chuckled, now fumbling with my car keys in the parking garage.

Being a practicing attorney in Chicago meant that I had to make myself available for a lot of pro-bono work to all of my 'Buzz Boy' friends whenever they got into trouble. My modest payment for my services, if I was lucky, was a steak dinner or maybe a round of drinks somewhere. In this case, it was breakfast at Mister C's Restaurant on Grand Avenue. We drove together to the restaurant, and we were seated in a booth next to the window facing the morning traffic.

"Good morning, boys," Dora, the waitress, said to us as we sat down. She was an older lady in her sixties who had been waiting tables at Mister C's since we were all in high school. Having breakfast at Mister C's was like eating in my mother's kitchen.

"Welcome back, Petey. How was the fishing trip?" Dora sarcastically asked.

Her smart-ass comments and comedy improv were all a part of Mister C's daily specials.

"Just great, Dora. It's always great to be back here at my favorite greasy spoon."

"Don't let Gus hear you say that," referring to the restaurant owner, who was the short-order cook in the mornings.

Petey was happy to be back home in Elmwood Park and didn't seem to mind Dora's sarcastic comments. We had all been having breakfast or lunch at that restaurant since we were teenagers in high school, and we were all qualified to probably own the damn place. Dora poured us some coffee without asking and pulled out her ticket pad to begin writing down our breakfast order.

"The usual?" she asked us both.

"No...I'm going to have steak and eggs today. Petey's buying," I said as I was putting a small container of cream in my coffee.

"Give me the same, Dora...medium rare, please," Petey said.

He started placing a packet of sugar in his black coffee and began stirring it loudly at our table as if to let everyone in the restaurant know that he was now home from his weekend vacation getaway at the Cook County Jail.

Petey had gone out with a few of his buddies for his birthday last Friday night at the Green Clover Lounge on Belmont Avenue, doing Black Label shots until 2:00 am. He then tried to drive the short distance home, knowing that he was close enough to probably walk or call one of his friends to pick him up.

At the age of thirty-two, Petey Rodriguez was finally a settled, blue-collar, upstanding citizen of society. Petey had been driving a truck for S&V Cartage in Chicago for the last ten years, and he had purchased a house on 75th Court in Elmwood Park almost five years ago.

He had gotten married to a girl from Blue Island named Lisa Marie Lopez eight years ago after getting her pregnant. They now had a little girl named Brianna, who was seven, and a little boy named Robby, who had just turned four years old.

Little Robby was my godchild. I just adored him and tried to spoil him whenever I was at Petey's house watching a ball game or having a few drinks in his 'man-cave garage. I always joked with the little boy that he was my namesake and had some big shoes to fill. I asked Petey and Lisa when he was born if their only son was named after me, but they said they only liked the name, which I never believed.

Petey's life was finally in order, despite his heavy drinking and sometimes drug use. His acute alcoholism was fast becoming a problem as he struggled with the many personal demons that we were all grappling with. We all went out for drinks every week, and our alcohol consumption was beginning to be a bad habit for all of us. It seemed that the more our personal problems escalated, the more whiskey we were drinking.

His occasional use of cocaine, as far as I knew, was done on very rare occasions. I had tried it a few times myself but realized I was far better off getting my personal highs from a crystal glass tumbler filled with Jack Daniels than a rolled-up dollar bill sticking out of my nose.

We made small talk at the table, discussing the extravagant accommodations at the Cook County Jail in Rolling Meadows.

"You're lucky they didn't send you to 26th and California," I casually mentioned. "You would have made a great bride for Bubba," I jokingly said.

"I know. Five gang-bangers in a jail cell all weekend was still better than rooming with Bubba downtown," he smiled, as our breakfast orders were now being served at our table.

"Steak sauce, boys?"

"Yes, Dora...please," I said, as she was refilling both of our coffee cups.

We both began eating our elaborate breakfast entrée's while Petey began talking about some of the things that were really bothering him. He seemed to be in a very pensive, reflective mood. I guess seventy-two hours stuck in a jail cell with five gang bangers will do than to someone, I would imagine.

"Dad has been cracking around my mother again," he casually said, putting some steak sauce on his breakfast.

I looked at him, rather shocked. "I thought he stopped doing that shit?"

"I thought so too. I went over to the house last week, and my mother was all banged up. When I asked her what had happened, she lied to me and said that she fell down the stairs."

I looked at him and shook my head. His father, Pedro, had difficulty finding work since he was fired from his truck driving job a year ago, and his drinking and abusive domestic behavior had been getting worse. His poor mother had become the brunt of Pedro's bad temper again since her son had gotten married and moved out of the house.

"Lisa and I haven't been getting along lately, either," he mentioned.

"What's going on at home?"

"She says I'm a lousy husband and father. She told me that I need to start spending more time at home or she's going to start looking for a boyfriend."

I smiled, "She's kidding, right?"

"I'm not sure. Lisa is not happy with my going out and partying. Says I need to stop or else."

"Or else what?"

"Lisa may be calling your office and requesting your services," Petey smiled.

"She knows I can't represent her. Besides, how bad is it getting?"

"It's going from bad to worse, especially after this past weekend. My wife didn't bother even to come and visit me in the joint."

A few moments of silence.

"Maybe you need to start laying off the juice, Petey."

"Really? I don't see you pushing the bottle away, bro. You've been doing more than your share of juicing too."

I hated to admit it, but he was right. I was doing more than my fair share of Jack Daniel's on weekends. The only difference, so far, is that I hadn't been busted on a DUI yet, even though there were several instances when I probably should have been. My drinking during that time was restricted to only Friday and Saturday nights, and I wasn't a full participant of the downtown happy hours at the nearby hotels on Michigan Avenue until later. We finished our breakfasts and, after Petey threw a twenty-dollar bill on the table, I dropped Petey off at his house.

"Send me your bill," Petey said just before getting out of my car, but we both knew that would never happen. I then watched him walk up to his driveway and enter his house from the side door. I sat there with my car idling in the street for a few minutes, in case Petey came running out of the house with his wife chasing him with a weapon in her hand. Of course, that didn't happen.

That Monday morning in May 1991 was the first indication of the foundation cracks that were now becoming increasingly apparent in Petey's personal life. His childhood problems with his father's violent temper and his abusive family home life while growing up was finally having an adverse effect on Petey's mental attitude.

193

He was bitter. He was angry. He felt as though he had been cheated out of his childhood. But instead of taking inventory of his moderately successful personal life, he started acting as though he wanted to do everything in his power to screw it up. Instead of partying less, he was partying more. Instead of staying home with his family, he was spending more nights out with his friends.

Petey Rodriguez was a tormented man, and as one of his best friends, I should have recognized it immediately and pushed him to get some help. But I had my own personal problems with my own family issues and my own demons at the time. I just figured that Petey was a big boy. He would have to be an adult and take responsibility for his own actions, I reasoned to myself.

A few months later, in August 1991, is when the bottom of Petey's life had finally fallen out. I was sitting in my office, getting ready for a divorce mediation meeting that I was having with a difficult Lake Forest couple that afternoon.

I'll never forget that day because I had just gotten a new cellular telephone, an OKI 700, and I was excited to start making cellular phone calls to all my friends and to finally throw away that annoying pager.

"Mr. Mazzara, you have a phone call from Detective Dorian from the Sixteenth District," my secretary and associate, Sandra, said over the intercom.

Detective Philip Dorian of the Sixteenth District of the Chicago Police Department had just been promoted from being a street cop in Jefferson Park. We had gotten to be good friends from playing on the same softball team that previous summer for a charity league, along with Petey, Billy, and Marco.

Johnny didn't hang out with us that much during that period because he was a resident at Chicago-Western Medical Hospital in Chicago. After Johnny graduated from Loyola Medical School a few years before, we didn't hang out as much with Johnny except on some weekends or special occasions.

Because Marco had just joined the Chicago Police Department a few years ago, he recruited us to play softball with him during that summer. We had all gotten to know each other very well, having done shots with Dorian and a few of his copper buddies at a few local bars. I had a great relationship with many of the Chicago P.D.

"Hey, Philly, what's up?"

"Robby, you may want to get down here as soon as you can. They're holding your buddy Petey over on Larrabee at the Eighteenth. I figured I would give you a courtesy call."

"Oh shit," I angrily reacted. "He's never going to goddamn learn. I keep telling him to stop drinking and driving, but he never listens to me anymore," I loudly ranted. I had just assumed he was picked up on another DUI. I paused for a moment, feeling my temper starting to rise.

"Just leave him locked up for a few days. I am getting so damn tired of bailing him out of jail every time he goes out drinking. He just doesn't appreciate the..."

"Rob...no. It's not a DUI," he loudly interrupted me.

A deep, cold chill started to run down my spine. There was a long moment of silence on the phone, as my worst fears were about to come true.

"Then why are you holding him? On what charge?" I innocently asked.

Detective Dorian paused for several seconds.

"Murder One."

CHAPTER TWENTY-THREE
Murder One

I raced over to the Eighteenth District on North Larrabee that afternoon upon hearing of Petey's arrest. I had to cancel the rest of my afternoon appointments to run to the police station to determine what had exactly happened and why.

Dorian didn't say much and didn't want to talk out of turn as to the circumstances of Petey's potential homicide charges. He knew of our close relationship, having played softball together and whiskey shots afterward, so he knew that I would be interested in helping out one of my best friends. I pulled my car into the parking lot off North Larrabee and raced into the police station, immediately being confronted by the desk sergeant.

"Can I help you?" said a burly man with a thick mustache and a very dark, ugly hairpiece.

"I'm here for Pedro Rodriguez."

"Are you his attorney?"

"For now, yes...I am."

He told me to sit down and wait while the detective handling the case could come out and greet me before bringing me downstairs to lock up. It took several minutes before Detective Bernie Bianchi came out to meet me.

"Good afternoon," a fair-skinned, fairly good-looking detective came out to shake my hand. I had met Bernie Bianchi a few other times, but I didn't know him as well as Detective Dorian.

"I understand you're here to see Pedro Rodriguez," he politely asked.

"Yes, I am."

"You are his attorney, correct?"

"I'm here to help him acquire representation. For now, I will act as his counsel."

"Very good," Bianchi replied, using his handprint to open the door and bring me downstairs to the District Eighteen lockup.

As he led me along to the lockup area, I was afraid to ask the next question.

"Who is my client accused of murdering?"

Bianchi stopped in his tracks and looked at me as if I had asked an incredibly stupid question.

"You mean you don't know?"

"No, Detective, I do not," I insisted.

He looked at me for about five seconds as if he needed a language interpreter to break the bad news.

"His father."

I became frozen in my footsteps and only stood there, speechless, just staring at the detective. He continued to look at me in silence, waiting for me to absorb the news.

"Are you kidding?"

"No, Counselor, I am not."

He continued to walk me towards the lockup area, using the handprint scanner to unlock the doors and allow me into the holding room. Petey was escorted in handcuffs and ankle chains out of his jail cell within twenty minutes and into the dingy conference room with only three very dirty, ceiling-high windows.

The walls bore a drab, green paint color that was so old it was starting to turn yellow. They had him dressed in a dirty, stained orange jumpsuit that looked like it hadn't been washed in weeks. His face was dirty and unshaven. His eyes were dark and completely bloodshot. Petey looked tired and withdrawn as if he hadn't had any sleep in the last forty-eight hours.

I stood up from the steel chair and table where I was sitting, and we both made eye contact, initially not saying a word to each other. We immediately hugged each other in the middle of the holding room while Petey was doing his best to control his emotions.

Petey was always the kind of guy who never displayed his emotions in public, probably another one of the wonderful traits passed down to him from his father. His terrible, unbridled temper was another one of his family characteristics that had never served Petey very well in his life. I had a feeling that his hot, violent rage had probably gotten him into this horrific situation.

"Petey, what happened?" I quickly asked.

My childhood friend then explained the exact events that transpired the prior evening:

Petey's father, Pedro, had been badgering his son to help him find a new truck driving job, preferably with his company. Knowing the way Pedro was, Petey was very hesitant to recommend him to his employer. He knew his father was very quick-tempered and didn't get along very well with other people, especially those with authority. Pedro had called Petey that early afternoon, and they agreed to meet at Stanley's Bar and Grill on West North Avenue at five o'clock. They both sat there for several hours, having a burger with fries and several shots of Black Label.

Petey did his best to avoid the subject with his dad, not wanting to let him know how reluctant he was to help him get a job with his company. After they paid the bar tab, it was almost nine o'clock, and they both walked outside into the parking lot. At that point, as Pedro was next to his car, he accused his son of being extremely 'ungrateful for all that he had done for him.

"Robby, that's when I lost it," Petey continued to say.

"I told him how much he had screwed up my life and what a terrible father he was to me. I also warned him about striking Mom again and that he needed to not take his temper out on her anymore."

At that point, Petey became silent. "What happened next?"

Petey then started to get emotional.

"He called me a fucking loser and that I never amounted to anything. He said he was sorry that I was ever born. He then grabbed me by my hair, the way he used to grab me when I was a kid. He then started hitting me with his fist as I tried to push him away. When he came at me again, I had my knife in my jeans pocket and used it to stab him several times. I must have stabbed him a dozen times or more. I couldn't stop. I was so angry. I just kept inserting that knife into his gut, over and over and over."

Petey then started openly weeping, which is almost thirty years, I had never seen him do before.

We held each other for several minutes until Petey had emotionally subsided. He seated himself on that cold, steel chair across from me at the table, and we were staring at each other silently for over several minutes.

"What do you want to do?" I asked him.

"I need you to defend me, Robby. I need you to explain to the judge and the jury that this was an act of self-defense. I need you to get me off that my stabbing him was a result of thirty years of physical and emotional abuse from a very violent, narcissistic human being."

I coldly looked at him.

"Self-defense is when you protect yourself from someone who is physically attacking you when your life is at risk. The question is whether your life was at risk, Petey, especially after stabbing him a dozen times or more in his stomach."

"You have to convince them, Robby. You were there; for almost thirty years, you were there."

I looked at Petey, tears welling up in my eyes.

"Petey...I'm not a criminal attorney, and we're going to need some help."

"But I need you, Robby; I need you to defend me!" he said loudly.

"You were there, Robby; YOU WERE THERE!" he screamed.

He then broke down again, his head buried into his handcuffed hands, crying profusely. At that moment, he looked completely helpless, tied up in chains and handcuffs, crying like a newborn infant uncontrollably, completely surrendering to the satanic demons which had practically taken over him.

I could tell that he was not the same Petey that I had grown up with. He was a broken, possessed human being who had allowed himself to be taken over by countless years of intense hatred and anger for his father. He looked completely powerless, totally vulnerable to the unholy circumstance that had brought him to this point of no return. I grabbed his handcuffed hands and clasped them together inside both of mine, trying to subdue him until he stopped sobbing.

By staring at Petey, I wasn't sure if he needed a criminal attorney or an exorcist.

After maybe ten minutes or more, I finally said to him, "Petey, I'm going to need some help. I can't do this alone. I need a criminal law expert, a criminal attorney who can help you better than I can."

At that moment, Petey was silently listening.

"I will be back here tomorrow, Petey. In the meantime, you need to stay strong. I will do everything that I can to get you out of here."

We both then got up as the jail guards came into the holding room to retrieve Petey.

"I'll be back here tomorrow," I told him.

"Promise?" he asked, staring at me with the eyes of a little boy.

"Yes, Petey...I will be back. You won't be alone." I promised him.

Petey was then escorted out of the holding room and back to his prison cell.

As I left the prison lockup and began to walk upstairs, Detective Bianchi was waiting for me by the doorway.

"Dorian just called me. Says that you and the prisoner are childhood friends."

"Yes...we are. I've known him since the first grade."

"Before you decide to help out your friend, Counselor, maybe you should have a look at some of these crime scene photos that I have on my desk."

"Okay," I slowly answered.

We walked together into his office, where he opened up a manilla file and then pulled out several color photos of the victim's body.

I almost went into shock. I couldn't even recognize Pedro's face as it was completely covered with blood. His facial features were gauged and severed, and his whole torso cut and sliced up as though it were a dead animal carcass.

"This was a brutal crime scene, Mazzara," Bianchi said as I only shook my head.

"' Lizzie Fucking Bordon' couldn't have done a better job. There had to be almost two dozen stab wounds in his stomach, chest, and face. I've never seen a murder victim with so many mortal stab wounds to his body," he followed.

I was speechless and without words.

"This was definitely *not* self-defense, Mazzara. Not by looking at these pictures. This was an all-out, cold-blooded murder."

I looked at the detective and tried to paint a good light on this.

"There obviously was a lot of anger there, Detective."

Bianchi started to smile, "And you think you can plead self-defense? Good luck with that one, Counselor," as he shook his head and returned the grizzly photos back into the manila file.

"I will need copies of those. I'll be back here tomorrow," I said.

"He won't be here, Counselor. We'll be bringing him to Twenty-Sixth and California early tomorrow morning."

I looked at him for a moment.

"Then I will be there."

After leaving the District Eighteen police station, I drove my car back to my office. Since I had my new cell phone with me, I dialed my office number while driving.

"Sandra...I'm going to need you to call my friend who specializes in criminal cases. Could you connect me immediately?" Within a minute, his office line was ringing.

"Michael Prescott's office."

CHAPTER TWENTY-FOUR

A Murder Trial-1992

The morning newspaper was sitting on my car's front seat as I was on my way to the Cook County Department of Corrections at 2700 South California early that morning. I only had a brief chance to read the article, which was on page one of the Chicago Sun-Times:

Elmwood Park Man Brutally Stabbed by Son

The article discussed how the two of them were having drinks at Stanley's Bar and Grill on North Avenue when the two had an altercation in the parking lot. There were no other witnesses who observed the attack and disclosed that the stabbing victim, Pedro Rodriguez, 61, of Elmwood Park, was dead at the scene. The alleged perpetrator, Pedro Juan Carlos Rodriguez, 32, of Elmwood Park, was arrested immediately at taken into custody.

I was in my office until almost eight o'clock last night, discussing this criminal case and potential defense with Michael Prescott, the criminal defense attorney I recommended to defend Petey. We both agreed that I would act as co-counsel on this case and assist Prescott on any of the complicated leg work needed to assist him in defending this intense criminal case.

It would only be the second time that I had met Prescott, having met him at a Justinian Society of Lawyers of Illinois function eight months earlier. The group is a not-for-profit organization of Italian American attorneys that assists one in another in networking and supporting the Chicagoland community. I had forgotten how good-looking and youthful Michael Prescott was. He could have easily doubled as a movie star with his Hollywood good looks and youthful appearance.

Prescott had recently defended several rather high-profile criminal cases successfully over the last few years, and I was very impressed with his resume of qualifications. Michael Prescott was a prominent criminal attorney with a downtown Chicago Loop law firm. He was also an international law expert and had defended several international law cases in Europe as well. He had also been an assistant prosecutor for Cook County for several years before joining his law firm on North LaSalle Street.

The traffic was rather jammed as I traveled westbound on the Eisenhower Expressway from my Michigan Avenue office to the prison. I eventually negotiated the traffic congestion and arrived at the parking lot on California Avenue. Prescott and I had arranged to meet in front of the jailhouse. We were both wearing blue suits coincidentally for our meeting at the urban prison and felt rather overdressed as we entered the filthy, time-worn jail.

We went through security and were escorted to the prisoner conference room located on the other side of the prison. We were told that Petey had just been transferred there at six o'clock that morning and was still getting settled in his new digs when we arrived. After almost thirty minutes of waiting, he was finally brought down in shackles and handcuffs.

"Hello, Petey…I'm Michael Prescott," as he introduced himself, shaking hands. We all sat down at the table while the criminal attorney withdrew his files and documents from his leather briefcase, along with a yellow notepad. He asked my friend to recite the events of the other evening, as Prescott took down detailed notes while I sat there and reviewed his files and documents. After summarizing the facts of this criminal case, I asked Prescott about Petey's self-defense option.

Prescott looked at his new client straight in the eyes.

"When someone is attacking you, and you're striking back to defend yourself, that would usually be self-defense. If you're the one with the knife, and you stab them once or twice to defend yourself, then that, of course, would also a viable option for self-defense," he explained.

"But twenty-six stab wounds across the victim's body, arms, face, and chest, is not normally considered self-defense, Petey. That is going to be the whole basis of the prosecutor's case against you and why they're holding you on first-degree murder without bail. The method and means by which you killed your father stem from some sort of psychological imbalance. The prosecutor is only going to contend that your hatred for your father, no matter what he did to you, did not warrant the procedure by which he was killed, especially by his own son."

"But I had a terrible childhood. I was beaten and abused throughout my whole life. My mother, up until last week, was still being physically beaten by my father. He abused us constantly."

"Even Robby can testify to that," Petey inserted.

"Does that give you the right to stab your father twenty-six times?"

We all looked at each other in silence for what seemed to be hours as Prescott was trying to come up with a valid defense. Prescott then came up with a good suggestion.

"Rob, what are your thoughts on a temporary insanity defense?"

I thought about it for a few minutes.

"Stemming from his intense child abuse from his father during his childhood?"

"Yes. He may need to go through some intense psycho-analysis from a qualified psychiatrist who could render an expert opinion in court, but that could be our best defense," Prescott was thinking out loud.

Another silent moment.

"Could you come up with witnesses who could testify to your intense problematic issues at home and the physical abuse you endured as a child?"

"Yes...could my mother testify?" Petey asked.

"Of course. Anyone who witnessed your physical abuse as a child."

In the meantime, the criminal attorney had a few of his law books inside of his large, leather briefcase. He pulled out one of them and looked up some of the legal terms and definitions for the temporary insanity defense.

"I've got it here," he said. He then began to read it out loud:

"Temporary insanity in a criminal prosecution is a defense by the accused that he/she was briefly insane at the time the crime was committed and therefore was incapable of knowing the nature of his/her alleged criminal act. Temporary insanity is claimed as a defense whether or not the accused is mentally stable at the time of trial."

Prescott continued after pausing for a moment.

"One difficulty with a temporary insanity defense is the problem of proof since any examination by psychiatrists had to be after the fact, so the only evidence must be the conduct of the accused immediately before or after the crime. It is similar to the defenses of "diminished capacity" to understand one's own actions, the so-called 'Twinkie defense,' the 'abuse excuse,' 'heat of passion' and other claims of mental disturbance which raise the issue of criminal intent based on modern psychiatry and/or sociology. However, mental derangement at the time of an abrupt crime, such as a sudden attack or crime of passion, can be a valid defense or at least show lack of premeditation to reduce the degree of the crime."

Then Michael Prescott looked at me.

"If we can play the 'child abuse card' along with the temporary insanity defense, we might be able to pull it off."

"So, the abuse excuse could tie into this legal defense if we can get witnesses to testify on his behalf regarding his horrific childhood," I plotted. I was starting to feel optimistic.

"Petey," Prescott said, "I want you to take this yellow pad of paper and write a composition of your whole childhood, an autobiography if you will. I want you to document every single time within your memory that your father ever struck, hit, or physically abused you. I then want you to make a list of all the witnesses who may have visually seen your physical abuse, besides your mother, of course."

Petey took the pad of paper from his lawyer, along with a pen. There was a shadow of a smile on his face. I knew that Petey had an undaunting task of trying to reconstruct his terrible childhood experiences and especially trying to write them all down on paper.

We all had very horrific experiences while growing up; some of those experiences lay dormant within the deepest, darkest realms of our memories, stashed away from our daily psyche, never to be remembered or revisited. Some of us were beaten, molested, and brutally discarded by some of our parents and especially our fathers, who were battling personal demons of their own. To go back, revisit, and resurrect those demons could be a very precarious task.

"We need to get you a psychological evaluation by a forensic psychiatrist who will more than likely testify that your abused childhood caused and instigated you to brutally stab your father when he attacked you the other night. Someone who is well acquainted with the

209

temporary insanity defense," Prescott stated, writing down more notes on his notepad.

"As co-counsel, I'm going to need you to assist me on all of this and to follow up with Petey," he said directly to me.

I knew at that point that I had my work cut out for me in taking personal charge of Petey's legal defense.

There were no promises and no guarantees. We all knew that this legal path of defense was Petey's only real hope against having a lifetime in prison.

It had been almost a year since Petey's arrest that past summer of 1991. It was now June 1992, and after several court appearances and status callings, the scheduled trial was set. We had both been working very hard, collecting and collaborating witnesses, evidence, and psychological evaluations from various experts regarding Petey's actual state of mind at the time of the murder. I had almost one hundred billable hours into this case, hours that I knew I would never see a penny.

My only reward would have been able to watch Petey walk out of prison once and for all. Although we would have our testimony from an expert forensic psychiatrist, this whole legal defense plan of attack was still a long shot at best.

We knew the prosecutor was more than willing and ready to paint Petey as a criminal monster with no control of his violent temper. We knew that the cross-examination of our witnesses would probably be pointed in that direction. We couldn't be sure that our defense method would be successful in this trial in front of twelve jurors.

That grueling long day of June 26, 1991, began at six o'clock in the morning at a coffee shop three blocks away from the Everett Dirksen Federal Building on North Dearborn Street. I arranged to meet Michael Prescott to review our trial strategies and review our notes regarding our potential witnesses and their probable testimonies. I would have to say that I was impressed with Prescott's method of defense and his intense analysis of this criminal case.

He left nothing to chance. By the time we sat down at that coffee shop on the morning of that trial, Michael Prescott had this whole criminal trial proceeding scripted as if it were some sort of rehearsed Broadway play. He knew each of the characters within his courtroom drama 'screenplay' and predicted the cross-examination responses from each of the witnesses that would be testifying in this case. The jury selection process began at eight o'clock that morning, before Judge Jorge Hernandez in Courtroom 1102.

We interviewed over thirty potential jurors before agreeing on twelve people, consisting of eight men and four women. Of the twelve, six were Latino, three were white males, and the others were African American. Because of our defense strategy, we both felt that a jury with a majority of Hispanic and black jurors would more than likely empathize with our line of defense. We also felt that we caught a lucky break with a Latino judge presiding over the trial. As the trial began, we called several witnesses, including three of my 'Buzz Boy' friends, Billy, Johnny, and Marco. They all testified to witnessing firsthand the beatings that Pedro had unleashed on little Petey when he was a young boy growing up in the neighborhood. We then called up his mother, Maria, who testified to the father's physical abuse of his son, along with the beatings which she endured during their marriage.

The prosecutor wasn't aggressive with any of his cross exams until we presented our psychiatrist, Dr. Jonathon Silverman, from Northbrook, Illinois.

He had been a forensic psychiatrist in Chicago for the past thirty years and had testified at many trials regarding the temporary insanity defense. While he stated that Petey's actions on the night of the murder were indeed acts of temporary insanity, the prosecutors got the doctor to admit that his 'expert testimony' was only based on the current facts of the case and that there was no evidence that our client had ever had any psychological episodes before the murder.

"Dr. Silverman, you testify to these types of criminal cases often, is that correct?" the prosecutor asked in his cross-exam. "Indeed," the psychiatrist responded.

"So, one would say that you're rather an expert at these testimonies, correct?"

"Yes."

"So, you are pretty familiar with the mechanics and qualifications of a 'temporary insanity' plea, are you not?"

"Of course."

"Dr. Silverman, are you being compensated to testify here at this trial?"

"Objection," Prescott jumped up and interrupted the prosecutor.

"No relevance to this case, Your Honor."

"The witness with answer the question," Judge Hernandez responded.

"Yes," the doctor replied,

"I am being compensated."

A moment of silence.

"Doc...how is your forensic psychiatry practice going up there in Northbrook?" the prosecutor asked.

"I no longer have my own practice. I am an associate with a medical group, and I am only called when I am needed. I've sold and retired from my medical practice five years ago."

"Really? So now you just go around, testifying at criminal trials regarding temporary insanity pleas, correct Doctor?"

"Objection!"

"Sustained. Counsel will keep the questioning relevant to the facts of this case," the judge responded.

"Yes, Your Honor."

A few more moments of silence.

"So, Dr. Silverman...I guess you're sort of a professional witness then, wouldn't you say? You do make a nice living at this, correct, Doctor? You go off running around to different courtrooms around the country, testifying for anyone who needs a professional opinion on a temporary insanity plea, isn't that right Dr. Silverman?"

"Objection again, Your Honor!" Prescott was now getting angry. I couldn't believe how that prosecutor could slip out that comment in front of the jury. "Sustained!" the judge angrily replied. "One more stupid question or comment like that, and you will be thrown out of my courtroom, Counselor!"

The prosecutor smiled at the three of us sitting at the defense table. He knew he had snuck out that comment for a reason, trying to discredit our expert witness into making him look like some kind of traveling, professional 'quack.'

"No further questions, Your Honor."

Dr. Silverman's responses to the cross-examination made our temporary insanity plea a tough sell to the jury. His responses to the prosecutor's cross-examination did not help us at all. The prosecutor's other cross exams of the subsequent witnesses made Petey look like some sort of angry, violent whack-job. He made our client look like a typical, angry alcoholic without any control over his aggressive temper on the night of the murder.

213

The Cook County District Attorney's office had also found four other witnesses who typically had drinks with Petey at the bars he frequented in the area, and they all testified to several of his public, drunken outbursts. His DUI arrests, although they were expunged, didn't help either.

Prescott got the judge to strike those statements from the court record. Attorney Michael Prescott gave an excellent closing argument to the twelve jurors, reiterating his abused, battered childhood and the frequent beatings he received from his father. He pointed out that any individual with Petey's past and personal background could suffer from an unreasonable moment of insanity when confronted with a violent situation.

In studying their reactions throughout the trial, I had gotten the impression that several of the jurors reacted sympathetically to Petey's abusive background and childhood, as several jurors were wiping away tears during the testimony of several of our witnesses. The jurors were then sequestered for deliberation.

The murder trial had taken a total of three-and-one-half days.

By the time the jurors returned with their decision eight hours later, we were all hopeful but exhausted. It had been a long, tedious road to get to this point. We had worked hard to get to this moment, and I wanted Petey to know that we couldn't have done anything else better than what we had done in defending him in this case.

"We've done our best," I said to Petey.

"It's all up to God now."

Petey only sat there with tears in his eyes. He continued to shake his head, periodically burying his face in his hands. Although he was sorry for being on trial for the murder of his father, I sensed that he was not remorseful for what he had done or how he had done it.

As Petey stood in between myself and Prescott, as I held his hand tightly, saying a prayer to myself, hoping for the best possible outcome. The head juror read their decision to Judge Hernandez, and I held Petey's hand as tight as I could. His hand was wet, sweaty, and shaking with fear.

I tried my best to grip his hand while the jury decision was being read:

"We, the jury, your honor, in the homicide death of Pedro Rodriguez Sr., find the defendant, Pedro Juan Carlos Rodriguez, Jr., guilty *of one count of first-degree murder.*"

CHAPTER TWENTY-FIVE

The drab, gray walls of the ten by twelve-foot prison cell were dreary and dilapidated, as Petey Rodriguez sat on the single mattress situated within the middle of the room. He had been at the Menard Correctional Center in downstate Illinois for the last three years, serving a sentence of twenty years to life in prison.

Because of the temporary insanity plea that Michael Prescott had tried in court for his father's murder trial, the judge and the prosecutor made a deal for a sentence of second-degree murder. This carried a minimum of twenty years to life in prison, but he would not be eligible for parole until after twenty years.

Based on the time served in his sentence, and as long as he didn't get into any trouble in jail, Prescott practically guaranteed that Petey would be out on parole after doing the minimum sentence.

But for Petey Rodriguez, surrendering twenty years of his life for the murder of his father was a very long sacrifice indeed. His wife had filed for divorce since his sentencing, and his children stopped visiting and writing him in prison now for quite some time. His Buzz Boy friends came to visit him now and again during the beginning of his sentence, with Robby coming there more frequently. But now, even Robby Mazzara was getting too busy with his own life and his problems to make the five-hour trip on Sundays to visit him from Chicago.

Petey was alone in prison. He had no friends to call or visit him, no family left to speak of, and very few acquaintances in jail.

His whole world consisted of his ten by twelve-foot prison cell, which he shared with another jail cellmate and was locked up in for almost every hour of the day. He got to go to the mess hall for breakfast, lunch, and dinner for one hour each day, with an hour in the exercise yard every afternoon after lunch. His only luxury was a small twelve-inch color television, which he could use funds deposited in his commissary to purchase cable TV.

His cell consisted of two bunk beds, which he shared with a South Side Chicago gang member from the Black Disciples named Andre' Becker. He was doing life for the murder of a twelve-year-old boy in Englewood in 1988, without any possibility of parole.

Petey had called his best friend Robby to begin the process of an appeal to his sentence, believing that perhaps, taking a temporary insanity plea may not have been the correct means of litigating his case. But Robby Mazzara assured him that he and Prescott had done everything in their power to litigate this homicide case that was charged against him. He strongly recommended to his Buzz Boy friend that a likely chance of an appeal, based on any misapplication of the law during his trial, was a long shot at best.

Petey was physically and mentally defeated. He struggled with severe manic depression almost every day, trying to get whatever physical activity that he could in the exercise yard for one hour daily. He had been weightlifting and doing some treadmill running in the indoor gym a few times a week. Petey also took out some books from the prison library and tried to pass his time reading when he couldn't be outside in the exercise yard.

But for the most part, living day to day in a ten by twelve prison cell with another inmate, a dangerous Chicago gang member, was difficult at best. The warden couldn't have paired him up with a more incompatible cellmate.

Andre' Becker was a significantly large, overweight, six-foot-four-inch African American Chicago gang member. He had no class, no personal manners, no etiquette, or any thought or consideration for anyone else in his cell or within the prison walls. He played his television and boom-box very loud, constantly drowning out Petey's TV to the point that it made him impossible to watch or enjoy any of his own programs. He a terrible body odor about him, and it seemed as though that no matter how often he washed or showered, his rotten, dead-animal stench accompanied him wherever he went. Andre' only had a seventh-grade education, and his black, city lingo English consisted mostly of the 'F' word and every other colorful adjective he could apply insert in between.

Because he was a gang member of the Black Disciples in Englewood, he had several gang member brothers who were doing time in Menard. There was a gang of about twenty-five of them that assembled in the mess hall and the recreation yard every day, verbally abusing and bullying the other inmates within the prison.

About six months prior, one of the inmates was found dead in the recreation yard. The inmate had been feuding with one of the Black Disciples gang members, and that several members had cornered the young inmate outside when one of the guards wasn't looking. He was brutally beaten with a ten-pound weight from one of the barbells used outside and was left for dead.

Because none of the guards saw who had severely beaten the young inmate, none of the other inmates testified against the Black Disciples members. The prison was on lockdown for several weeks because of the incident, but no one was ever punished for the prison murder.

As Petey laid in his upper bunk one late afternoon, he thought about his life. He thought about his two young children and the wife who had now abandoned him, not wishing to wait for him in jail. He thought about his years growing up in Elmwood Park and all of his Buzz Boy friends.

218

Petey thought about his last visit from Robby Mazzara two months ago:

The prison conference walls bore a drab, green paint color that was so old and dirty, and it was starting to turn yellow. As he sat down on that cold, steel chair, he waited to hear the familiar voice of that favorite Buzz Boy that he hoped would make this incredible nightmare go away, coming down the hallway towards the conference room.

As he hugged his best friend from across, Petey felt elated to finally have a visitor come in to see him.

"How are you holding up?" Robby had asked him on that muggy summer afternoon.

"Not well, Robby. They cram us in this small ten by twelve jail cells two at a time, and our living quarters are cramped. It is inhuman the way they lock us up here. I don't know how much longer I can last," Petey pleaded to his best friend, almost crying by the sound of his voice.

"You gotta get me out of here, Robby. I can't take it. You gotta get me transferred out of here."

"That's going to be difficult to do, Petey. You're considered a dangerous criminal, convicted on second-degree murder charges. They locked you up with the worst felons in the system."

"Robby, I can't do this. I need some living space at the very least. I've got this huge, three-hundred-pound gang-banger for a cellmate, and he's making my life miserable."

Petey paused for a moment.

"You've gotta get me 'outta here, Robby, please," he pleaded. "Talk to Prescott. There is gotta be something he can do."

"I'll try, Petey. I will plead with him again and see if he can change your place of servitude. But it will be up to the judge, Petey. According to Michael Prescott, when he approached the judge

219

about where you would be serving your sentence, the judge insisted on your doing time here at Menard."

Petey became silent, practically overcome with emotion. At that moment, Robby grasped Petey's hand, assuring him that he would do whatever he could. He then tried to change the subject, hoping to bring a lighter note to their prison visit.

"Petey, do you remember that fight I got into with Jakubowski in the fifth grade? Do you remember how badly you wanted my baseball cards?"

Petey suddenly smiled.

"Yes, and I would have probably got them too if Billy wouldn't have given you those brass knuckles."

"Really? You rat! You really wanted me to get my ass kicked?"

"If I could have gotten your baseball cards 'otta the deal, absolutely! You had the best baseball card collection in the neighborhood," he smiled.

"Some Buzz Boy pallie you are," Robby laughed, knowing that reminiscing about the old days in the neighborhood was the only way for Petey to take his mind off of his current troubles.

"Whatever happened to those baseball cards, Robby? They gotta be worth a ton of money now."

"Yeah, no kidding. Those and my Superman comic book collection. Once I went away to college, I never saw them again in my house," Robby replied.

He had always suspected that his mother probably either threw them out or his father sold them out from under him just for spite.

"Do you remember when we used to go to the clubs together in high school? Do you remember going to church, all dressed up to go clubbing, and Billy made us go to church to kiss the crucifix on Good Friday?"

"Yes, Petey. I remember. Those were fun times."

Petey looked at his best friend, now tears in his eyes.

"We had a great childhood whenever our asshole fathers weren't beating the living shit out of us."

"I know," Robby agreed.

They both looked at each other, and they were silent for almost five long minutes.

"Do you have any regrets," Robby asked his Buzz Boy pallie.

Petey thought about it for several long seconds.

"My only regret is that I didn't do this when I was a kid, Robby. I would be tried as a juvenile, and I would be out by now on good behavior."

Robby thought about it and shook his head. It was incredible that each of their fathers had managed to push their sons to the mental edge of no return. The only solution, they had all reasoned, was to physically take their abusive fathers out of their lives and push them as far away as possible.

Far away from each of them. Far away from physically and mentally torturing their young lives.

"We should have all aced our fathers," Petey whispered loudly, making sure no one was within earshot of their conversation.

"They deserved nothing less than the brutal depths of hell," he declared.

Robby grasped his hand as their visit together was about to end.

"I love you, Robby," he said to his best friend.

"I love you too, Buzz Boy," he replied.

They then hugged each other over the long visitation table that no prisoner was allowed to go around.

At that moment, Rodriguez was escorted in handcuffs and ankle chains into his jail cell away from the conference room.

That was the last visitor that Petey had received over two months ago. Since that day, he had not heard from Robby, despite his attempts to reach him regarding his prison relocation progress.

As Petey laid in his bunk bed on that Sunday afternoon, he realized that he could no longer take it anymore.

If he couldn't escape the Menard Federal Prison alive, he would find another way to escape and end his suffering.

As Andre' Becker loudly played his boom box, totally oblivious to the needs of his cellmate, Petey had absorbed enough.

He suddenly jumped down from his bunk bed, and grabbing the boom box, slammed it as hard a possible, breaking into a million pieces on the concrete floor of the prison cell.

"Hey, you fucking nigger! When I say lower that fucking boom box, I mean shut this fucking thing off, you fat, fucking bastard," he loudly ranted at his roommate.

At that moment, big Andre' Becker, who was at least twice Petey's size, grabbed him by the hair and slammed his head against the jail cell's steel bars several times.

As Petey was screaming and trying to escape the gang-bangers wrath, big Andre' slammed Petey's head against the bars a few more times, loudly cursing him with words rhyming with the phrase 'you fucking cracker' a few more times.

Hearing the screams from Petey's prison cell and all of the commotion, the jail guards quickly entered the cell and separated the two prisoners. With three large gashes in Petey's head, he was quickly taken to the medical station downstairs to the first floor of the penitentiary. Although Petey received six stitches on his forehead from his confrontation's gash wounds, he at least had the luxury of spending the night in the medical infirmary, away from his cramped, ten by twelve prison cell.

But he rightfully knew that once he was released from the medical infirmary, that his life was definitely in danger.

Three days later, Petey's dead body was found in the corner of the outdoor exercise yard. His head had been gashed several times by the barbell weights that were located in the middle of the recreation area. Of course, nobody saw what happened, and nobody knew who would have assaulted and violently killed Petey Rodriguez.

His funeral at St. Angela's Church several days later was a simple one, attended by almost forty people, including his long-time friends, a few family members, and of course, his Buzz Boy fraternity. Everyone, especially Robert Mazzara, felt guilty for not realizing how dangerous leaving Petey at that Menard Correctional Facility really was. Nobody comprehended how dangerous it was for him, especially with his sharing a prison cell with an extremely violent gang member.

Petey was crying for help, begging to break away from the long-term mental anguish he was suffering while doing time at Menard. Petey had to find a way to escape if it was even by death. Petey Rodriguez knew the consequences of confronting his dangerous, gang-banger cellmate, but he was desperate.

Perhaps his death was a suicide of sorts. He knew that he could never survive a confrontation with his gang-banger cellmate. He knew that he could never physically overtake him in a physical fight. And like the young prisoner's death before him, Petey knew that there would be gang retaliation for his verbal disrespect to their Black Disciple gang leader.

But Petey Rodriguez also knew that he had to escape his confinement and incarceration, if even through death.

He was interred at St. Joseph's Cemetery on Thatcher Avenue in River Grove. Billy, Marco, Johnny, and Robby were the pallbearers. They all pitched in to cover his funeral expenses, including his internment and the small, granite stone erected at his gravesite.

Robby returned to the cemetery a few weeks later after the funeral to make sure that his best friend's granite memorial was properly placed at his grave. When he found the grave marker, he took out Petey's Buzz Boy medallion that he had acquired from all of his personal belongings that were forwarded from Menard. Using a small tube of epoxy, he placed the medallion hard onto his granite tombstone, holding it tightly for several minutes.

Wiping the tears away from his eyes, he lovingly read the inscription next to his name, along with the craved angels holding trumpets on each side of his granite marker. It simply said:

Petey Rodriguez
_____
Best Buzz Boy Ever

CHAPTER TWENTY-SIX

The Death of Elvis - 1999

I was sitting at the Clover Leaf Lounge on Diversey that hot, summer Friday night having a Jack Daniels on the Rocks after work. It had been a stressful week, and I told Annie I would be stopping by to have a few drinks with some friends. The Clover Leaf had become a hang-out for several of my Buzz Boy buddies. I never had to hang out too long before running into Marco, Billy, or Johnny to show up and pick up a few rounds.

Three months ago, Annie and I had bought a new house in River Forest at 1301 Park Avenue and paid a hefty $1.1 million for it. It was an older estate home with five bedrooms, a built-in swimming pool with a cabana house, and 6,500 square feet of living space. Annie had always wanted a bigger house, and even though we only had two small daughters, she wanted the larger home to entertain guests and have more parties. Diana and Annette were both in grade school at the time, and Annie was looking to live close by to Trinity High School for girls, which is where she eventually wanted to send them. It was a beautiful house in a convenient location, near the train station and close to St. Vincent Ferrer Catholic Church, where the girls were now enrolled in grade school.

I had to admit that at the age of forty, my life was definitely in order. I had a beautiful wife that I was still totally in love with, two healthy, beautiful daughters, and a successful family law practice on Michigan Avenue. I joined the River Forest Country Club and tried to get on the course twice a week when my pushy clients weren't nailing me to the cross in my office.

But truth be told, my demons were calling. I found myself drinking more, with a few cocktails during the afternoon and several more after work. I was looking for any excuse to hit the downtown happy hours from four to six o'clock and kept a bottle of Scope mouthwash in my suit coat pocket at all times.

That didn't stop my wife Annie from taking notice. She had mentioned a few times that my drinking was getting a little excessive. But I explained to her many times that the pressures of all of the divorce cases, depositions, and court discoveries with all the high-power couples coming into my office, I was under a lot of pressure. Stopping at the Clover Leaf Lounge on Friday nights were my moments of refuge, as I could always count on one of my Buzz Boy pallies to show up for a drink or two.

I had heard the Marco was working at the Eighteenth District and on duty that evening, and Johnny was on call, probably working at the hospital. So, I figured Billy would probably stop by as soon as he got off of work.

I arrived at six o'clock from the River Grove train station and walked over to the Clover Leaf Lounge on that Friday night. It was rather crowded with the usual suspects, so I figured it was only a matter of time before Billy showed up.

I was on my first JD on the Rocks when Billy came over to sit next to me at the bar.

"What's up, Robby?"

"Hey Billy," I said, smiling. I hadn't seen him in several weeks.

"Are you getting this round?" he innocently asked, knowing that he would probably be drinking on my tab that night.

I nodded my head, as Doreen the bartender, came over and poured him a double shot of Johnny Walker Black.

We started making small talk as the Cubs game was blaring from several televisions that had the game on in the bar. After his third shot, he put his arm around me and told me that he was having difficulty sleeping.

"What's going on, Billy?"

"My dad just doesn't want to stay dead. I'm haunted by him almost every night when I try to go to sleep. Whenever I close my eyes, I still envision my father beating me, hitting me with belts, baseball bats, and other objects. I still see him hitting my mother at the dinner table. My dreams are continuously haunting me."

Billy was telling me all of this because he knew that I was having the same kind of nightmares, and I had mentioned to him that I was having a hard time as well.

"Well, at least you made peace with Papa Casimir before he drowned," I happened to mention.

Billy looked at me, then ordered another shot. When he got it, he swallowed it immediately, as if it was the last drink he was ever going to have. He then started his confession.

"Robby, I have something I need to get off of my chest."

"Really? What's up?"

"Robby, I killed my father."

I looked at him, at first thinking that he was either kidding or extremely drunk.

"What?"

227

"I killed him, Robby. When my father had his heart attack on my boat, he fell off the fishing boat and struggled to swim. He got up closer to the boat, and I gave him the boat ore to grab onto to pull him back in. I was about to pull him into the boat. But at the last second, I let go of the boat ore."

I looked at him, speechless.

"I allowed him to drown, Robby. I let him drown."

I was confused at first, not knowing whether he was actually kidding or confessing the truth. Billy's eyes were now full of tears, and he started getting emotional. He ordered another round of drinks for the both of us, and we sat there in silence for the next five minutes. He then looked at me again.

"I killed my father."

It was several years since Papa Casimir's death, and we had always believed Billy's story, and the way his father had 'drowned' during that fishing trip in Lake Geneva had finally come to light. By the time Billy was married and had two children of his own, his past and his demons started to catch up with him. We were sitting at the bar once, having drinks, when Billy finally explained to me how he was being 'haunted' by his father. He said that he seldom ever had more than a few hours of sleep every night and that the demons of his childhood had come to mentally abuse him once again.

He spent the rest of the evening explaining to me how he had 'let go' of the paddle that his father was holding in an attempt to rescue him on that faithful day in Lake Geneva. He said that he felt possessed and that he couldn't bear the thought of pulling his father back into the boat after the way he had abused him all of those years. In his mind, he had killed his father, and he now couldn't sleep at night.

After he explained all of this to me, I looked at him, and I suddenly remembered that unsolved murder of Johnny's Orozco's stepdad, Joe LaFatta. I recalled his body being washed up off of Lake Michigan one day several years ago, and I was curious.

"Billy, do you remember that washed-up body of that guy we all beat up as kids, who used to be married to Johnny's mom?"

Billy Kozar turned three shades of white when I asked that question.

"What do you think happened to him?" I brazenly asked.

Billy looked at me in silence. He then finished his drink and quickly ordered another.

"I saw an older man fishing on the pier off of Evanston Beach one afternoon. As I was launching my boat, we started making conversation. He seemed like a nice older man and asked if he could come out with me on my new boat to go fishing. He didn't remember who I was until we were about a half-mile away from shore."

I looked at him intently while ordering another Jack Daniels on the rocks.

"While we were out on the water, he then said some pretty shitty things about Johnny and the four of us, mentioning that if he had not been so drunk, he would have easily killed the five of us without any problem."

"So what happened?"

Billy looked at me and only said, "the less you know, the better."

Being that Joe LaFatta's body was ridden with stab wounds, I figured that Billy had something to do with his murder. Billy was dangerously angry at that time, and it didn't take much to get him to the point where he would use his switchblade on anyone to really pissed him off. It didn't take a genius to figure out that he had cut him up pretty good with his knife and threw him off the boat and onto Lake Michigan.

In his thirties, Billy Kozar became a very haunted man. He started drinking heavily, just like the rest of us, only now he had become a wife-beater like his father until Julie finally left him. He had been taken into custody a few times by the police for domestic violence. His wife had placed a restraining order on him several times until they finally separated and divorced.

At the age of forty, he was no longer the cool, soft-spoken tough guy from the movies. He was now an over-weight, balding shadow of the man that he once was, having physically suffered from years of self-deprecation and alcohol abuse. Billy looked twenty years older than his actual age, and he was mentally beginning to lose it. His violent temper and mean streak got him into several fights at the bars he frequented, and I was constantly pleading with the judges in Cook County to give him a hall pass from his assault and battery charges.

On that Friday evening, we had several drinks apiece, and I had Annie leaving me voicemails on my cell phone. I knew I had to get home as it was past eight-thirty, and I still hadn't had any dinner.

I closed out the bar tab, and Billy and I walked outside of the bar. He offered to drive me home but knowing that he was just as drunk as I was, I decided to call a taxicab.

He gave me a long hug and whispered in my ear, "I love you, Robby, I love you."

"I love you too, Buzz Boy," I said, smiling as I got into the taxicab.

That was the last time I saw him alive.

Three weeks later, during that summer of 1999, my brother Buzz Boy, Billy Kozar, met his final end.

The once Elvis Presley look-a-like got into an altercation with the wrong guy in the Clover Leaf Bar on Diversey Avenue. After the disagreement spilled into the parking lot, Billy Kozar pulled out his switchblade while the other guy pulled out a Smith and Wesson .38 revolver and pulled the trigger. He had made the mistake of bringing a knife to a gunfight, and Billy didn't stand a chance.

A .38 caliber bullet hit Billy in his chest, and he bled to death on his way to the hospital.

I remember getting a call from Detective Marco Pezza from the Sixteenth District at two-thirty in the morning, informing me that Billy had gotten into a deadly altercation and had died at the hospital. Marco was pretty broken up over the phone.

Marco was on duty that evening and rushed over to Resurrection Hospital that night along with Dr. Johnny Orozco, who was off duty at the time. By the time I had gotten there, Billy's body had been taken to the morgue, and we were asked to go over there and identify him.

There three of us stood as Billy's face and body were uncovered by the white sheet used to cover dead bodies. I remember my eyes being blurry from all of the intense tears and shock I was experiencing at that moment, as I was having a difficult time focusing on his lifeless body. Marco had asked the coroner for his belongings, and along with his wallet, his switchblade and brass knuckles were his car keys. Attached to his car keys was his 'Buzz Boys' medallion, which we still all carried with us. Marco asked me to hold onto it for a while until after his family was contacted and his funeral arrangements were made.

Billy was the second Buzz Boy to die amongst us, and we were all pretty broken up. The three of us were all pallbearers, carrying his body into St. Angela's Church in Elmwood Park.

William Thomas Kozar was buried at St. Joseph's Cemetery in Chicago off of Cumberland Avenue on that rainy, summer day in 1999. We all stood together, the three of us, realizing the tragedy that Billy had endured from the effects of all of our violent and abusive childhoods. Billy had self-destructed from the demons of his own father. It was as if Casimir Kozar had pulled his son into a grave next to his, revenge for not pulling him out of the water. We all stood there as Billy's body was buried in a cemetery plot between his mother and his father's graves.

About two months later, I was still carrying around Billy's Buzz Boy medallion with me as I visited his gravesite on that fall day in October. A small, four-inch by ten-inch marble grave marker was placed there on the ground, with his simple name and years of his birth and death. I had gone to the Ace Hardware store earlier that day and purchased a small tube of clear epoxy. After saying a short prayer to myself, I applied some epoxy onto the back of his Buzz Boy medallion and placed it on his gravestone.

With the flask of Jack Daniels that I had always carried with me, I made a quick toast to Billy there at his grave, then sprinkled the rest of the whiskey onto his tombstone. I thought about the times we played together on Cortland Avenue. I thought about the way he coached me during that fight with Jakubowski in the fifth grade. I thought about all the times we went out together, partied together, laughed together, cried together, drank together at the bar complaining about our horrific childhoods. I thought about the way we had achieved forty years of old age together. I placed a packet of his Marlboro Lights onto the grave and said goodbye to him for the last time. As I walked away, I couldn't have walked more than two hundred yards when I thought I heard someone calling me. I quickly turned around where Billy was buried.

There Billy was, standing at his own grave, the same way he looked in high school. He had his black leather jacket on, his black tee shirt and cigarettes, nodding his head at me with that cool smile of his.

Elvis never looked better.

CHAPTER TWENTY-SEVEN

My Father's Death - 2004

The traffic on I-94 going eastbound was rather light that evening, as I was driving most of the night to St. Anthony's Hospital on the westside of Chicago. I was coming in from downtown Chicago and had just gotten word from my younger brother Jimmy that my father, Alberto Mazzara, was gravely ill. His neurological disease had taken a toll for the worst, and he had been suffering a slow downturn in his health. He had been in the hospital for several days, as pneumonia had taken over his 81-year-old body. The complications of his Parkinson's disease had left his body almost totally paralyzed. His intense disease was an illness that he had been struggling with for over twenty years and now had taken a toll, disabling most of his bodily functions.

I had not spoken to my father since my wedding day. I had been estranged from my father since that day when he arrived at the church to start a fistfight with me before the ceremony. In all the years after, he never called. He never checked on my family or me. He never bothered to acknowledge me and the horrific treatment inflicted on myself, my mother, and my brothers.

When my two daughters were born, he never came to see them at the hospital nor visit them at home. He didn't show up to their baptisms, never called to ask how they were doing, or checked on the welfare of my family.

In all the years of my adult life, he never apologized nor felt any remorse for the terrible abuse that he inflicted on our family. My father was an abusive, ego-centric, narcissistic bastard. And yet, like most of my friends and especially myself, we all were conflicted. It was as though we couldn't make up our minds as to whether our abusive fathers deserved to be forgiven. Or spend an insurmountable amount of time and wasted energy hating their guts. It was a conflict that haunted all of us throughout our adult lives, and I personally couldn't make any peace with it.

As I was driving to the hospital that evening, I had debated long and hard about whether I wanted to be at my father's deathbed. There was a part of me that would have rather stayed as far away as possible from him and that gloomy, drab hospital room. I didn't want to think about his dying without ever making peace with me, his family and acknowledging all of his past sins.

And yet, there was the rational side of me that realized hating my father exuded way too much energy. I needed to find some peace with whoever and whatever was deep inside of my father's soul. I knew that I had always struggled to overcome the inner torment and violence that was so prevalent in my childhood. All of my insecurities, all of my anxieties, and my personal demons were created and exemplified by my father.

He had recently closed his tool and die company, which further contributed to his private miseries. He couldn't accept responsibility for the failure of his sixty-year-old business. He had even blamed his business failure on the dismal fact that neither of his remaining two sons wanted to part of his business.

My brother Jimmy had become an electrical engineer, working for the Motorola Company in Schaumburg. And like me, he continued to struggle with the terrible, abusive memories of our childhood. The only difference was that he had a better relationship with my father than I did. He was at least speaking with him, while I refused to have anything to do with him whatsoever.

Realizing that his comments and emotions were always toxic, I rightfully turned my back on him and walked away, never speaking to him or having a relationship with him. With all the events going on in my life, my father continued to remain stoic. He refused to participate in the ebbs and flows of my life, refusing to witness the triumphs and tragedies that have been so much a part of these last twenty years. I had withdrawn his exclusive right to control and dominate me, and I'm he was bitter.

I turned off the Fullerton exit and drove two miles west to St. Anthony's Hospital. It was a warm Saturday morning in May, just after 4:00 am, and I was only allowed to enter the hospital at that early hour through the emergency room entrance. After checking in with a few of the nurses, I was instructed to go to the intensive care unit on the eighth floor on the hospital's west wing.

As I entered Room 822, there laid an old, balding shadow of a man, with tubes and wires protruding from his dilapidated body into complicated monitoring machines. These were devices that made beeping noises, measuring everything from his heart rate and blood pressure to his brain waves and breathing functions. He was a pale shadow of the intensely strong, larger-than-life man that I once knew, lying helplessly in his hospital bed...waiting for death to come. My father was once the epitome of strength. His legendary success in his life and his business only accompanied his arrogance and his uncontrollable temper, for which I took the brunt of as a very little boy.

There was no one else in his private room in intensive care, but only monitoring machines and a very dim light near his hospital bed. The whole intensive care ward smelled of bodily fluids that I couldn't describe, and I was having a hard time keeping myself from getting nauseated. The eighth floor of the hospital was deafeningly quiet, and to my surprise, no one else from my family was there. I sat on the chair next to his bed, my heart beating out of my chest with the stress and nervousness of my sitting all alone next to my father's deathbed. As the machines continued to make their faint, beating noises, I noticed my father opening his eyes. I then grasped his hand.

"Mike? Mike?" he kept saying my dead brother's name.

"No, Dad, it's Robby."

He looked over towards me as I sat at the chair next to his bed, as I was still totally afraid even to touch him. At first, he seemed to glare at me, and for a scared moment, I wanted to walk out of that hospital room and return to the suburbs.

Then, I noticed tears welling up in his eyes, struggling to find words to speak in his final moments of life. He had the age spots and bruises of old age, as his face looked scared and war-torn, untouched by a razor blade in several days.

I bravely touched my father's hand, wondering if he had the strength to withdraw it. He seemed to grasp my hand as I touched his tightly, and then I immediately knew that, at the very least, he was open to hearing my voice.

"How are you feeling, Pop?"

He didn't answer but only looked at me as tears were now streaming down his face. My eyes were starting to well up as well, as I was having

237

trouble focusing on him lying there, so helpless in his bed.

A nurse came to interrupt our lack of conversation as she took his vitals on his right arm. I tried to release his left hand in mine, but he found the strength to hold it as he continued to look at me. His once deep, intensive hazel brown eyes were bloodshot and looked almost a pale blue, while he was struggling to say the few words that we never exchanged in our total intertwining lifespan of fifty or more years.

"It's going to be a beautiful day outside," I struggled to say, trying to make conversation regarding the warm spring day. I had remembered so many times trying to talk to him years ago and only managing to have the subject of the current weather in common.

Tears then began streaming down my face as I was having difficulty focusing on the man I tried so hard to love, hate, and forgive my whole life. At that moment, the little eight-year-old boy inside of me stood up from the chair, and I put my right hand on his unshaven face and pressed my face next to his. The familiar smell of his skin, a body scent that I hadn't smelled in over forty years, overcame me.

But there was no reaction, no words, no thoughts of remorse, or requests for forgiveness. I must have been sitting next to his hospital bed for more than an hour. He only occasionally glared at me as if he wanted me to go away during that whole time.

Watching him lay there in that hospital bed, being defiant without any remorse, suddenly made me angry. Not even on his deathbed could my narcissistic father acknowledge the hurt and pain he had inflicted into my childhood.

My hatred, my bad memories, and my personal pain began to overwhelm me at that moment. Next to his bed on a hospital chair were two large pillows. I looked at those pillows, and the very thought of taking revenge against this man started to overtake my mind.

There were no nurses around, and the hospital floor was practically empty.

I walked over to that chair and grasped those two pillows. I realized that, in my father's frail condition, putting those pillows over his face and suffocating him would be a quick death.

No one would see me. No one would hear him take his last breath. No one would hear him scream with those heavy pillows over his face.

I walked over to his bedside, holding those pillows with both of my hands. At that moment, my father looked over at me as if he had already known what I was about to do.

Suddenly, he started to cry out loud, coughing up blood and saliva out of the side of his mouth. He started gaging and was struggling to breathe. The heart monitor was starting to jump erratically, and the breathing machine began making beeping sounds. I dropped the pillows that were in my hands onto the floor. At that moment, a nurse rushed into his room.

He began breathing intermittently, and another nurse came to assist the other caregiver. She pulled the steel file holder's charts attached to the wall, which clearly said "A. Mazzara - Do Not Resuscitate" in bold letters. As the two nurses administered and adjusted his IV, my father gave me one long last look, a look that I would never forget...as if to silently say goodbye. I stood there,

239

just watching him in silence, waiting for my hatred to subside.

He then only closed his eyes, and the heart monitor flat-lined.

God saved you, I thought to myself.

It was as if God knew what I was about to do, and He decided to beat me to it. Someone upstairs didn't want me to have the mortal sin of murdering my father in that hospital room on my conscience. Maybe Petey or Billy were both up there watching me, and they suddenly interceded from my taking my father's life at that very moment.

My feelings about this man that I tried so hard to love without question or condition overcame me, and I started to get emotional. I was still conflicted about him, knowing that it was possible to love someone with all of your heart and fervently hate them at the same time.

At that moment, I could feel his soul immediately leave his body, as a cold chill that I had never experienced overcome me. I could feel him watching me from above, as his spirit was rising from his dead body and surrounding me, bringing a faint cold wind across the room. My eyes began to well up as I leaned over and kissed his still warm forehead, leaving the tracks of my tears against his skin.

"Goodbye, Pop," was all I could manage to say, as the blurred vision from the tears in my eyes made it almost impossible for me to see. At that moment, I could feel his essence, grabbing me, pulling me, squeezing my arm, slapping, and punching my face as he did so many times to me as a child.

I struggled to leave him alone in his hospital bed. It was though all of my anger, all of my

240

anguish, and all the intense, frustrating pain that I felt as a child had finally left my body and had transcended upwards towards his spirit.

And then, while Alberto Mazzara's lifeless body was still lying on his bed...I turned and walked away.

CHAPTER TWENTY-EIGHT

Dr. John Orozco - 2005

Physician, heal thyself.

A biblical proverb meaning that people should take care of their own defects and not just correct the faults of others.

The class brain, the class nerd from Elmwood Park, was a physician and a Buzz Boy. But not just any Buzz Boy. He studied hard, overcame many personal and financial obstacles, and became a doctor.

He was one of us.

Johnny Orozco was the smartest one of all of us Buzz Boys. He graduated in the top ten of our Class of 1977 from Holy Cross High School, went to the University of Illinois, and Loyola Medical School, graduating with high honors in 1985.

He was the pride of his mother, of course, and all of our families and friends in Elmwood Park. Everyone in town wanted to get tickets to his graduation ceremony, held at Donnelly Hall in downtown Chicago. Although he was only limited to six tickets, he was able to sneak a few more passes so that there were twenty of us there at the large auditorium to watch him get his doctorate in medicine. I remember all of us screaming, shouting when his name was announced, as Loyola University's Dean of Medicine placed his doctoral garments around his neck and then handed him his medical degree.

"Doctor Buzz Boy," we used to kid around and call him after several drinks at the bar. We were all very proud of Johnny, and watching him grow up alongside us and succeed was the highlight of all of our lives.

He decided that he would become a cardiologist and had tilted his internship and medical studies to where he could pursue that specialty. Petey, Marco, Billy, and I were all very proud of him, knowing that we were probably forever indebted to his intellect, his superior study habits, and how he was able to allow us to grasp onto his coattails in helping us to pass most of our classes. We all admitted that there were numerous times at St. Angela's grade school and Holy Cross High School that we would have flunked out if not for Johnny's help and assistance.

Johnny grew up to be the smallest one of all of us. The four of us grew to be between five feet, ten inches, and over six feet two inches tall. Johnny was barely five feet, six inches, and one hundred and forty pounds. He was a smaller guy and thus tried to overcompensate for his lack of height by doing physical things that the rest of us wouldn't think of doing.

He started running track and cross country in his senior year in high school and became very proficient at running the mile in under five minutes, breaking the school record. He would regularly run marathons in college and medical school, and to say that he was in excellent physical shape was an understatement.

Because of his intense studies, we didn't get to see a lot of him during college. I was away at Michigan State, so I didn't see him beyond summer vacations and winter and spring breaks. We would call each other once in a while. We still managed to maintain a good friendship while he was finishing his medical studies and went on to his hospital residency at Chicago-Western Medical Center.

Johnny met a gorgeous nurse working there by the name of Allyssa DiSantis. She was a shapely brunette with a bubbly personality that meshed

243

very well with Johnny's sometimes shy and introverted character.

They were both married at St. Angela's in Elmwood Park during the summer of 1988. Needless to say, all the Buzz Boys stood up at his wedding, with Billy Kozar as his best man. There was a reception at the Fountain Blu Restaurant in the city, and we all gave Johnny and Allyssa a wonderful wedding send-off.

But something was going on with Johnny that we didn't find out about until a few years later.

During his medical studies at Loyola, Johnny would lift cadavers in his anatomy classes and other students assisting him. With the constant heavy lifting, he managed to severely throw out his back. His back pain had gotten so bad that he could not do the long-distance running that he was so used to doing, and he started taking pain pills.

At first, he took Tylenol-3 prescription pain killers, which had a mild amount of hydrocodone in them. After a few years, having gone to several doctors for treatment, he started taking some higher-quality opioids.

I remember sitting at the bar with him on Friday night with Marco and Billy after work. We were talking and enjoying a few shots when I suddenly watched him take two pills out of his pocket and pop them into his mouth, along with his drink.

"Johnny, what's that you're taking?"

"Oh, just some aspirin. I have these headaches that never seem to go away."

At first, I thought nothing of it. It wasn't until years later that we all realized that Johnny was severely addicted to pain medication. He prescribed himself opioids by using his friends, whom he would write prescriptions for, and have them filled at the local pharmacy. I was even asked to do it a few times. I didn't ask questions. I figured that he was in a lot of severe back pain, and I felt sorry for him.

"Why don't you go see a back pain specialist who can help you with your back problems?" I asked him several times.

"Oh, MD's don't know shit about back pain," he would say. "Besides, I'm seeing a chiropractor who is helping me with my back," Johnny always replied. Years later, we found out that he never went to see anyone, not trusting them with his back ailments.

They say that doctors make the worst patients, and Johnny definitely fell into that category. Instead of getting help, he continued to take opioid pills for almost twenty years, continually popping them three times a day.

Needless to say, Johnny's luck finally ran out in acquiring the pain meds that he needed, so he then turned to something much stronger:

Cocaine.

At the age of forty-two, Johnny had become a drug addict and prescription pill user. As a result, he became involved in several malpractice lawsuits involving some routine bypass surgeries that went completely wrong, and he could no longer afford the malpractice insurance premiums.

The medical specialty group of cardiologists on Western Avenue near the hospital bought him out, essentially kicking them out of their medical partnership. They just didn't want the exposure of his sloppy methods of practicing medicine anymore.

245

About that time, Johnny and I were meeting over at Diamond Lil's Bar over in the Bucktown neighborhood on North Milwaukee Avenue. He asked me to have a drink with him one Friday night, just the two of us.

"What's going on, Johnny?" I asked him when I arrived at the bar. He was already sitting there gulping down his second drink.

I hadn't seen him in about a year before that meeting, and I went into a very mild state of shock. I didn't recognize Johnny at first. I had to take a double look at him, as he did not look anything at all like he had in his youth. He had gained a significant amount of weight and looked as though he was over two hundred and seventy-five pounds. With his short stature and protruding stomach, he could have passed for a beachball with arms. Johnny was now almost completely bald. He looked significantly older than his forty-five years with the deep wrinkles on his face and discolored teeth.

As we started talking, he started to confess to me some of his recent problems.

His wife Allyssa had left him, and she took his two daughters, ages 15 and 12, along with her. She was suing him for divorce. He also told me that he had been kicked out of his medical group and was in the process of losing his medical license in the State of Illinois. His five-bedroom mansion in Oak Brook was in foreclosure, and he was in a tremendous amount of financial debt. He had talked to a bankruptcy attorney in the prior week and was considering filing in the next few days.

As he explained all of this to me, I asked him how he let his promising life and career get so out of control.

Johnny glared at me as if poisonous venom were protruding from his eyeballs.

"You didn't have to watch your mother whore around the neighborhood to put food on the table," he viciously replied.

"You, Petey, Marco, and Billy used to complain about your fathers. You guys used to all bitch about how bad you guys had it having to live under the same roof as your asshole fathers," Johnny retorted, anger leaking out of his voice.

"You guys all got beat up by your dads. At least you all had dads. All I had as a kid were my goddamn mother's boyfriends who would come over every night and fuck my mother's brains out while she thought I was sleeping in the other room."

Johnny went on to describe how many times he would hear his mother screaming and moaning in the bedroom while she was in bed with different men. He would go to sleep almost every night, hearing all of the sound effects of his mother's sexual conquests in the other room.

Except for Joe LaFatta, his very brief stepfather, we were never aware of any of the problems Johnny was having at home growing up. Between the five of us, Johnny complained the least. All of us Buzz Boys sort of envied Johnny in high school, as he didn't have a hot-tempered, abusive father to kick his ass around while he was growing up.

As it turned out, Johnny was suffering from other problems, most of them surrounding his mother's promiscuity and her struggle to keep food on the table and pay the rent every month.

At that moment, I looked at the other end of the bar and saw a familiar face. I remembered his being a detective, as he used to play on our Chicago

P.D. softball team years ago, along with Marco and Phil Dorian. By that time, we both locked eyes. I could tell he was struggling to remember my name as I was his. He then got off his barstool with his drink in his hand and walked over to where the both of us were sitting.

"You're a divorce attorney, right?"

"Yes, I'm Robby Mazzara. We played softball together years ago. You were playing with Phil Dorian, I remember."

"Oh yes. Nice to see you again. I'm Dennis Romanowski with the Eighteenth District."

As we shook hands, he interjected.

"You're good friends with Detective Pezza, correct?"

"Marco, yes. We've been lifelong friends."

I then introduced him to Johnny, and we all shook hands and ordered another round of drinks.

"We all grew up together," Johnny interjected.

As Detective Romanowski was enjoying his vodka, he then delved deeply into his memory bank.

"I remember you guys. Your softball team was called the 'Buzz Boys,' right? You guys were pretty good, as I recall."

Johnny laughed. "Yes, Billy was hitting that ball out of the park, remember Robby?"

"Yes, and Petey was awesome on first base. You and I were pitching and catching, remember?" I recalled to Johnny and smiled.

A chill went down my spine as I nodded my head. The memory of all of us playing in that police softball league was a wonderful memory from years gone by. It was a beautiful recollection from a simpler time when we were young when we were all struggling young adults. It was a time when we were all learning to let go of our miserable childhoods and embrace our future lives.

At that moment, I would have paid a million dollars to play softball with all of my Buzz Boy brothers again. It was a happier time when the five of us were the best of friends, where we had each other's backs. Indeed, we were the Buzz Boys.

We made more small talk for another hour or so until Romanowski excused himself. He had mentioned something about losing his best friend recently and was forced to spend his usual Friday watering hole sessions drinking by himself.

"We'll see you Buzz Boys later," the detective exclaimed as he put a twenty-dollar bill on the bar counter to cover the second round of drinks.

I remembered that night at Diamond Lil's very well because, at the end of the night, Johnny asked me for a loan.

"How much do you need," I curiously asked him.

"Can you lend me five thousand dollars? I'm several months behind on my mortgage, and the bank is threatening foreclosure. I have the house for sale, and I'm hoping I can pay the minimum amount of outstanding interest until I can sell the house."

"Aren't you filing for bankruptcy?"

"Well yeah," Johnny sheepishly responded. "But I know I gotta pay you back. We're lifelong friends."

I pulled my checkbook out and wrote him a check for five thousand dollars, which he promised he would repay back within the next month. I knew better, though, and unfortunately, I was right. That monetary loan was a generous donation to a very down-on-his-luck Buzz Boy.

After his messy divorce, I came to find out later that Dr. John Orozco had moved down to Miami, Florida. He had an opportunity to join a cardiology medical firm at Miami-Mercy Medical Center and get his life back on track. By that time, he had been in a drug rehabilitation facility and was finally recovering. Marco Pezza had gone down to Miami to see him a few years ago. He said that Johnny had gotten his life back on track and was living with his new girlfriend, a Cuban girl named Zoraida.

He liked to call her 'Mi Cubanita,' and according to Marco, she was a gorgeous Latino at least twenty years younger than he was. We all came to find out later that she was no help to him in getting over his drug addictions, as she was an intense drug addict herself.

But Marco said that Johnny looked much better. He had lost some weight, started wearing a hairpiece, and according to him, wasn't partying hard or doing drugs anymore. He had gotten the impression that Johnny was finally getting his life back on track. According to Marco, Johnny seemed very happy.

But because Johnny owed me money, he must have felt ashamed to call me. I called him a few times and left him several messages, but he never returned my calls. I never had the chance to talk to him again after he left Chicago for Miami, and unfortunately, we lost touch.

Then a few years later, I got a phone call in the middle of the night.

CHAPTER TWENTY-NINE
A Lonely Funeral-2007

Miami International Airport was bustling with travelers as I had grabbed my suitcase from the American Airlines luggage carousel downstairs in Terminal Three. It was a warm summer day in that tropic Florida city, and I immediately was assaulted with the humidity and hot weather as I exited that terminal.

I was looking for Marco's black rented Cadillac, which was supposed to be parked somewhere on the airport's arrivals section.

Marco came to Miami almost immediately after hearing of Johnny's overdose death. With his mother dead for several years and no other relatives or family to claim Marco's abandoned body in the Little Havana neighborhood, Marco was the only one who could take charge of our Buzz Boy pallie and make the necessary funeral arrangements.

Dr. John Orozco was found dead in his parked car, several hundred yards away from the ocean pier near the Little Havana section of South Miami. He had been dead in his car for over twenty-four hours of an apparent cocaine overdose.

Apparently, his 'Cubanita' girlfriend had introduced him to the white powder again after his drug rehabilitation, and Johnny's life began spiraling out of control. After being on the other end of several of his abusive, violent temper episodes, his girlfriend had finally left him. The Miami police had several domestic violence calls from their small house on Euclid Avenue near the Art Deco section of South Beach, and Johnny had been arrested several times. There was now a standing restraining order filed against him in the Dade County Courthouse. Johnny had a lengthy court record of his illegal drug possession and violent domestic tantrums over the last two years.

I saw a black Cadillac CTS beeping the horn as it pulled up in front of me at the airport arrival section.

"Jump in," Marco said, as we gave each other a quick hug while I threw my suitcase into the back seat.

Marco easily maneuvered the luxury car out of the airport traffic, and we were soon on the interstate expressway.

"How was your flight?" he politely asked, which is always the first question everyone asks, including cab drivers, when you're getting picked up at the airport.

"Great, if you like turbulence," I remarked.

"Thank God for juice. A cute airline stewardess was handing me miniature bottles of Johnny Walker on the airplane," I smiled, as I had saved a few of them in my suit coat pocket.

"Thank God for Johnny Walker," Marco laughed. By that time in my life, I was drinking quite heavily, looking for any excuse to throw a shot or two of whiskey into my morning coffee, my lunchtime lemonades, and my afternoon Diet Coke breaks.

"How did this happen?" I asked Marco as he was driving down the expressway to our hotel on Collins Boulevard.

"What do you fucking think, Robby? He found a young gold digger to siphon out his money and turned him back onto the white powdered shit again," my Buzz Boy best friend said with total disgust in his voice.

"I thought he was off of that shit. You said so yourself."

"I thought he was," Marco loudly exclaimed.

"According to one of his medical partners at the hospital, he was clean for a long time. But apparently, he and his girlfriend were having issues, and she got him hooked again into doing 'eight-balls' on a daily basis. He hadn't been to work at the hospital in over two weeks, and his partners were covering for him and his appointments."

"When is the last time you talked to him?"

"Two weeks ago. He sounded a little distraught, explaining that his girlfriend had moved out over a month ago. Johnny said that he was sorry that he let her move in, apparently clipping him for over one hundred thousand dollars in cash."

"She stole from him? Are you kidding? How the hell did she do that?"

"Johnny mentioned that she got some of his personal checks and starting helping herself, starting with smaller amounts of three and five hundred dollars apiece. She later graduated to larger numbers, using all of it for her own drug use," Marco recalled his last conversation with Johnny.

"He didn't catch on for a long time because she had him strung out on 'coke' too. He didn't realize what was going on until his bank starting calling him because his checking account was constantly overdrawn."

I looked at the clouds of that blue Miami sky encircling the downtown buildings and skyscrapers while Marco explained the circumstances of Johnny's death. I wondered while he was talking how such a beautiful, tropical city like Miami could

253

have dealt such a treacherous end for a Chicago cardiologist who once had so much promise for his life.

Johnny Orozco was only forty-eight years old, an age when one's life was still in high gear and had the earning power that others could only dream of. I had heard through the grapevine that he was making over $350,000 a year, which was plenty of money to start one's life over in a beautiful city like Miami.

But, like the rest of us, Johnny had terrible demons. Demons of his mother bringing strange men home in the middle of the night. Demons of his mother waitressing at Mister C's restaurant in Elmwood Park while he would sit and sleep in a booth and drink cokes, waiting for his mother to finish her night shifts. Demons of his mother's boyfriends severely beating and sexually abusing him when he was a very little boy.

Johnny had severe psychological issues that spilled into his regular use of opioids and pain killers, then later graduating to cocaine. Like Marco and Petey, he had abandonment issues and had difficulty controlling his violent temper later in life.

Johnny Orozco was a broken soul, and his deep, dark depression and drug use took the best of him.

"When the cops found him, it looked like he had done a line of coke on his dashboard and passed out," Marco explained.

"The crime labs said that he must have gotten hold of some tainted shit because he probably passed out and died right then and there."

I continued to look at the Miami skyline.

"He had been dead for almost twenty-four hours, sitting in that car with the windows closed on that abandoned street in Little Havana. His body was starting to decompose." At that moment, we were now in downtown Miami and were about to pull into the Marriott Hotel on Collins Boulevard.

As I grabbed my suitcase from the backseat, Marco hit me with a surprise.

"Could you help me with some of these funeral expenses until we can settle Johnny's estate? I had to put his cemetery plot on my credit card, and I still have to take care of the funeral chapel."

"No problem," I immediately said, knowing that Marco was having severe issues of his own, including his marriage, his job, and other personal problems.

We later came to find out that Johnny's home on Euclid Avenue was actually a rental house, not owned like Johnny had told Marco during his last visit. His 2007 Chevrolet Corvette was a three-year lease rental, and most of his other belongings were paid for with his credit cards, which had been recently shut off. He had taken out large equity loans against his medical practice partnership and had very little equity in his cardiology medical group. He had stopped paying the premiums of his one-million-dollar life insurance policy years ago, and there was very little money in his personal savings.

Bottom line: Johnny was broke.

Dr. John Orozco, the once very successful cardiologist who grew up with us in Elmwood Park, had died in Miami, in a desolate neighborhood in Little Havana, penniless at the age of forty-eight years old of an apparent drug overdose. Despite all of his personal problems, Johnny always refused to get help. He believed that the old adage of *'physician heal thyself'* didn't apply to his own life and that he had everything under control.

For being so smart and so intelligent, he was also extremely proud and stubborn. Johnny believed that he could never face his friends in trying to overcome his personal, emotional, and financial problems. It was as if he chose to die alone in his white Corvette in that seedy part of town, with traces of white powder still smattered across his dashboard.

On my insistence, we found a Catholic church not far from the Coconut Grove neighborhood in South Miami for his funeral mass.

St. Peter The Apostle Church laid out his body in a closed casket in the vestibule of the church before the funeral mass. The undertaker stated that his body was too decomposed to have an open casket, and I could have counted the number of people on both of my hands that had come to pay their respects. Not even his ex-wife or his two daughters came to his funeral service.

Marco found a nice, single plot for him at Our Lady of Mercy Cemetery on NW 25th Street. We thought about bringing his body back to Chicago and burying him back there near his mother. But the costs of transporting his body back to Chicago seemed quite exorbitant. Since his ex-wife or children didn't seem to show any interest in mourning Johnny's death, we both figured it would be better to bury him where he lived the last few years of his life.

I went to the monument engraver the same day that I had arrived in Miami and paid extra for Johnny's gravestone to be immediately placed at the gravesite after his internment. I didn't want to fly back to Miami and continue to grieve. I had been in Miami for a very short period of time, and I had seen enough. I had no desire to return to the 'Magic City.

For some unusual reason, Johnny's overdose and death had hit me hard. Here was another Buzz Boy, once a victim of his family's misplaced love, lack of morality, and physical abuse, dead at a young age.

After Father Pollack said some final words and blessed his casket at the gravesite, I got extremely emotional. Watching his body being lowered into his final resting place and then observing the cemetery workers throwing dirt on top of his casket was too poignant and traumatizing for me to watch. Marco escorted me back to his car until the burial was over.

After about an hour or so, when everyone had left the gravesite, I got out of the car and walked back to Johnny's grave. I had taken off my suitcoat and tie, and I was tightly gripping my bottle of water as I approached the newly covered grave. I was crying so hard on that hot afternoon; I was afraid I would become dehydrated.

The granite marker was immediately installed, and it was engraved exactly the way I asked them to inscribe it. There were two angels on each side of his name with the inscription:

Greatest Buzz Boy
Dr. John Orozco MD

_____

Suzie-Q

I had the last part of his tomb inscription placed there as a tribute to my school fight with Jimmy Jakubowski in the fifth grade. Johnny was always a Rocky Marciano fan. He grew up devouring every single boxing book that was ever written about him and the sports subject of boxing. Although he had probably never thrown a punch at anyone in his life, he was always a boxer-wanna-be. I knew he would have appreciated the famous description of Marciano's right hook being inscribed on his gravestone.

Marco had met with the Miami Police Department and, as a matter of professional courtesy, acquired all of Johnny's personal belongings inside his impounded Corvette. In it were several of his lab coats along with some miscellaneous clothing, some medical books, a pictorial 'History of Boxing' book in the back compartment, and his car keys.

Of course, attached to his car keys was the Buzz Boy medallion I had made in shop class at Holy Cross. Marco gave me the copper medallion, knowing that we would perform the same ritual tradition that we had done for Petey and Billy.

Having brought along a small tube of epoxy, I applied some onto the back of the copper medallion. I then pressed it against his granite tombstone as hard as I could for several long minutes. Making sure that the copper medallion couldn't be removed, I put my hand on his grave maker and closed my wet, tear-soaked eyes.

I imagined the little boy with horn-rimmed glasses from the fifth grade. He was standing by St. Angela's Grade School's school doors as I was being escorted to the principal's office, about to be suspended for that championship school fight with Jimmy Jakubowski.

There was little Johnny, smiling with his clenched fist, whispering...*Suzie-Q.*

CHAPTER THIRTY

Death of an Angel - 2010

The sun was beating sharply upon the glistening sand as I gathered my folding chair across the beachfront. I was trying not to fumble with my Corona beer, trying to be extra careful not to spill my extra-large lime, shoved halfway into the bottle, onto the hot, grainy sand. The sounds of summer were everywhere. The noises of seagulls chirping across the blue Lake Michigan water, the music of young boys playing Frisbee across the cottage next door, the melody of cars whisking by along the road interweaving along the open beach.

It was a beautiful July afternoon. I could only hope for more summer moments like today, only wishing that they would last for an eternity. I had just arrived at my rented cottage and had just unpacked my suitcase after driving five hours from Chicago to Ludington, Michigan. It was a quaint, small two-bedroom wooden structure located on top of the sandy, white beach that took me six months on a tourist waiting list to rent for seven days.

My love and my recent memories of the summertime on Lake Michigan were never a secret, and the only relaxing moments in my life were my limited time on the water. Spending time in a beach house overlooking Lake Michigan was always a lifelong dream.

Annie and I had spent so many of our summers with our kids growing up along the pure, blue Lake Michigan waters. Our limited time together during those summers was spent mostly on the beach, memorizing every new freighter, every sailboat, every majestic yacht that had darted across the distant Chicago shoreline. Those moments of our marriage became utopic, life-long memories.

I just couldn't ask for a more beautiful July afternoon, and yet, as I settled into my folding beach chair and forcefully pushed the fresh lime into my cold, wet Corona, my stomach was in a million knots. I could feel my inner anxiety turning my guts over and over, only to make my stomach and my inner pain more prevailing with every gulp of that cold, bottled beer. I could not stop thinking about the real reasons for why I was so anxious, so angry, so down, so damned depressed.

My lovely wife, Anna Maria, the love of my life, was gone.

Annie had contracted a brain tumor one year ago. Her brain surgery and aggressive radiation, her drug therapies, and hormone replacements had left only a shell of the women I had once fallen in love with and married. She had gained a tremendous amount of weight and had a large scar on the right side of her head that extended across her scalp. Because she had an aggressive form of glioblastoma, the oncologists recommended that she have brain surgery. Annie had been aggressively fighting this disease to the point where if she was sleeping on the couch or in our bed in pain, she was in the hospital for several days at a time while recovering from the aggressive chemotherapy treatments.

From the very beginning of her diagnosis, she was in awful pain. Annie had to go through six weeks of radiation just to shrink the rest of her tumors enough to perform the surgery. Within several months, her cancer had already spread to her liver and her lungs.

Although the radiation and chemotherapy managed to slow the rapid spread of cancer in her body, the intense tumor treatments were so strong that she would spend days at a time at Chicago-Western Medical Center to recover from her cancer therapies.

On top of all of that, Annie had fallen into a deep, dark depression. The drugs that she was on had bloated her face and body to the point where she was almost unrecognizable. She spent most of her days crying until the doctors had her on high dosage milligrams of Prozac and Lithium. Watching her suffer was the hardest experience I ever had to go through.

Finally, that past April, Anna Maria had fallen into a deep coma. Two days before she died, she had awakened just long enough to give her final directives.

"Take care of the girls," she repeatedly asked me.

Diana and Annette were twenty and eighteen years old at the time and were still too young to permanently lose their mother and their best friend.

"Don't forget me," she would continuously say.

I sat next to her bed for days at a time. I had finally said 'Ti amo' to her while her eyes were still closed, and she was barely conscious.

"I love you too," she finally said before closing her eyes.

On April 17th, she was still in a coma when she finally took her last breath. She was only fifty years old.

We had her funeral at St. Angela's Church in Elmwood Park, where we had both grown up and spend the second grade together. I buried her in a cemetery plot at Queen of Heaven in Hillside. Because there were several plots available, I guess I had a lapse of judgment and purchased three of the cemetery plots next to hers. I morbidly figured when our final moments on earth came to an end that we would all have a family cemetery plot together.

But those last three months were torturous. I was battling such a severe form of depression that even the excessive dosage of antidepressants wasn't working, and I had finally stopped taking them. They were leaving me lethargic, and I was spending most of my days walking around in a daze. My law practice began to suffer, as several of my legal associates had difficulty picking up the slack that my excessive mental absence was leaving.

On that July weekend, I finally decided to leave. I left my two daughters alone at home, asking a neighbor next door to check on them periodically. I had to escape. I had to run away from the depressive and emotional tattering that had left me completely useless to my law clients, my employees, family, and two daughters.

I was now drinking more than ever. I was purchasing Jack Daniels' cases at a discount from the nearby liquor store and was consuming a fifth of whiskey each day. Every evening, I would pass out on the couch with my shirt and tie still on. I was neglecting my two girls, who also were suffering from their mother's death. I was disregarding my legal practice, and my family law clients were definitely noticing. I was in a deep, miserable, gloomy state of mind, and I couldn't find my way out.

There I sat on that beautiful July afternoon, trying to enjoy those Lake Michigan moments that I remembered having with my wife and children. I had worked so hard my whole life, and I was watching it all slip away.

But I just didn't care anymore. The most important moment every day was now the early shot of Jack Daniels that I was putting into my morning coffees.

I just couldn't put all of this behind me. The Prozac medication was having limited success on my mental state of mind. I started going through intense therapy, visiting with Dr. Pisani twice a week. My therapist was just a paid-for friend who listened patiently to my limitless bellowing of self-doubt and deprecation.

The depression had gotten so bad at times that I discussed suicide with my trusted, overcompensated psychiatrist. He upped the medication, scolded me for entertaining such terrible thoughts, and told me to call him in the morning. The dark, repressive moods had made me believe that everything in my life wasn't worth anything to me any longer.

I really didn't want to live anymore.

The smell of the salty air seemed to complement the white cap waves that rushed along the long, sandy beachfront. The sounds of the seagulls, fighting for every morsel of food, darting back and forth within the water, made for an almost perfect summer Saturday afternoon. And yet, the inner voices of my demons, preying on my every good thought and my every good intention, seemed to be consuming me. I gulped down the last swallow of that cold, thirst-quenching nectar in my hand and walked back into the cottage.

I had unpacked my bags when I arrived and had left an important component of my belongings still within my suitcase. Within the zippered portion of my Samsonite luggage, packed neatly, was a black, cold, Lugar .38 revolver. I could say that I brought this gun along for a lot of different reasons. I had purchased it at a local gun shop for $359.00 last week, and I never had the time to fire it or even learn how to shoot. I would have been hard-pressed to tell anyone where the safety switch was, let alone the trigger. I stared at it for several, long minutes.

Perhaps, after all...I needed to end all of this. What a perfect day to die, to end my life, then along the beachfront, along Lake Michigan, on such a perfect Saturday afternoon. All the demons banging in my head, all the problems of my wife's death, potential bankruptcy, overdrawn checking accounts, disgruntled clients could all, so suddenly, so simple, just go away. One pull of that magnificent trigger and every single problem, every single degrading emotion, torment, and pain would go away forever, never to bother me, never to torment me or leave me distraught ever again.

I picked up the revolver, making sure the six bullets were in the chamber like the gun salesman showed me. I pushed down on the safety switch and pointed the long, endless barrel towards my face. I could taste the metal, the acidic smell of cold steel in my mouth, so eagerly, so ready to do the function for which it was purchased to do.

I took one last long look out the window, one last long gaze at the gorgeous, sunny beachfront surrounded by the chirping seagulls.

I closed my eyes.

Suddenly, my cell phone started to ring. Who could be interrupting me while I was trying to kill myself? I kept hearing the phone ring over and over as if it would never stop.

I begrudgingly put the gun down.

"Hello?"

"Robert? Whatcha doing?"

It was my mother...of all times for her to call.

"Nothing, Mom. I just got here in Ludington. I was unpacking."

I was just about to kill myself before you called Mom.

"How is the weather there? I have been watching it rain here all day."

She was calling from Marco Island, where she moved to after my father died. Despite having a miserable, abusive marriage, my parents had managed to put together a nice retirement plan for the both of them. Papa Alberto worked hard, pinched his pennies, and they saved, and saved, for almost fifty years. There was never a new car for my parents, a nice vacation, or a new restaurant for an occasional meal outside my mother's dinner table.

Besides all of the abusive fights, there was the constant bickering of money, watching their grocery bills, being very careful to cut out every coupon. They were never late to any sale. My folks were frugal, almost to a fault, never letting the word "happiness" get in the way of their monetary goals. Now, after my father's death, she was living in a two-bedroom condo in Marco Island, bored and miserable.

"The weather here is gorgeous, Mom. It's sunny and 85 degrees."

And to think that, a moment ago, I was admiring the weather one last time.

"What are you going to do all alone, by yourself, for one week up there?"

And, of course, that was my mother being nosey as usual.

"Not sure yet, Mom...maybe I will find some trouble to get into."

"Do you really need to find trouble? You just buried your wife. Could you give yourself a break, please?"

My mother thought that I was ready to run into some local bar and start chasing skirts again. She had no idea how despondent, depressed, and dejected I was feeling. I did a good job of hiding my inner demons away from her, knowing that she would worry herself sick. She had no idea how mentally distraught I was... sick enough to take my own life.

"I will be careful, Mom. "

"I love you," she said so eagerly as if to erase every evil demon that was lurking in my brain. I felt my eyes start to well up.

"Love you too, Mom." I quickly pushed the END key on my cell phone and placed it gingerly on my dresser.

I continued to gaze at the black loaded revolver laying so eagerly on my bed. Back to the business at hand, I thought to myself. I stared at the gun for a few more moments, my mother's last words still ringing in my ear, over and over and over.

Maybe this wasn't a good day to die after all. Maybe this was a good day to go to the bar and practice being some foolish alcoholic, allowing myself to be over-served. Perhaps, as they say, alcohol is the answer.

266

Besides, I thought to myself, and this was such a nice, cute little cottage. All the ornate seashells were placed so nicely along with the room, with cheerful paintings of the lake and children playing on the beach. Why splatter the bedroom with all that red, messy blood?

It just didn't make any sense. I pushed the revolver safety clip back on and placed it neatly in the top dresser drawer. To be used for another day, I thought to myself.

I showered and dressed up in my best, casual Lake Michigan attire and proceeded to find my way to the nearest local watering hole.

CHAPTER THIRTY-ONE

The Sandbar Inn- Summer, 2010

The blaring sounds of the jukebox seemed to overtake the darkness of the drab saloon as the bright Ludington sun overshadowed its doorway. I pulled my car into the parking space in front of the bar and walked very gingerly into the dark, shadow forecasted doorway. I was not familiar with what I would see inside the entrance but could hear the Fleetwood Mac music reverberating off the walls.

My eyes adjusted to the darkness as I found my way to a barstool and waited patiently for the attention of the bartender. She was an older blonde lady who looked as though she was slinging drinks as a part-time gig to make up for her social security checks' shortfall. The make-up on her face was over-done, and I had a hard time distinguishing the red blush and blue eye shadow and what could have been over-applied war paint. She noticed me at the end of the bar and walked over and smiled.

"Welcome to the Sand Bar Inn," she politely said with a smile. "What can I get you?"

"Jack Daniels on the rocks, with a splash of water."

What the heck. I was feeling daring. I figured I would start easy and slowly work myself into a belligerent state of drunkenness. She mixed my drink in front of me, and I peeled off a twenty-dollar bill from the wade of singles I had rolled up in my shorts pocket.

"Start a tab, please." I innocently requested, hoping she didn't see the other small bills I had attached to my twenty.

"Oh sure," she smiled as if to play along.

I figured that if I was going to be thinking about depressing subjects like suicide, I might as well use up what cash I had left to spend. I certainly can't enjoy it once I'm gone. I took a few swallows of watered-down whiskey, hoping that someone would walk over to the jukebox and make another selection other than Fleetwood Mac. I looked around the drab, seedy bar, noticing a few televisions playing either the Cubs game or some slow, quiet golf tournament. The place looked like it hadn't seen a coat of paint since Humphrey Bogart was headlining movies at the cinema down the street.

There was a faint smell of old stale cigars as if the 'No Smoking' laws didn't apply to beach town taverns. I took another swallow of my drink and noticed a woman sitting quietly at the end of the bar. She was hidden away at the corner, away from the doorway, away from the Fleetwood Mac music. She was holding her wine glass in front of her face as if to try to hide her appearance. I fixed my gaze at her, not caring whether or not I was embarrassing either her or myself. She was mindlessly staring at the Cubs game, blaring out on set in front of her, trying to ignore my stares.

She was a pretty brunette with long, wavy dark hair, maybe in her forties. Her brown, chestnut eyes contrasted her light blue blouse and the gold necklace reflecting the sunlight from within the bar. From behind her wine glass, she looked stunning. I held my breath and patiently waited for her to put her drink down, hoping to get a glimpse of whatever she was trying to hide. She looked like a modern version of Ava Gardner and just seemed totally displaced by the dark, worn surroundings of the Sand Bar Inn.

She kept lifting her wine glass as if to be pretending to take long, slow swallows. I felt myself

269

being hypnotized as her diamond bracelet-clad wrist kept picking up her wine glass...up and down...up and down...up and down.

"Maybe you should take a picture." The over-painted bartender snidely smirked as he was waiting for me to order another refill. I was starting not to like her.

"I'll have another one...and give the lady at the end of the bar another glass of whatever she's having."

"Yeah...that'll work," she sarcastically said.

Now I wanted to reach over the bar and slap her. A few minutes passed before 'Trixie,' the smart-ass bartender, brought over my drink and then hers. At first, the dark brunette at the end of the bar pretended not to notice the additional beverage, as 'Trixie' explained that the idiot on the other end with a staring problem was sending her a refill. She then started to smile in my direction, and I felt a slight chill take over my body. As if to be entranced, I walked over to the end of her bar and invited myself next to her bar stool.

Amazing! How bold we become, I thought to myself, when you actually realize that you have absolutely nothing to lose for a moment in your life.

"I'm Rob Mazzara," I said loudly, making sure she could hear me over Fleetwood Mac. "Are you a Cubs fan?" I asked, rolling the dice.

"Yes," she smiled, "Another hopeless season."

A slight pause in the conversation.

"I'm Elizabeth Laughlin," as she held out her hand.

"Thank you for the wine," she graciously said.

"If you're going to get drunk in this little beach town, you're going to have to work a little harder. It's going to take a lot more than just sipping red wine," I advised, sounding more like a philosopher than a broken-down divorce lawyer.

"I'm in no hurry," she smiled.

Her voice sounded like the sultry sound of a Hollywood starlet, stepping onto a red carpet before a barrage of flashing cameras. I was having difficulty taking my eyes off her, as the glow from the Cubs game seemed to dance a flickering light into her dark brown eyes. I happened to look down below her waist and noticed her faded, tight blue jeans with two holes placed strategically above her knees.

She was attractive, definitely hot.

"Are you from around here?" she asked.

I was wondering for a second if I had one of those slow, Michigan Militia accents.

"No...from Chicago. I take it you are, too, if you're torturing yourself watching a Cubs game."

"Yes...a hopeless Cubs fan indeed."

Her smile started getting warmer and more radiant as the level of her Pinot Noir started descending. We started making small talk, trying to talk over the Fleetwood Mac songs that kept playing in the background. The jukebox must have been playing the "Changes" album as I recognized some of the songs playing over and over.

She began to tell me that she was from Lake Forest, Illinois, and was currently separated from her mega-rich, extremely successful husband, who was an insurance executive for one of those high-end insurance companies.

"So what's a nice girl like you doing here in Ludington?" I asked, feeling the second splash of Jack Daniels taking its effect.

"My sister has a cottage here not far away on the lakeshore, so I decided to use her place and find some peace and quiet."

"So what's your excuse?" she asked.

"Here to escape the reality of the big city," I lied, not telling her my real intentions.

"Couldn't have found a better place. This beach town is the only place in the world where I can relax."

She continued to tell me her life story about how she was in an abusive marriage for the last twenty years and probably continued the marriage for all the wrong reasons. She had two teenage daughters in high school at some North Shore prep academy and had all the comforts and luxuries that a seven-figure annual income could offer. Without exaggeration, she said, and in no uncertain terms, she had it all. But the Lake Forest mansion or the brand-new Mercedes convertible parked outside was not coming close to the happiness and the emotional peace she was looking for.

Although some of us would tend to argue, she made it very clear that all of her husband's wealth and money could not buy her love. After all the years of physical, verbal, and emotional abuse she had endured, she came to despise him. She looked for every reason and opportunity not to be in the same room, let alone the same house, with her husband. She had finally asked him to move out last month and was in the process of shopping for a good

Chicago divorce attorney who wouldn't empty out her purse.

After telling her that I had a family law practice, she looked at me very innocently and asked,

"Do you handle divorce cases?"

"I don't think you would want me as your divorce attorney. I haven't been doing a very good job for my clients lately."

I was fumbling through my wallet and noticing that I didn't have a business card.

"You can look me up on the internet. I'm on Michigan Avenue."

I pulled out my Apple iPhone and started to fumble with my internet connection on my phone. Although I successfully connected to the internet without local Wi-Fi, I couldn't connect to my office website for some strange reason. She patiently watched me as I tried to prove to her that I was, indeed, a Chicago attorney with a legitimate address and telephone number.

"This internet isn't working right." I finally said, exasperated that my website or office wasn't showing up anywhere.

"That's okay. I believe you." She was trying to console me as I had a very frustrated look on my face.

We ordered a few more rounds, and I was starting to feel the effects of the alcohol. We talked about our children. We talked about our broken marriages and our spouses. We were both laughing and giggling at each other's stupid jokes. I looked at my watch and noticed that we had been sitting at the bar talking and drinking for over four hours.

"Are you hungry?" I innocently asked, not wanting to let this beach town tavern turn such a laid back, enjoyable Saturday afternoon turned into evening.

"Sure," she said. "There is a cute oyster bar about three blocks away. I think it's called Emma's. I've been there once before. Great food."

"Why not!" I exclaimed. After all, with the effects of the whiskey lingering in my brain, I needed some food to sober up and keep myself from saying or doing something stupid.

I paid off 'Trixie' with the rest of my waded singles, and we walked outside of the Sand Bar Inn onto the sidewalk, as close together as we could without making contact or holding hands. On several occasions, as we were walking those short blocks to Emma's, she would inadvertently touch my shoulder as she was talking, as if she was asking me to grasp her hand. I just didn't have the nerve. We walked into Emma's Oyster Bar and got seated next to a window overlooking Lake Michigan, and the ferry boat docked nearby.

"What a beautiful ferry boat!" she exclaimed.

"The S.S. Badger makes two trips a day, back and forth from Manitowoc, Wisconsin, bringing over cars and travelers, over Lake Michigan, into Ludington. Every day at 7:05 pm, all the bells in town ring, letting everyone know that the car ferry has arrived." I mentioned the matter of factly.

"Such a quaint little beach town."

Elizabeth took a deep sigh as if to try to exhale all the problems and pressures that lingered inside of her. The waitress came over and took our dinner order, and we sort of gazed at each other, wordless with nothing to talk about. Several long, quiet seconds ticked by, as if they were hours, until I finally asked her.

"Are you seeing anyone, now that you're separated, I mean."

She sort of looked at me as if I was very bold by asking the question.

"I've done a little dating. I'm very picky."

We exchanged more conversations about our personal nightmares, and we had a lively discussion during dinner. When the waitress brought over our check, I reached into my wallet pulled out my American Express card, figuring that I wouldn't have any problem using it that evening. The waitress returned to our table to tell me that my charge card didn't go through and noticed I didn't have any other credit cards.

I went into a mild shock. How could I leave Chicago and not have any more credit cards in my wallet? I looked deeper inside one of the slots of my billfold and found the secret hiding place where I kept a folded one-hundred-dollar bill. Thankfully, it was still there. I removed it and used that to pay the check.

Elizabeth then looked at me quite innocently.

"I need some company tonight," Elizabeth said in such a way that I knew exactly what she was referring to.

"Yes....." I slowly said. "Me too."

She grasped my hand from across the table, and we quickly got up and walked, hand in hand, toward the door. I could feel the sweat exuding from her hand and got the impression she was as nervous as I was.

"Just so you know, I don't do this with everyone I meet in this beach town."

I got the impression that, deep down, she was suffering, and her soul was as devastated as mine was. She was reaching out, almost desperately, to find the same answers I was continuing to look for but couldn't find. We walked hand in hand along the sidewalk to our parked cars, hoping that she would follow me to my quaint little cottage just down the road. It was amazing how this day had ended, I thought to myself. I went from almost killing myself and committing suicide at the beginning of this day to bringing a beautiful lady that I just met home to my rented cottage.

It all seemed like a dream.

CHAPTER THIRTY-TWO

The Ludington Lighthouse – Summer 2010

The warmth from the morning sun radiated through my cottage window as I struggled to open my eyes and gather my surroundings. My eyes were still squinting with sleep as I looked over and realized that I wasn't alone. Her flowing dark brown hair was expanded across her pillow, as nothing but her bare breasts and shoulders were exposed over the covers. I began to remember the night before, as we made love prohibitively throughout the moonlit night. Her soft touches, her kisses planted so carefully onto the small of my neck and the middle of my back, felt as if an angel had been sent down to comfort me from all of my problems of the past. She looked gorgeous, even at six o'clock in the morning. I tried to move carefully out of bed and begin my journey to the kitchen when I heard her rollover.

"Good morning," she said softly as if the night before was starting to slowly sink in.

"Good morning. How did you sleep?" I innocently asked.

"You know you have a snoring problem, right?" she replied.

"I've was told that from my late wife. My snoring drove her insane."

She giggled as I reached for the floor in search of my Tarzan-style underwear. I rose up from the bed and grabbed my shorts, laying on the chair, parading briefly across the bedroom. I felt her eyes watching me, checking out my modest figure.

"You know, for an old guy, you have a great body." She complimented.

"Thanks. One of the perks of being suddenly single or a widower. The stress of loss seems to curb your appetite."

"So I have that to look forward to?"

"You have no worries," I reassured her.

She was now sitting upright on the bed; two pillows were supporting her back. I was trying hard not to stare at her as her perfectly proportioned breasts were exposed above the covers. Her near-perfect body could only be found in a glamour magazine as she began to stretch her arms across the air and gather her thoughts.

"I normally don't do this." she started to explain. "In fact, I don't think I've ever done this before."

"Do what?" I was trying to pretend I didn't know what she was talking about.

"You know." A few moments of silence before I commented.

"Then why did you?"

"You looked like you needed rescuing."

I kind of stared at her, wondering if she knew the real reason why I escaped Chicago. I started to gather my thoughts and began to concentrate on the task at hand.

"I wonder if these Ludington cottages come with coffee." I thought out loud.

"There's a Starbucks down the street," she suggested.

278

I walked over to the kitchen and fumbled through the kitchen cabinets until I found a red, plastic half-can of coffee. There was a sparkling clean coffee pot sitting on the counter near the sink, so it only seemed natural for Mrs. Folgers and Mr. Coffee to be paired together. After finding the coffee filters, the brewing coffee pot was well at work. I heard Elizabeth fumbling through my closet and slamming a few drawers in the other room, and thereafter she emerged wearing only one of my freshly pressed white shirts.

"I'm afraid I can only offer you black coffee."

"That will do."

She opened up the screen door and emerged outside onto the patio, facing the soft, harmonic waves of Lake Michigan. Wearing only my shirt, she found her way onto one of the two Adirondack chairs facing the lake and sat there, enjoying the fresh-water air and the morning sunrise. I walked onto the patio bearing only my white shorts and two cups of black coffee.

"So ..." as I sat down next to her at the next available chair.

"Why are you REALLY here?" she inquisitively asked.

"The truth?"

"Yes, I can take it."

"I came here to kill myself," I said matter-of-factly. She stared at me motionless as if to not be surprised.

"I found the gun in your dresser drawer. Great taste in revolvers."

"Thanks." I didn't know how to react.

There were several minutes of silence as we both listened to the waves rush in and out of the beach in a perfect rhythm.

"You said last night that you were in therapy."

I was starting to regret some of the things I had mentioned to her after my fourth or fifth drink.

"Dr. Pisani doesn't know I'm here. Besides, I made sure his bill was paid before I left."

A few more minutes of silence.

"So?"

"So what?" I was waiting for her to finish her sentence.

"What's stopped you?"

I thought long and hard before responding, not wanting to keep the conversation too serious.

"I didn't want to lose my security deposit, with the extra cleaning and coroner costs and all..." I tried to make light of it but couldn't get her to laugh at my half-witted reply.

"My hourly fees are much cheaper than your shrink's." She was winking her eye at the same time.

"I've spent a fortune. With all the fees I've paid to my shrink, I could have bought this beach house."

"Paid in full, I'm sure," she replied.

There was something mystical about her as she stared off at the beach, hypnotized by the waves rushing in and out off of the perfect white sand. She seemed to be in tune with my feelings, with all of my disparity and all of the stress that came with it.

Her voice was a soothing song of endless comfort, as if she were trying to reassure me that everything was going to be okay. She seemed to know me only after one passionate night and seemed to understand the terrible, dramatized world I was trying so hard to escape.

"You do realize that, once you check out, you can't come back." she slowly said.

"Come back to what?" I retorted. The caffeine from my black cup of coffee was starting to kick in.

"Do you really believe that you wouldn't be missed? That you haven't made a difference with anyone in your life?"

"My two children will miss their ATM machine."

I went on to tell her what a good father I was to them, about how I never missed a dance recital or a girls' softball game. But I was constantly chastised, for all of the late-night hours at the office, all of the client meetings, and working all hours of the night to prepare for client trials. All the drinking didn't help either, I said. I was blaming myself for her death, and she could see the guilt written all over my face."

"Do you really think it was your drinking that killed her?" she asked, referring to my survivor's remorse.

"I'm sure it was part of it, with all of the late-night happy hours and coming home half in the bag. My wife Annie tolerated my drinking and battling my demons, and she kept it all in. All the many years of pent-up anger and stress finally took its toll on her in the form of her brain tumors."

281

She looked at me, dumbfounded by my explanation.

"Rob, people don't give other people brain tumors."

A long moment of silence.

"I wonder sometimes. I'm sure all the stress that I placed on our marriage didn't help."

"It's too bad you don't realize how important you are to everyone around you," she replied.

I stared at her for a long while. My eyes became fixated with hers as if we had been talking our whole lives.

"You seem to know this for a fact?" I asked her. She innocently looked at me and nodded her head. We were almost done with our coffees when she innocently asked:

"Ever wonder what this world would be like without you?"

I started to laugh out loud.

"Is your real name Clarence?" I joked, referring to the frumpy angel opposite Jimmy Steward in 'It's A Wonderful Life' movie.

"Just call me Clarisse!" She had an infectious laugh as if the whole world around us didn't matter.

"I will bet that you have done some very wonderful things with your life, Mr. Mazzara."

I took all of what she had to say in, and her soothing voice seemed to bring a calmness that I had never experienced. We were both enjoying the warm, freshwater breeze that came blowing in with every wave that rhythmically danced along the beach. We sat in our chairs in silence, mesmerized by the white cap waves of Lake Michigan.

"Have you ever been to the lighthouse here?" she asked.

"Not in a long time," I replied.

"It's a wonderful walk along the break wall, over to the lighthouse beyond the water."

"Okay. I'm in. By the way, you're not taking me over to Martini's Bar afterward, are you?"

"How many times did you watch that movie?" she jokingly asked.

"More times than I can count."

"Relax, George Bailey. My plans for you are much bigger than Mr. Potter's."

With that suggestion, we both rushed inside and showered, dressed, and prepared for our long, romantic walk towards the Ludington lighthouse.

———————————

The waves from Lake Michigan were splashing hard against the rocks as the agitated water continued to rise above the breaker wall. The Great Lake surges seemed unusually strong, its white caps splashing over the half-mile long walkway to the Ludington Lighthouse. Elizabeth gripped my hand as we walked along the concrete reef; her hand seemed so warm and secure as we made small talk about the weather, the beach town, and the status of our lives.

"When is the last time you've been inside a lighthouse?" she asked.

"Probably not since I was here with my kids. Never had the time to walk up a lighthouse and look out at the water." I replied.

"Lighthouses are amazing. I love lighthouses. They are so symbolic, so serene, so summertime." She explained.

We walked hand in hand along the concrete break wall, dodging the large waves that were hitting the huge concrete rocks and boulders stacked neatly alongside the lighthouse reef. We arrived at the lighthouse, and as we began to sit down along the steel wall. Elizabeth then magically pulled out a bottle of prosecco from her large purse, along with two plastic glasses.

"Do you always keep a bottle of prosecco in your purse?"

"I picked up a bottle on our way in."

Not remembering when she would have had the time to go to the store to pick up a bottle of liquor, I was dumbfounded. We had been together all morning, but I decided not to dwell on it.

"You've came prepared."

Her timing couldn't have been more perfect. We propped ourselves up against the steel, blue-painted lighthouse wall, protruding with is large rivets and steel-reinforced beams holding the lighthouse intact. She opened the bottle of prosecco and gingerly filled our plastic cups.

"Here's to something new," she toasted.

I felt myself forgetting every single problem I ever encountered in my life, as I was surrendering my heart and my soul to Elizabeth. She was the perfect combination of everything; her laughter, beauty, intelligence, affluence, way about her, and the classy way she carried herself; it was all so intoxicating. We made more small talk and quickly finished our refreshing green bottle.

I was trying very hard not to become so smitten with her whole package but falling immediately in love with her was just so relaxing, so exhilarating, and so easy to do. Being with her that July afternoon seemed to be so incredibly insatiable, so magically right.

We walked inside the lighthouse, and there was a fee of ten dollars each, which I reached into my wallet and paid. We walked up toward the narrow, spiral stairway going up the lighthouse, slowly, as we ascended 57 feet to the very top of the steel-plated structure. Once we were at the top, we could see the eastern shores of Lake Michigan at the end of the breakwater along the Pere Marquette harbor. If we looked hard enough, beyond the mist of Lake Michigan, we could see the shores of Manitowoc, Wisconsin on the other side. The views on the top were gorgeous, yet so simple, so peaceful, so majestic.

"Are you starting to feel better?" Elizabeth asked.

"Yes. A feeling of peace is starting to come over me," I confessed.

We were alone on the top of the lighthouse, overlooking the Lake Michigan view, when she asked me another personal question, one that made me feel very uncomfortable.

"Have you ever tried to kill yourself before?"

I hesitated, as I didn't know how to answer her question.

"I've often thought about it."

There was a pause.

"My psychiatrist, Dr. Pisani, stopped me many times from taking more sleeping pills."

"Good thing. I am happy that all of that is behind you," she expressed. She then came closer and kissed me, making sure that she could feel my passion at the very top of the lighthouse.

"Have you ever made love in a lighthouse before?"

Before I could even respond, she strategically placed her hand over my crotch, and she felt my throbbing member, and she grabbed my other hand and pulled it inside of her jeans. She felt so incredibly wet, and I was totally excited and partially nervous about making love inside of a public place, a place as open and communal as a lighthouse. As I noticed that no one else was coming up the stairs, she quickly pulled down her jeans, sat on one of the circular steps, and pulled me inside of her.

I was so nervous, so turned on, and so excited all at the same time. I kept plunging her harder and harder on the lighthouse steps, making sure we were both quiet. We moaned and groaned in each other's earlobes as I kept pushing myself inside of her, harder and harder. Elizabeth was dripping wet, and her juices were beginning to splatter on top of the spiral stairwell. I thrusted myself inside of her one more incredible time, and we both climaxed quickly without making a sound.

She smiled, pulled her jeans up, and caressed me closely, and giggled as I struggled to buckle up my pants.

"Is the mile-high club next?" I asked.

We both started laughing as we descended the lighthouse stairs, still noticing the no one was entering inside. We had the Ludington lighthouse to ourselves for five minutes, and it was absolutely wonderful.

Elizabeth and I continued to enjoy the rest of our day, walking around the main street of Ludington, relaxing on the grass near the pier, and talking about our dreams and our lives.

Those last few days with her were a carefree distraction from the personal depression and intense feeling of loneliness that I was experiencing without my wife.

On the last day that we were together, we spend the day at my rented cottage. We swam in Lake Michigan together, splashing each other with the warm, wonderful waters of the Great Lake. It was as if we were baptizing each other, wishing each other the good fortunes that awaited us after that summer afternoon. We made Sunday sauce and ate pasta while drinking more wine and making love several times that day. I took it for granted that we would probably continue to see each other again after we both returned to Chicago that week.

As she was leaving my cottage, I realized that I didn't have any of her personal contact information, so I asked her for her telephone number. She only smiled and gave me an intense, long, good-bye hug.

"It's been a wonderful few days," she softly said.

"Always keep me in your heart, and don't ever forget me."

She looked at me with big, hazel brown eyes that were now welled up with tears. It was as if she didn't want to let me go but felt that she had to.

"Please don't ever do anything to harm or hurt yourself."

She gave me one last, very long kiss.

And just like that, she turned and walked away. Elizabeth permanently disappeared, away from Lake Michigan, away from my cottage, away from my life.

I tried in vain to find her when I returned to Chicago, to no avail. She had probably given me a fake name, as there was no one living in Lake Forest with her name and description. I looked up her name on the internet, but there was no such person with that name living in the Chicagoland area.

Elizabeth had mentioned while we were together that she often took the CTA train downtown to Chicago. So I went as far as to sit in my car in the Lake Forest train station parking lot, desperately waiting for someone who looked like her to step off the train. For hours, I walked around Lake Forest into all of the shops and stores that aligned Western Avenue. I asked a few salespeople working at the Macy's store if they had ever heard of her as I described her and mentioned her name. I was praying that she would suddenly appear out of nowhere.

Elizabeth Laughlin was nowhere to be found. Like a fallen angel, she had suddenly disappeared from my tragic life. I then only realized that she briefly came into my life for one sole purpose; to prevent me from killing myself during those few summer days in Ludington.

I could now only close my eyes and think of those brief, warm days in July, making love to a beautiful angel inside of that enchanting Ludington lighthouse.

CHAPTER THIRTY-THREE
Sixtieth Birthday- July 2019

I was parking my black Maserati into my parking space at my home on that hot summer day. I had gotten home from my office early, and I decided to go home to my West Loop loft and take it easy.

I had been in court most of that day on a divorce case, representing the husband. My client, Paul Hartman, was worth about eight million dollars with three grown children. He was in a thirty-year marriage and was suing his wife for a divorce. Both myself and the wife's attorney had pretty much had the whole divorce estate settled except for the alimony agreement, which my client refused to pay.

As we were going back and forth between both the husband and the wife, the Cook County judge decided to grant us another two-week continuance, with strict orders that a settlement is agreed upon or a trial date would be immediately set.

By the time I arrived home at my West Loop loft on North Peoria Street, I was exhausted. That day was supposed to be a special day, but I was not anywhere in the mood to celebrate.

That last day of July was my sixtieth birthday, and my two girls had been threatening to take me out to dinner and celebrate with me on that Wednesday night. Because I couldn't drink anymore, going out didn't sound like much fun with just my daughters.

As I was exiting the elevator and entering my loft, my cell phone was already ringing.

"Happy Birthday, Daddy," my youngest daughter Annette sounded so excited on the phone.

"What birthday? Are you sure you have the right number?" I was kidding around, trying to play stupid.

"Come on, Daddy. Don't pretend this isn't your special day. We need to take you out tonight. It's not every day that you turn sixty."

"Don't remind me. I am not excited about getting older. Besides, birthdays are way overrated."

"Daddy," Annette sternly changed the tone of her voice.

"Diana and I are going to be at Bar Siena at 7:30. Meet us there for dinner so that we can celebrate."

"Annette, honey, I can't drink anymore, you know this. Besides, I am really exhausted. Let me rest tonight, and we can go out this weekend."

"No, Daddy," Annette insisted. "We are celebrating tonight. We're not taking 'no' for an answer. We'll see you at Bar Siena at 7:30."

As a first-year law student at Loyola University, my youngest daughter was going into the right profession. She was beautiful and charming like her mother and extremely tenacious and pushy like me. When she made up her mind, there was no changing it.

I can't say that I wasn't flattered when she said she wanted to become an attorney like her old man. With all of the stress and problems of being self-employed, trying to pay the bills, acquiring clients, and getting them to retain me and pay their invoices, I must have done something right.

290

My oldest Diana was definitely a Daddy's Girl from the minute she was born. But Annette was my 'Baby Girl.' My wife and I had spoiled her, especially when she used to pout and look at me with those large, saucer-like, hazel brown eyes. Every time she would ask me for something, as much as I tried to resist, I would always melt. Little Annette knew how to play her old man, and I was continuously helpless to her charms.

It was already 4:30, and since Bar Siena was only five blocks away from home, I figured that I had plenty of time to take a nap and get a few hours of rest before going over to the restaurant on Randolph Street.

I turned the television on and laid down on the couch, probably falling asleep right away.

The next thing I know, it was already 7:20 pm. I had knocked off on the couch and now had only ten minutes to shower, get dressed, and rush over to the restaurant.

If Superman were in a telephone booth, he couldn't have done it faster. I had showered, got dressed in a casual button-down shirt and light sport coat with a pair of new dress jeans. I put on my new Allen Edmonds shoes and grabbed a taxicab to go five blocks from my house to the restaurant. I arrived there at 7:35.

Annette was already in front of the restaurant waiting for me, looking extremely upset.

"You're late, Daddy," as she gave me a birthday kiss on my cheek. Somehow, I felt like a high school freshman coming home late after my curfew.

The hostess met us at the front door. Holding a menu, she pretended to lead us to our table in the other room. Annette took my hand and led me inside the restaurant. At that point, I was already suspicious.

"Where is your sister? Where is our table?" I immediately asked. She continued to grasp my hand tightly, making sure that I didn't meander off to the bar somewhere. She led me into a room where the doors were closed.

As the doors were opened, I was immediately assaulted.

"SURPRISE," coming from loud voices everywhere, as the 'Happy Birthday' song came on the loudspeaker. The room had to be filled with over one hundred people, and everyone started singing 'Happy Birthday.' I had never received so many handshakes, hugs, and kisses all at once in my whole life, and I was in mild shock. My eyes immediately started welling up with tears. My oldest daughter Diana then came over and kissed me.

"Surprise, Daddy! Happy Birthday! I love you," she continued to hug and kiss me while Annette had both of her arms around my waist.

'Daddy's Girl' and 'Baby Girl' were holding me so tightly that I had a hard time maneuvering myself to greet all of the guests that had arrived. It was as though they were afraid of my leaving them. They had both developed abandonment issues since their mother had passed away, and I always tried to reassure them that as their father, that I wasn't going anywhere.

"I love you, Daddy," Annette continuously repeated as all the guests from all over the room were congratulating me. I was so elated with emotion; tears were streaming down my face. As I glanced around the room, my friends from Elmwood Park, employees from my office, my in-laws from

Milwaukee, and many other friends with their spouses were there.

But most especially, was my Buzz Boy best friend, Marco Pezza. He was practically the same age as I was, as his sixtieth birthday was coming up in September.

Marco came up to me and hugged me tightly, giving me one of his bourbon-flavored kisses on my cheek.

"Hey pallie, you made it."

"I love you, Marco," I immediately responded. We continued to hug each other as we were practically crying in each other's arms. We were the last two Buzz Boys left from the old neighborhood in Elmwood Park.

Billy was shot to death at a bar. Petey died in prison. Johnny had overdosed in Miami. Marco and I were the only two Buzz Boys left, and we both felt as though we were hanging on to each other by a thread.

Marco had just lost his job as a detective with the Chicago Police Department and was under investigation for shaking down and accepting bribes from prisoners under his arrest. He was struggling to keep his marriage together. She had asked him to move out of their Addison home, which was currently in foreclosure. He had recently filed his second bankruptcy in ten years. I only knew this because I was friends with the bankruptcy attorney he was using in Cook County, where he had filed.

In my fourth year of surviving stage three prostate cancer, I was extremely paranoid about my health. I had stopped drinking and smoking, and it seemed as though the demons in my life and my past were almost physically forcing me to go back to my old life and have another drink.

And then, of course, there was my wife, Annie. She had been dead now for almost ten years, and not a moment of my life since her passing has ever come and gone without my thinking about her. Her death from glioblastoma at the age of fifty was a tragic loss to not only myself but to my teenage daughters at the time. We all missed Anna Maria, my dear wife, and their loving mother. We had struggled as a family to get over her loss for a very long time and move on.

With Diana now in her final year of medical school at the University of Illinois and Annette finishing her first year of law school, I felt as though everyone, including myself, were all in a very good place. It seemed as though all of my past demons and my abused childhood were all behind me. With the death of the other Buzz Boys and the death of my wife, it seemed at that moment that every tragic minute of my past life had faded away in the rear-view mirror.

At that instant, on my sixtieth birthday, I felt a final peace come over me, knowing that the rest of my life with my two beautiful daughters would only be clear sailing from then on.

I had no idea that more tragedy was on the horizon.

We all sat down for an elaborate dinner of tortellini soup, chicken Caesar salad, pappardelle pasta, rib-eye steak, and double-baked potatoes. For dessert, we were all served my favorite treat, a large tiramisu sheet cake, with what looked like sixty very small candles, all conveniently cramped and lighted on top.

After singing 'Happy Birthday' once again, I was very proud of myself. I was able to blow out all of those candles in one deep, swooping breath.

After dinner, we had all gathered at the bar and the outside veranda for cocktails. As several of us were standing around drinking (I had a Sprint with lime), Marco caught my attention. He just didn't look like himself.

I could tell that Marco was under a tremendous amount of stress. He was working a security job at a high-end jewelry store in Northbrook while trying to fight off the investigation initiated by the top Chicago P.D. brass regarding allegations of his being a 'dirty cop.' If he were found guilty, he would probably lose his police pension, which would literally shoot his almost thirty-five-year career with the Chicago P.D. right out the window.

I motioned Marco to follow me outside with our drinks, and we stood on the second-floor veranda facing the Randolph Street traffic.

"Marco, are you okay?"

He only looked at me and smiled.

"I don't know how much more I can take, Robby," he said as he was probably sucking down his fourth JD on the Rocks.

"They're coming at me from all angles, Rob. I got my wife coming at me from one direction. I've got the CPD coming at me from another direction. I'm struggling to keep my security job at the jewelry store. The bank is up to my ass for the late mortgage payments. My credit cards have been shut off. I'm trying to scrape up a thousand dollars to retain my bankruptcy attorney so I can get some of this debt off my back," he was struggling to explain.

At that moment, I reached into my pocket and pulled out some cash. I had luckily cashed one of my paychecks the day before, so I had plenty of money on me at the time.

"Here, Marco, here's a thousand bucks. It's an early birthday gift," I said, remembering that his birthday wasn't until the middle of September. I counted out the money from my stash and put ten Ben Franklins in his hand.

Marco got defiant, "No, Pallie. This is your birthday. You're not supposed to be giving me gifts."

"Don't worry about it, Marco. It's only money. It's our friendship and our good health that is the most valuable. We can always make more money."

Marco looked at me with tears in his eyes.

"Thank you, Pallie. I'll give this back to you soon."

"Don't sweat it. As I said, it's an early birthday gift. Use it to get you by or use it to retain your lawyer."

He then gave me an intense hug.

"I love you, Robby. Remember, we'll always be Buzz Boys, and we will always have each other's backs, no matter what."

"Yes, we will. We always have since grade school, Marco. We're BFFs," I said with a smile, putting my arm around him.

We both chuckled at my acronym, knowing that it was a term only women used to describe their best friends. We then started standing around awkwardly as the other party guests were drinking at the bar.

"Have you seen your father?" I sheepishly asked, knowing that this was a very sore subject.

"Are you kidding? He won't even take my phone calls. That old man has more money than he'll ever know how to spend. I tried to ask him for help, but he has flat out refused," Marco responded with anger.

"That old son-of-a-bitch ruined my fucking life," he started to lament.

"He killed my mother, Robby. He made Mom kill herself. He molested all of us. He beat the living shit out of me, my brother, and my sister. That fucking bastard belongs in hell!"

Marco started getting emotional as he was finishing another of his Jack Daniels on the Rocks.

"That's all in the past now, Marco. We can get through this now. I promise you. I will help you do whatever you need to do to get through this," I said, hoping at the time that I couldn't bear the loss of another Buzz Boy.

Then I swallowed hard.

"You need to let go of the past."

He only looked at me with tears in his eyes.

"I can't, Robby. I just can't."

Suddenly, Marco got angry. He placed his empty drink glass on the bar counter and walked away from me. Within less than a minute, he had left my birthday party and was gone. He didn't even say goodbye.

"Where did Uncle Marco go?" Annette approached me and asked, noticing that he was no longer around.

"He's going through some personal problems, and he had to get home early," I reassured my daughter.

The symptoms were all there. Three months later, I was still reliving those moments of that last conversation with Marco in my mind. I was replaying our dialog from that evening in my head, over and over again. I should have seen the signs.

Marco was on the verge of a very intense, very violent breakdown. Knowing him better than anyone else, I should have seen it. His anxiety was written all over his face.

Along with his volatile temper and other personal demons, he was now a circus act, walking a high wire tight rope. My Buzz Boy pallie was a thousand feet up in the air without a trapeze circus net to break his fall. He was a dangerous time bomb waiting to explode.

After my party at Bar Siena on that hot July evening, I never saw Marco again.

CHAPTER THIRTY-FOUR
Funeral for A Friend -October 2019

I had arrived at the Cumberland Chapels on West Lawrence Avenue to discuss the details of Marco Pezza's wake and funeral. I had called his sister, Rosaria, to express my condolences, and she wished for me to assist her in burying both her oldest brother and her father, Vincenzo Pezza.

Because they were all estranged, we decided to bury them both out of the same funeral chapel and have two separate funeral services, with two different burial plots at different cemeteries.

Marco's youngest brother Anthony was killed in a car accident in 1996 and was buried next to his mother at Queen of Heaven Cemetery in Hillside. Since there was an available crypt near her mother and brother, Rosaria decided to intern her brother close to her mother Cira and her brother Anthony. Since she also was estranged from her father, Rosaria decided not to have his funeral and holy mass at St. Angela's Church. She opted for quick service at the Cumberland Chapel, with his interment being private. Her father, she decided, would be buried in a small plot at St. Joseph Cemetery in River Grove, far away from the wife and children he had so viciously abused during his lifetime. According to Rosaria, her father wasn't worthy of being buried next to his family.

I had suggested that she have her father cremated, but Rosaria said she was still very afraid of her father, even in death. She was fearful that he would come back from the dead and haunt her for the rest of her life. It seemed that even in death, mean old 'Papa Enzo' still had a horrific grip on his only surviving child. She knew that her abusive father was capable of anything while alive, and she certainly didn't trust him in death.

The funeral was a solemn mass at St. Angela's Church in full, Chicago Police Department regalia. He had two police department officers standing guard over his casket while several hundred mourners filed past his coffin. The whole Eighteenth District was at his funeral, with purple bunting hanging over North Larrabee Avenue's station. Although he was suspended and under investigation by the Chicago Police Department, he was still recognized as a CPD member and part of the Eighteenth District family.

I stood with his sister next to Marco's casket, on her insistence.

"You were like a brother to him," Rosaria said to me several times, for which I was grateful.

Detective Philip Dorian from the Sixteenth District and Detective Dennis Romanowski were also there to pay their respects. I asked them both to be pallbearers to Marco's funeral, along with four other patrolmen, also from the Eighteenth District. Because it was a City of Chicago police department funeral, there were specific rituals that were always done for officers who died in the line of duty. Even though Marco's actual death was a murder-suicide, the Superintendent of the Chicago Police Department deemed that his death was a 'death caused in the line of duty, despite his fragile mental state. This determination allowed his family to receive the death benefits normally paid to widows and survivors of veteran Chicago police officers.

As the pallbearers put on their white gloves and stood next to the casket, I stood behind his coffin, following it up the church steps of St. Angela's with the Scottish bagpipers following closely behind. We followed the coffin to the front of

300

the church as the canter sang the "Ave Maria" in a loud, glorious tenor voice. The traditional song seemed to reverberate from St. Angela's Church's magnificent walls, with its ornate stained-glass windows, containing its sacred sounds for all those who came to witness the ascension of my last, lifelong friend and brother Buzz Boy.

As the priest presided over the funeral mass, my mind drifted elsewhere. At that moment, I was having 'survivor's remorse,' wondering why my best friend Marco was chosen to suffer the mental anguish and consequences of his childhood sexual abuse and why I was spared on that day. I sat there in total contempt, vehemently blaming our fathers' brutal sins and for the death of another one of my best friends.

I became extremely angry. Why weren't our fathers stopped from handing out the physical abuse we had to endure as young children? Where were the agencies like the Department of Children and Family Services back in the 1960s and 1970s, stopping abusive fathers and mothers from physically and sexually abusing their children? Why were women like Johnny's mother allowed to keep their kids while running a low-level prostitution service out of her bedroom? Where were all of our families and friends from the neighborhood that noticed us coming to school with black eyes, broken noses, and large bruises on our bodies? Why were so many parents, especially Papa Enzo, allowed to walk free in society after his children tried to testify against him for all of the physical violence and emotional abuse he inflicted on his family?

Why were these monsters never convicted in our neighborhood, in our village, in our state? There were so many other children who were raped, beaten, and taking advantage of at such a young, vulnerable age. There were so many children like us Buzz Boys, who grew up alone and isolated, only having each other to understand our inner torment. We all grew up to be either drunks or drug addicts, sometimes both, thanks to our psychotic fathers and mothers' gruesome sins.

At that moment, my rage was beginning to overcome me, right there in the middle of my best friend's funeral mass. For a brief moment, I wanted revenge. But since all of the abusers were now all dead, there was no one left for me to kill.

Johnny's mother was dead, dying from ovarian cancer several years ago. Billy's abusive father had drowned right in front of Billy in Lake Geneva. Petey and Marco both personally killed their abusive fathers. My father was the only one allowed to die a peaceful death in the hospital, staring at me with a pillow in my hand.

Did he deserve it? Should I have used those hospital pillows and put them over his face, stopping him from breathing? Perhaps God saw my intentions and took my father away at that very moment, keeping me from taking out my vengeance and retribution against him.

As the funeral mass concluded, I stood behind the Chicago P.D. pallbearers as they carried my best friends' casket out of St. Angela's Church in Elmwood Park. As we were leaving, I said goodbye to the church most of us Buzz Boys had been baptized in, had made our First Communions in, had served as altar boys in, and buried our estranged parents. As we were leaving the church, I looked at the last three pews in the back of the church where my Buzz Boy brothers and I used to horse around during Holy Mass in the middle of the week in grade school.

I helped load Marco's body onto the long, black hearse waiting at the bottom of the church's steps. I was accompanied by my two daughters, Annette and Diana, and we all grieved all together in my car. We followed the funeral procession, passing Marco's house on Cortland Avenue in the old neighborhood, and then onto Queen of Heaven Cemetery in Hillside. When the parade of cars finally arrived at the cemetery, the funeral hearse pulled up in front of the many aisles of neatly arranged marble crypts, each row named after an obscure saint.

I assisted the other pallbearers, following the coffin to Marco's final resting place. An open marble crypt at the fourth row in the middle, whose stone slab had already been removed, awaiting the arrival of my best friend's body. The priest mumbled a few more prayers as each of the gatherers placed a red rose on top of the dark brown, silver-trimmed casket. All the mourners, including myself and my two daughters, stood silent as the unique forklift lifted the coffin, with two undertakers alongside it, and slowly pushed Marco Pezza's body into the empty marble crypt in the fourth row.

We all watched my best friend, the last Buzz Boy beside myself, become forever entombed. I said the Lord's Prayer, wishing eternal rest for his soul. As my face was soaked in tears, I silently waited for the rest of the mourners to leave until myself, Annette and Diana were the very last ones facing Marco's gravesite.

My daughters became familiar with the Buzz Boy ritual that I had started since Petey's death several years ago. I put my hand into my suit coat pocket and pulled out the copper medallion. I then placed it onto Marco's gravestone, along with a small tube of epoxy, applying some on the back.

This had become a very sad tradition.

With my eyes drenched with tears, I pressed the medallion as hard as I could onto the granite tombstone for a few minutes until the epoxy adhesive immediately dried. I then tested it, making sure that the Buzz Boys copper medallion couldn't be removed. I then took my hand, along with Annette and Diana's hands, and we all placed them together onto his granite crypt, reading his inscription:

Marco Pezza

An Officer & Buzz Boy
Who Valiantly Served
The City He Loved.

We all cried together for several long minutes, saying our last goodbyes. We then left the aisle of crypts behind us, walking arm and arm together toward my black Maserati parked along the side of the mausoleum.

I kissed each one of them on their foreheads and told them how much I truly loved them. At that moment, I realized something very real and very tragic in my lifetime:

I was going to way too many funerals.

Every human life's story always ends in death, and the stories of my Buzz Boy fraternity brothers have all ended in the same but very tragic way. I have had the blessing and the burden in my life to grow up with four very beautiful human beings.

We were five wonderful souls who all started the same way. A long time ago, we were all little boys, running, laughing, playing, joking, and learning to touch each other's hearts with the love, the camaraderie, and the loyalty that none of us would have experienced had we not grown up together in that small, quaint little neighborhood on Cortland Avenue.

My beloved Buzz Boys taught me at a very young age how to live, how to laugh, and how to love. We all enjoyed life surrounded by the simple pleasures that made our lives whole despite the personal tragedies and setbacks that we all had to endure.

But one by one, our intense, satanic demons came to defeat us. Not having unconditional love from our parents and especially our fathers, we were sent into an extremely difficult world to navigate.

We never felt loved. We never felt safe. We were never convinced that we were all special. We were never nurtured to believe that we were one of God's extraordinary children. We only felt that we were hapless byproducts in our parents' lives, getting in the way of their own selfish needs and bad decisions.

We lacked the self-confidence and self-love necessary to give us the inner strength that we all needed to survive.

We developed addictions that we used to cover up the lack of love and self-esteem that was always missing, qualities that we struggled to find and replace. We instead found other means to fix our inner problems, allowing those inner demons to come in and defeat us.

But why God had chosen me to bear witness to all of this and allowed me to bury my wife and my four best friends was still a mystery to me. Was it because I sought psychological and emotional help while the others did not?

Maybe I was just lucky.

That old adage '*There by the grace of God go I*' may have held true to my life at that moment. But nothing gave me the right to survive, while all the ones that I truly loved from my childhood passed through this world at a very young age.

I had lost my wife. I had lost all of my best friends. And with that final Buzz Boy funeral, I thought that I had endured all of the severe, extreme, emotional grief that I was ever going to persevere and survive in my lifetime.

I never suspected that my final ordeal would be the worst one of all.

CHAPTER-THIRTY-FIVE
Auld Lang Syne- New Year's Eve, 2019

I was in my law office on that frigid Tuesday morning on New Year's Eve. I was dressed in my casual blue jeans and Polo shirt and sweater, as I was happy to dress casually for work on that day. Since New Year's Day was a legal holiday, I usually gave my employees both days off to rest up and enjoy the holiday season's remainder before hitting it hard later on. We had a lot of pending family litigation to address, with various court appearances, affidavits, discovery orders, and depositions later that week that were scheduled, so I wanted my associates to enjoy what little time off they had left before returning to work. Of my current total of over fifty-two employees, there were a few of us who decided to come in and get caught up on whatever work could be done without the office telephones ringing off the hook.

As I looked out of the window of my office on top of the Hancock Building, I could see all of the traffic building up on Michigan Avenue down below, as if the end-of-year celebrations were beginning to escalate at a very early hour. It was not even two o'clock in the afternoon, and I could already envision all of the celebrations that would soon begin on that evening.

I had no plans for New Year's Eve. Since my annual year-end date with Dick Clark on 'ABC's New Year's Rockin' Eve' was no longer around, I had to make myself comfortable staying home alone and trying to warm up to Ryan Seacrest. We had regularly gone out to New Years' Eve parties when Annie was alive, usually to a neighbor's house or a restaurant nearby in River Forest. But since moving away and living in the West Loop, I no longer had any interest in dealing with the amateur drunks that were usually running rampant on New Year's Eve And since I used to be one of those amateur drunks myself, my staying home and away from all of them made even more sense.

At that moment, my office desk phone rang, and looking at the caller ID, and I knew I had to take the call. It was my daughter, Annette.

"Hello, Honey."

"Hey, Daddy. Whatcha' doing there at the office, slaving away on New Year's Eve?"

"One of us still has to work for a living to finance your exorbitant education at Loyola, my dear," I said with a smile. She shouldn't have sounded surprised, as I had always made it a habit of going into the office on New Year's Eve and working at least half a day.

"Do you have any plans tonight? Any hot dates?" she chuckled over the phone, as she knew that I had given up on dating a long time ago.

"The only date that I have is with Ryan Seacrest tonight, honey."

"Gee, Dad, that's too bad. Michael and I were hoping you would come out with us for dinner at Dei Edoardo's Ristorante on Lake Street in Oak Park tonight. We have reservations for seven o'clock."

Michael Grossman was the new young man in her life, as Annette had been dating him for the last few months. I had met him several times, and he seemed to be a very likable, polite young man. He was a third-year law student at Loyola University and was always very courteous and respectful. He was from an affluent, Jewish family in Glencoe and seemed to mesh very well with our very small, close-knit Catholic family. There was only one thing about her new boyfriend that really troubled me:

Michael Grossman had a drinking problem.

The two of them came over to my loft on Christmas Eve while my daughter Diana and I made an extensive, 'Seven-Fishes' Christmas holiday feast for all of us to enjoy. Michael hardly drank at all during dinner, having only one glass of wine. So, I was beginning to believe that he had cut back on that habit at my daughter's insistence.

We all then went to Holy Family Cathedral downtown for midnight mass. Even though her new boyfriend was Jewish, he didn't seem to mind sitting through the long, religious ritual.

Midnight mass on Christmas Eve was always a religious tradition for my family. I remember Annie and I brought the girls while they were little to midnight mass every Christmas Eve. The two of them would bring their pillows and blankets and fall asleep in the pews while the Christmas choirs were loudly singing their magnificent holiday carols. We had always told them that they had to come to mass at night with us while Santa Claus would drop over at our house, fill up their stockings, and bring their Christmas gifts.

One time, I had one of the neighbors, Al Mancini, come over to the house and put the girl's gifts under the tree while we were all out at midnight mass. When we finally arrived back home from mass at one-thirty in the morning, they were delighted to see their gifts under the tree. Santa's cookies and a glass of milk were even consumed.

That holiday stunt cost me a high-end bottle of Jack Daniels (Sinatra Edition), not because of his coming over to put the gifts under the tree. But because he had to force himself to consume a whole glass of milk and eat several chocolate chip cookies baked by my daughters, especially for Santa.

"Diana is coming with her boyfriend, Chuck. They're going to a party afterward."

"She's not working at the hospital tonight?" I referred to her having to work in the Emergency Room over at Chicago-Western Hospital that night, as I was sure she would be needed there during these holidays at the hospital. My daughter Diana was doing her residency there at Chicago-Western.

"No. Diana has the night off, believe it or not," Annette exclaimed.

My first reaction was to take a pass. Besides not wanting to go out on New Year's, I didn't want to be the 'fifth wheel' while both of my daughters were with their boyfriends enjoying dinner together.

"That's okay, honey. You guys go ahead and have fun."

"No, Daddy. Please come and meet us there. Diana wants you to come out with us too. She says she is going to have a very busy month at the hospital, and we may not get another chance to visit with her again for a while after tonight."

The thought of my baby girl begging and pleading with me to do anything was always more than I could bear. She distinctively knew from the very minute she was born that she had me wrapped around her little pinky finger.

"Oh, alright. But we're not staying out late. And, of course, I'm not drinking."

"We all know this, Daddy. Meet us at the restaurant at seven," she instructed.

"Bye Daddy, I love you," as she always ended every phone call.

I wrapped up whatever I was doing at the office and drove back to my loft on that New Year's Eve. I decided I would spend the rest of that afternoon relaxing on the couch and watching some college football. The Sun Bowl, with Florida State Seminoles and the Arizona State Sun Devils, was going to be playing on TV, so I figured I would watch the football game before going out.

I had no idea of the incredible horror that was awaiting me that evening.

CHAPTER THIRTY-SIX
Winning Demons

It was a little after seven o'clock when I had finally arrived at Dei Edoardo in Oak Park. The Eisenhower Expressway traffic started to get a bit jammed in both directions, as potential New Year's Eve partyers were preparing for their year-end activities.

The snowflakes were starting to accumulate on my windshield as the Weather Channel called for two to four inches of snow to accumulate that evening. Another reason to cut out early and stay home for New Year's Eve. As I had walked in, I saw my two daughters sitting at the bar with their boyfriends, having drinks and casually talking when I approached them.

"Happy New Year," I immediately kissed both of my daughters as their boyfriends got up from their bar stools and gave me the traditional 'man hug.'

Diana and her boyfriend Chuck came over from the bar and hugged me. My oldest daughter was well dressed in a black sleeveless dress and had her dark curly hair up but was wearing very little make-up, which was unusual for her. Her boyfriend was wearing a dark dinner jacket and a white button-down shirt and looked very stylish as always.

Her boyfriend Chuck was a third-year pediatrics resident at Chicago-Medical and was always very polite and gracious. Annette's boyfriend, Michael Grossman, immediately smelled like alcohol on his breath, while I noticed a crystal tumbler on the bar with a bourbon drink of some kind.

"Glad you could make it, Daddy," Annette smiled with excitement as the four of them were waiting for a table.

"Can I get you a drink, Mr. Mazzara?"

"Yes, a Seven-Up with a Lime would be great."

Annette looked at her boyfriend.

"Daddy doesn't drink, Michael. Remember?"

"Oh yes, I'm sorry."

"Have you been at the bar long?" I inquired about my youngest daughter's boyfriend.

"Yes, been here since five o'clock. I was in the area, so I got here a little early. Picked up Annette at the train station not far from here on Lake Street."

Annette then chimed in. "We're going to a party not far away from here after dinner."

I immediately got the impression that Annette's boyfriend had been drinking at the bar quite excessively before I had gotten there. He laughed and joked with others sitting there at the restaurant bar and seemed to be in a very festive mood.

I immediately darted a very concerned look to Annette, and based on our eye contact, and she knew exactly what I was concerned about. We didn't say anything as the five of us got a table towards the back of the quaint Italian restaurant.

Dei Edoardo's was one of those cliché type restaurants typical in their old-world cuisine and décor. The tables are all covered in red and white checker cloths, with straw-covered wine bottles hanging from the various areas of the bar and

313

ceiling in the restaurant. It had been several years since eating there, and I remembered the food being pretty good. The restaurant was packed with seated patrons, as everyone seemed to be getting themselves ready for more party plans later in the night.

As we all sat down, the kids ordered a bottle of wine, except Michael, who managed to get another refill of his bourbon on the rocks.

We all chatted about our jobs and our busy lives. Annette was looking forward to going back to classes at Loyola in the next week. Diana's final year of medical school at the University of Illinois was going to keep her busy with her clinical and internship. She was spending time in various departments but mentioned that she would probably specialize in either Emergency Room or Internal Medicine.

I noticed that Annette's boyfriend was gulping down his bourbons quite excessively as he ordered another drink as our entrée's had arrived. By then, Grossman was starting to slur his words, and it didn't take a genius or a breathalyzer test to figure out that he was starting to get very intoxicated.

"How are you guys getting to your party tonight?" I inquisitively asked Annette.

"We're driving. I will probably be the designated driver tonight."

I looked directly at Grossman.

"I hope so."

"Don't worry, Mr. Mazzara, I feel great right now. I'm okay."

Then I sounded like a concerned father.

314

"I don't think you should be driving tonight."

"Oh, don't worry, Daddy. Michael is very responsible about this sort of thing."

For some reason, I decided not to push it that night, as I didn't want to ruin the evening with my concerns regarding his excessive drinking.

Looking back on that night, I probably should have handcuffed him in the bathroom somewhere or physically disabled him from continuously ordering more drinks.

We all finished our dinners, and the kids easily polished that bottle of Pinot Noir. Annette's boyfriend ordered another bourbon, but by then, I took Annette's word that she would be the designated driver for the evening. I graciously paid for dinner as the young waitress brought back my American Express card, and I left her a large cash tip.

We all got our coats, with Diana and Chuck valeting their car. She had said that they were stopping at a party in Lincoln Park but would not be staying late and would probably be in bed before midnight.

We all kissed each other goodbye and wished one another a wonderful New Year.

"Happy New Year, Daddy," Annette said as she hugged me.

"Both of you call or text me when you get home tonight, please."

These were my usual instructions to my children whenever we went out together, and they were usually pretty good at following my directive.

I had self-parked my car on the side of the restaurant, not trusting the valets with my

Maserati. As I was getting into my car, I noticed Grossman and my daughter getting into his Cherokee Jeep vehicle after getting the keys from the valet.

But Grossman was getting into the driver's side, and Annette was casually getting into the car. I was probably two hundred yards away, and I made eye contact with both of them as they were pulling away. As he was putting his vehicle into drive, he smiled and waved to me, then quickly pulled his car onto the heavy traffic on Lake Street.

What happened to my daughter being the designated driver? Why was she allowing him to drive, especially after having several drinks that evening?

A cold chill ran down my spine, and at that moment, I felt completely helpless. As I got into my car and turned on the ignition, I called Annette on her cell phone.

There was no answer. I texted her.

No response.

I then sat in my car and auto dialed her number several times, with no answer. She had probably muted her phone during dinner, and there was no way for me to contact her.

A dark, sickening feeling came to my stomach, and I was starting to feel nauseous. I had a distinct feeling that something very terrible was about to happen.

I drove my car southbound on Harlem Avenue, and I was stuck at the traffic light on Harlem and Madison Avenues. As I was sitting there, I noticed the traffic immediately in front of me being suddenly jammed ahead, and the vehicles ahead of me were no longer moving. There were loud sirens now going on as an EMS ambulance was trying to make its way from behind me and was practically driving on the sidewalk, struggling to get to the scene of the accident.

I was probably sitting in my car for about thirty minutes or more before the traffic started moving again, narrowed down to one lane going southbound.

As my car came close to the expressway intersection and Harlem Avenue, I noticed the traffic accident ahead of me, and I suddenly went into shock.

A Jeep Cherokee SUV had slammed underneath the side of a large truck, which looked like it was making a left-hand turn. The car looked as though it had been well caught underneath, and there were several ambulances and Chicago Police squad cars with flashing lights, trying to direct traffic.

I took a very good look at that Jeep SUV.

It was Grossman's car.

I fervently tried to park my vehicle on the side of the road and then ran up to the officers who were directing traffic onto the expressway.

"What happened?" I asked the patrolman, who was trying to keep me from approaching the vehicle.

"I'm sorry, sir. You need to get back into your car."

"But what happened? I think I know those people in that car. I think my daughter is in that car."

The CPD patrolman looked at me, then motioned another patrolman to come over. He then

317

said something to the copper, and he escorted me onto the side.

"Do you know these passengers? There were a man and a woman in the car?"

"Yes," I immediately said. "The woman in that car is my daughter."

"They were just taken to the hospital, over at Chicago-Western."

"Are they ok?" I asked the policeman.

Just by looking at the smashed vehicle slammed underneath the tractor-trailer, it didn't look good at all.

"You need to get to the hospital, sir. That's where the accident victims have been taken."

I could tell that the patrolman didn't want to tell me the victims' condition in that vehicle. I ran back into my car and called my daughter Diana.

"Honey, we have to get to the hospital. Annette and her boyfriend have been in a serious car accident."

I could hear the shock in Diana's voice. There was a silence of more than several seconds.

"What happened, Daddy?"

"They are both at Chicago-Western. I will meet you there."

I jumped into my car and made my way to Chicago-Western Medical Center on North Ashland Avenue, trying to maneuver my way around the traffic going eastbound towards the city. There were several more traffic jams as I was having a terrible time trying to negotiate my way to the hospital. I parked my car near the emergency room entrance and ran into the ER.

As I had arrived there, Diana and Chuck were already there in the waiting room. Diana's eyes were drenched in tears, and her boyfriend Chuck was sitting next to her, his head buried in his hands. At that moment, Diana rushed into my arms and started crying copiously on my shoulders, and I knew that the worst happened.

"She's gone, Daddy. She's gone," she continuously kept crying.

At that moment, Chuck came over and grasped my arm as if to keep me from collapsing and slowly walked me over to the chair in that waiting room.

"I'm so sorry, Mr. Mazzara. I'm so sorry."

I was crying out loud, and I was nauseous, trying to process all of this information. An hour of all of us crying continued at that reception room until I finally had the strength to ask Chuck what had happened.

"The tractor-trailer was making a left-hand turn, and Grossman's car slammed into its side, with the top of the car being cut off by the truck. They were dead at the scene," he softy explained.

I later came to find out that my daughter and Grossman were both decapitated in that car accident and that his alcohol level was 2.0, over twice the legal limit.

I continued to sit at that chair in the hospital waiting room, completely frozen. I was in total shock, almost unable to move. I continued to cry to myself sitting there alone with my daughter. Her boyfriend, by that moment, had taken charge of the situation and talked to the various other attending residents and doctors about getting whatever information he could. He then made the arrangements for the coroner's office to pick up the bodies, as they were quite interested in finding out how drunk Michael Grossman was.

I was probably sitting in that same chair in the emergency reception room for several hours. I didn't arrive home at my loft until almost three-thirty in the morning. I only managed to walk over to my couch, and I just sat there, alone and despondent.

I was alone, and I was angry at myself. I was angry that my daughter allowed Grossman to get into that car and drive that evening. I should have done more, realizing how drunk Grossman really was.

It was almost ten o'clock that morning when I walked out of my loft and walked several blocks to the liquor store, and purchased several bottles of whiskey.

I had quit drinking and hadn't had a drop of alcohol in several years. But at that moment, I just didn't care. I sat at my dining room table and poured myself a drink. With the New Year's Day football games playing in the background, I continued to indulge with my once best friend and favorite demon, Jack Daniels.

My cell phone was ringing off the hook, but I didn't give a damn. My baby girl was dead, killed by her drunk driving boyfriend who didn't care to keep himself and my little girl safe. As far as I was concerned, he had killed her. He had killed himself. Grossman allowed himself to drive and slam into that tractor-trailer on New Year's Eve, paying no attention to his actual condition to drive.

I should have stopped him. I should have tackled him. I should have beat the shit out of him and physically stopped him from getting behind that fucking stirring wheel. I should have prevented that accident from happening instead of watching the two of them climb into that SUV and drive away.

I sat on that couch for two days, drinking myself into a complete stupor. I cleaned myself up just enough to attend the funeral and bury my daughter.

I then returned to my couch and poured myself more shots of Jack Daniels. I had been defeated. I had been beaten. I lost my wife. I lost my Buzz Boy best friends. I lost my baby girl. This was too overwhelming and more than I could bear.

After sixty years of fighting and struggling and coping with all of the tragedies in my life, I decided that I had enough.

My terrible, satanic demons had finally won.

CHAPTER THIRTY-SEVEN
Dressed For a Funeral -January 2020

It was the rush hour going home, as the Big Timber Westbound train was about to arrive at the Western Avenue train station on a cold, January evening. At least forty or more people were standing and waiting in the train depot, trying to keep warm in the cold winter weather. They were all watching their breath crystalizing in the sub-freezing temperatures.

Those people were all probably going home to have dinner and enjoy their families after work. On that Tuesday night, they were all about to witness a horrible, gruesome event that no human being should ever be allowed to observe.

An older man in his early sixties parked his black, late model Maserati in the train parking lot across the street. He made sure that his car keys were openly displayed on the driver's dashboard and the car was unlocked. He was well dressed, wearing a black suit, dark tie with white stripes, and a crisp white shirt. Bundled in a gray cashmere London Fog overcoat, the gentleman looked as though he could be dressed to go to the Chicago Lyric Opera that evening on Wacker Drive.

In reality, he was impeccably dressed for a funeral.

On that early evening, he continued to look at his gold, Rolex watch to make sure that he was on time for that train's arrival. The gentleman entered the train depot filled with potential train passengers trying to stay warm and shielding themselves from the brutal winter cold. He quickly walked past the ticket counter, realizing that he didn't need a train ticket on that winter day.

It was 5:50 pm.

At 5:56, the sound of the train going westbound from the Chicago's Union Station towards the western suburbs was about to approach its first stop on Western Avenue. Many people began to line up outside the train depot, getting ready to enter the train cars in a single file.

The well-dressed gentleman, not wanting to miss the train, quickly walked one hundred yards ahead of the train depot, making sure that he would be the first to greet the fast-approaching the Metra-Big Timber train.

At 5:57 pm, as the train was rapidly approaching the depot, the 60-year-old man suddenly jumped onto the railroad tracks. He then stood erect on the tracks in front of the Metra train, waiting for the high-speed locomotive to arrive.

As the Metra train began feverishly sounding its horns, he only stood still, looking away towards the other direction as the train hit him. His body was instantly dismembered and dragged over twenty feet across the tracks as all train bystanders and passengers looked on in horror.

There was blood splattered all over the front of the Metra train, as people still inside of the train depot began screaming. There were infinite cries of 'Oh my God' reverberating within the closed walls of that train depot. Words of shock and horror were continuously loudly exclaimed by all those who bore witness to that gruesome event. Two older witnesses fainted at the sight of the victim's decapitated and mutilated body scattered all over the railroad tracks. Many of the train passengers ran out of that Western Avenue train depot, unable to bear witness to the horror of that unexpected horrific suicide on that Tuesday evening. Several other passengers dialed 911.

Within minutes, several Chicago EMT ambulances were immediately called, and the Chicago Police Department squad cars arrived at the scene, filled with patrolmen and detectives. One of those was Chicago P.D. Detective Philip Dorian from District Sixteen. As he exited his squad car, he immediately knew that he was investigating another gruesome train suicide. As the other patrolmen tried to push the train passengers away from that horrific, bloody location, Dorian approached the halted train. He immediately noticed the dismembered victim's body parts still scattered across the train tracks.

Philip Dorian then took a deep breath. These gruesome crime scenes were the absolute worst, as he knew he would soon be on the train tracks, helping the other patrolmen gather whatever scattered body parts they could gather, strewn and distributed across both sides of the halted train.

"Do we know the identity of the victim?" he asked one of the patrolmen.

"We haven't found anything with the victim's identification just yet," responded the Chicago patrolman.

As the victim's body parts were quickly being gathered by one of the patrolmen, a dismembered arm, drenched in blood, was immediately recovered along the side of the tracks. When the young Chicago patrolman recovered the body part, he immediately noticed that the bloodied severed arm was still wearing what looked to be a gold, Rolex watch.

The young Chicago copper looked in both directions, making sure no one at the crime scene was looking. He then took the very expensive, gold Rolex watch off the dismembered victim's arm and put it into his pocket. The copper then placed the body part into the black bag of human debris that he was still gathering.

One of the witnesses described the older, well-dressed gentleman who stepped onto the train tracks. He stated that he had parked his black Maserati across the street. When the Chicago copper pointed out the parked vehicle across the street in the parking lot, he immediately gave Detective Dorian information. Dorian walked over to the parked car, noticing that the Maserati was unlocked, with the key fob sitting on the car's dashboard. As he looked inside, he found the victim's wallet was neatly placed in the glovebox. It was as if the well-dressed suicide victim wanted to make sure that he was easily identified at the crime scene. As Dorian opened the wallet and read the victim's driver's license, he loudly gasped in disbelief.

"Oh, dear God," he loudly said to himself.

He immediately grabbed his chest as the intense, sudden shock physically overwhelmed him for several long minutes. He buried his head in his hands, saying several prayers out loud. It was as though he were praying over the poor man's soul, asking God to forgive the victim for committing the ultimate cardinal sin and taking his own life. There were now tears streaming down from his eyes as he continued to shake his head. He noticed that attached to the Maserati key fob was a copper medallion. Dorian had seen that medallion before. He knew who it was and now knew why the distressed victim had suddenly decided to take his own life.

"Why?" he said several times as he continued to cry out loud.

Dorian was emotionally distraught, as he then started banging his clenched fist several times on the Maserati's dashboard.

"Why?" he continued to copiously cry out loud.

The 60-year-old suicide fatality was a longtime, personal friend.

CHAPTER THIRTY-EIGHT
A Buzz Boy Forever-February 2020

Four weeks later, on a quiet Sunday afternoon, a young woman arrived at Queen of Heaven Cemetery in Hillside, Illinois, on that mild, February day. The heavy snow had recently melted, leaving the streets of the cemetery pavement wet and soaked. The sun was now shining brightly on that day, as the forty-five-degree temperatures began to bring a taste of spring to that very mild winter. The bright sun was casting the shadow of her car onto the green grass as she parked in front of the section of monuments that she was there to visit.

She had just gotten off her hospital shift as a medical resident at Chicago-Western Medical Center and was very apprehensive about going to visit those graves on that day.

'Section 31, plot 171,' she said to herself, reading the directive on the piece of paper that was given to her by the cemetery office earlier over the phone.

The young woman had been severely disturbed and traumatized for the last four weeks, and she was not physically able to attend the recent funeral or the internment of her loved one. She could not absorb the horrific emotional trauma of suddenly losing and burying another family member. There was a closed casket funeral at St. Angela's Church in Elmwood Park. It was a beautiful service, and she was told that over five hundred people came to pay their respects to the well-loved, well-respected, but very heartbroken, tormented soul. The young medical resident approached the gravesite, as a large, granite monument with her family surname was boldly engraved into the stone marker. It had just been erected several days ago, and the young medical resident had not been to the cemetery to visit the family plot until that day.

There were three granite grave markers neatly placed in front of the tombstone, each bearing her dear relatives' names.

Her mother's name, her sister's name, and now...her father's name, all neatly lined in a row.

She remembered the long-standing tradition that her father had started years ago. Still wearing her hospital lab coat, she put her hand into her pocket and pulled out a copper medallion. She then placed it onto her father's gravestone, along with a precut piece of adhesive, epoxy tape attached on the back.

As her eyes were now drenched with tears, she pressed the medallion as hard as she could onto the granite tombstone for a few minutes until the epoxy adhesive immediately dried. She then tested it, making sure that the Buzz Boys copper medallion couldn't be removed. The young woman started to cry for several long minutes copiously. The emergency room resident-physician was now...all alone. Alone in front of those headstones. Alone at that cemetery. All alone in her life.

She was incredibly bitter, realizing that the selfish act of her father's suicide had left her completely helpless and emotionally drifting. There was now no one else in her life to assist her in navigating her future lifetime problems.

Her father would not be there to see her medical residency's final years to see her pass the medical boards and become a licensed physician.

Her father would not be there to watch her get married and walk her down the aisle.

She was no longer Daddy's Girl. Her father would not be there to witness the birth of his grandchildren and to bear witness to her happy life. A life that he wanted so much for her to have, free of the inner torment that he suffered from as a child, struggling to grow up in Elmwood Park. Her dad was always grateful that neither of his children would ever bear witness to the abusive family environment that he, his brothers, and his close friends had to grow up in.

The young resident physician wondered how she would now cope. She had lost her mother to glioblastoma, a deadly brain tumor. She had lost her sister to a car accident. And now, she had just lost her father to suicide.

"Why, Daddy? Why? I'm all alone now. Why did you leave me? You promised you wouldn't!" she loudly cried.

It was as if a long collection of spirits and ghosts had gathered before her to listen to her heartbroken screams. There was anguish in her voice, knowing that the promises that her father had always made to her were now forever broken. She was now a total orphan, without a mother, a sibling, and now a father to watch over her and guide her in her young life. The young woman closed her eyes and pressed her hand onto the gravestone, hoping to suddenly feel an immediate connection to his spirit. She hoped to instantly experience her deceased father's troubled soul one last time. The resident physician then bent down and kissed the grave marker.

"Goodbye, Daddy. I hope you're happy now. I hope you're at peace and in heaven with Mommy and Annette."

Diana Mazzara re-read the engraved, poignant inscription on her father's gravestone one last time:

Loving Husband & Father
Robert A. Mazzara

Miles To Go Before I Sleep
A Buzz Boy Forever

After several long minutes, the bitter young woman stood up and got into her blue Toyota Camry. Starting her car, she took one last look at the cemetery around her. She then drove away from the family plot, quickly exiting Queen of Heaven Cemetery and merging onto the east-bound traffic.

The sun that Sunday afternoon was blinding, with the sun rays reflecting off her windshield as Diana drove off towards her townhome in Jefferson Park. The young resident brushed off her tears with her right hand. She wanted to leave that cemetery as quickly as she could. There were too many spirits there...too many ghosts. There were too many wonderful, lost memories of loved ones she would never be able to embrace again. It was as though her whole life was now buried at that cemetery, and she needed to escape.

With her car recklessly changing lanes, she stepped on the accelerator. Diana put on her sunglasses, not looking for any upcoming traffic in her rearview mirror as she was thinking out loud:

There will be no more cemeteries. There will be no more death.

She never returned.

MORE GREAT BOOKS BY CRIME NOVELIST EDWARD IZZI:

Of Bread & Wine (2018)

A Rose from The Executioner (2019)

Demons of Divine Wrath (2019)

Quando Dormo (When I Sleep) (2020)

El Camino Drive (2020)

When A Rook Takes the Queen (2021)

The Buzz Boys (2021)

New Book Releases Coming Soon:

They Only Wear Black Hats (Fall, 2021)

Evil Acts of Contrition (Spring, 2022)

His novels and writings are available at www.edwardizzi.com, Amazon, Barnes & Noble, and other fine bookstores.